Shaun's an outsider. He has a dark past and an even darker habit of cutting himself and burying his emotions under his skin. The only thing he's got going for him is his guitar and a head full of lyrics.

When Jesse moves to town, bringing big bright smiles and warm blue eyes into Shaun's dark life, he insists they become friends.

But that's going to be a problem for Shaun. He's never had a real friend before. Oh, and he's also finding himself hopelessly attracted to Jesse's undeniable charm, which is definitely not going to work out.

Being gay isn't brutal and Shaun has an image to uphold if he's ever got a shot at becoming the death metal God he knows he's destined to become.

DEEP CUT

Permanently Black and Blue,
Book One

C.R. Scott

A NineStar Press Publication

Published by NineStar Press
P.O. Box 91792,
Albuquerque, New Mexico, 87199 USA.
www.ninestarpress.com

Deep Cut

Printed in the USA
First Edition
April, 2020

Print ISBN: 978-1-951880-84-2

Also available in eBook, ISBN: 978-1-951880-83-5

Warning: This book contains sexually explicit content, which may only be suitable for mature readers, self-harm, suicidal ideation, child abuse, murder/suicide, rape, drug use, homophobic slurs, and witnessed necrophilia.

To my husband, Aaron

Chapter One

For the first time ever, Jesse almost had a room to himself.

The new house had four bedrooms. It was their house this time, so they could do whatever they wanted with it. They kept the bunk beds though, and as usual, Jesse got stuck with the top while Sam got the bottom.

Already, the room was covered in half-emptied boxes, clothes, various personal items, and discarded fast-food wrappers.

Jesse hung over the edge of his bed so he could see the tiny screen on their TV. His younger brother, Sam, had convinced him to do two-player in *Call of Duty*. He'd wanted to finish unpacking his stuff, but after an awful lot of complaining on Sam's part about how completely *bullshit* it was internet wouldn't be installed for almost a week, he'd agreed.

They were wasting a perfectly good Sunday evening and had been for the last few hours. Jesse sat with a blank stare, zoned out, the controller hanging loosely from his hands, when a soft voice from the doorway snapped him to attention.

"Jesse, I wanna come up."

Brian stood in the doorway, a pout on his little round face. He picked his way into the room and stood directly in front of the TV.

"Get out of the way!" Sam's hands were occupied. He nudged the three-year-old with his foot.

"Stop it," Brian whined. "Jesse!"

"You should be in bed," Jesse sighed.

"I can't sleep. Lissa won't stop crying." Brian stepped over a pile of clothes and started up the ladder.

Jesse rolled his eyes, but he dropped the controller and crawled to the edge of the bed. He lifted Brian off the first rung and dragged him to the top bunk.

"Oh, man! I got you," Sam laughed as he blew Jesse's character away on-screen.

"Fuck you, I wasn't paying attention."

"Dude, Brian, go sleep with the twins. We're busy," Sam said as he started a new game.

"No."

"Leave us alone! Go back to your room!"

But Jesse knew that wasn't happening. Just as Brian had mentioned, he could hear baby Melissa wailing in the other room.

Monica shuffled past their door. She had PJs on, and her hair was bedraggled. The baby quieted somewhat, but that was just because she was getting attention. As soon as Monica tried to go back to bed, Lissa would start up again.

Brian watched Sam and Jesse shoot each other up. After a while, his head started nodding. The toddler slumped onto Jesse's pillows and was soon fast asleep.

"So...are you nervous about starting school?" Sam asked abruptly.

"No." It was the truth. What was there to be nervous about? "We've been to a million other schools before. This one's no different."

"I guess," Sam said. "But...I don't know. Those other schools were different— Crap!" he cried as Jesse's character skillfully sniped his.

"Should've ducked," Jesse snickered. He earned a middle finger for his efforts.

As they waited for a new game to load, Sam returned to the topic of school. "This is different," he said again. "Like when we were living with Joey, that was temporary."

"Mmm, another of Mom's boyfriends," Jesse agreed.

"Yeah," Sam said. "But there's no boyfriend here."

"That's a good thing, right?"

"I don't know. What if we hate it? We're stuck here," Sam said tightly. "This is our home now."

Jesse hadn't thought about it like that. They'd been moving around since before he could remember. They'd stayed with friends and moved in with Monica's many, *many* boyfriends. But Monica's dad, their grandfather, had died about six months ago and he'd left them this rundown house in the middle of nowhere. Monica had considered selling it, but after a bad breakup with Joey, the last asshole boyfriend in Detroit, she'd decided to move them halfway across the country to make this hole-in-the-wall their own.

Nothing was ever set in stone, but from the way she talked about it, they'd be here for a while.

"It'll be fine," Jesse said.

"But what if—"

"Dude!" Jesse shot Sam in the head as he ducked out from behind a crumbling wall. "Are you going to play or what?"

It was a lame attempt at distraction, but it worked. Sam kicked the frame of the bed. The top bunk shook. "I'm gonna kill you," he said.

Beside him, Brian stirred and moaned in his sleep.

Jesse sighed. He brushed a hand through Brian's blond hair and lulled him back to dreamland as the next game loaded.

*

Sam and Jesse didn't go to sleep until two in the morning.

Unfortunately, Brian was up at the crack of dawn. He accidentally kicked Jesse in the shin as he crawled out of the bunk and lowered himself down the ladder.

Jesse clutched his leg and hissed in pain. He blinked a few times in the bright morning light. He could hear voices downstairs. He decided to abandon the idea of sleeping in. He got up and followed the toddler down to the kitchen.

"Mommy, I'm hungry," Brian said as Jesse came in the room.

The kitchen was full of boxes. Cookware, dishes, utensils, and other such items spilled out of them, half-unpacked. Monica had cleared them away from the stove and was attempting to make pancakes while she balanced Lissa on her hip. When she saw Jesse, she sighed in relief.

"Come take the baby."

Melissa sniffled as she was handed off. She buried her curly red head against Jesse's chest and shoved her fingers in her mouth.

"Hello, cranky." Jesse smiled and toted the baby to the kitchen table. He pushed some boxes aside and found a seat across from Tyler and Allison.

"Morning guys."

The twins looked up from their Nintendos. They gave Jesse identical sunny smiles.

"Hey, Jesse."

"Hi."

"What are you guys doing?" Jesse asked, more to keep them distracted than out of actual curiosity. The twins loved talking.

Of course, they felt completely different about Brian, and when he tried to worm his way between the twins to get a look at what they were playing, Allison shoved the toddler away. When he tried again, Tyler hit him.

"Ow!" Brian's blue eyes welled up with tears.

"Jeez, guys, is that necessary?" Jesse waved Brian over. He picked him up so he could sit next to Lissa.

"You're such a whiny little baby," Tyler said.

"Am not," Brian complained.

Jesse tried his best to keep the peace.

Luckily, Monica was done with breakfast, and she yelled up the stairs for Sam. By the time she started serving the slightly burnt pancakes, Sam had dragged himself into the kitchen.

"Too early…" he groaned. Robotically, he took Melissa from Jesse and sat her in the high chair. She cried at the mishandling, but it was a common enough occurrence that it caused little reaction.

Brian got into his own chair between Jesse and Sam, and Monica took the last chair available at the head of the table. She ignored her own breakfast in favor of spooning mush into Melissa's mouth.

"Jesse, I need you to watch the kids today. I've got to head to the school and get everyone's classes sorted."

Jesse sighed, but he nodded. Being the oldest at eighteen sucked. He babysat *all* the time. He didn't know why he'd thought it'd be any different here, but he'd hoped.

"I can take care of myself," Sam pouted as he cut up Brian's pancakes.

"Me too," Allison said quickly, following whatever the older and wiser Sam had to say. Tyler would have agreed as well, but his mouth was full of syrup and practically glued shut with the sticky stuff. Jesse struggled not to laugh at the sight.

"Me too!" Brian screeched happily.

Monica, Jesse, and Sam cleaned up the younger kids after breakfast, and then the two older boys took everyone upstairs to get dressed. Monica left to take care of business soon after, and they were left on their own.

The twins wanted to play outside, so Jesse ushered everyone out the back door so he could keep an eye on all his siblings at once.

Sam looked awfully unhappy, but since there wasn't much to do by himself, he didn't protest. He took out his soccer ball and started kicking it to Allison and Tyler. When Brian cried at being left out, they turned their impromptu game of soccer into a monkey-in-the-middle type of deal. Jesse knew he should stop them. Brian was becoming upset, but Jesse had his hands full with Lissa. He decided not to get up.

They were in the middle of nowhere out here. There was nothing but woods in one direction and fields in the other. There was a farm way off in the distance, but besides that, their only other neighbor was about a mile down the road.

Jesse could see the house from the backyard. It was a brown, beat-up rambler with ugly lawn decorations among the hedges.

He wondered if there were any kids there his own age. Hoped was more like it. If he had a friend living just down the road, maybe being isolated all the way out here in the boonies would be a little more bearable. He was already going crazy from being stuck with his family for the last few days. Even if he hated the new school, at least it'd be an opportunity to get out of the house and away from his little brothers and sisters.

"Guys, cut it out!" Jesse yelled once the roughhousing had gotten out of hand and Brian began to cry in frustration. "Play nice!" he cried. He gave Sam a sharp look, and with a guilty look on his face, the younger teen called an end to the mean games.

Sam was thirteen, perfectly capable of looking after two five-year-olds or one three-year-old, but when he had to look after all three at once, he seemed to lose a few years of maturity. Sometimes he just needed to be reminded he wasn't a baby anymore.

Being mature was incredibly boring after all. Sadly, Jesse knew a lot about that.

*

When Monica came home later that evening, she had good news. Well, maybe not good news to most of the children in the house, but news nonetheless.

"The school wants everyone to start immediately," she said over dinner. It was fast food again, the quickest and easiest way to feed five hungry kids. Poor Lissa was stuck with more mush from the Gerber jar. "I also went in to check on my transfer at the hospital. I start in a few days."

Monica was a registered nurse. She said it was her calling to help her fellow man. The fact that she picked up more men there than anywhere else proved she took her job *very* seriously.

"So, tomorrow, I'll go have a look at daycare," she continued over Brian's cry of distress.

"No!" he complained, but no one listened to him.

"When do we start school?" Jesse asked.

"Bright and early Wednesday morning," Monica said cheerfully.

Sam groaned with disappointment. "But that's the day after tomorrow!"

He and Monica argued for a bit, but Jesse didn't listen in. He was glad. Maybe he wasn't thrilled about the homework and note-taking and all that other fun stuff, but it'd be nice to talk to someone his own age. Allison and Tyler seemed to feel the same way. They bent their heads together and started whispering excitedly.

"It's so unfair," Sam bitched later that night. "If Mom wouldn't have gone to that stupid school today, I bet we could have gotten another week off."

Jesse shuddered at the thought. "You're making too big a deal out of it. It'll be fine."

"That's easy for you to say," Sam said. His bottom lip stuck out petulantly.

"What's that supposed to mean?"

"You're always popular. No matter where we go," Sam said. "*Nobody* likes me."

"That's not true." Jesse knew it wasn't true. Sam had friends! He even kept in touch with some of them online.

"I'm so ugly."

Oh.

"Are you talking about girls?" Jesse asked. He couldn't help himself. He started to smirk.

Sam blushed bright red. "No," he said quickly.

Jesse snorted.

No, Jesse didn't have a hard time with girls. He wouldn't say he was overwhelmingly popular with them, but he wasn't afraid to talk to them either. He dated lots of girls.

He didn't know what to say about the "ugly" comment though, as he didn't think he was all that good-looking either. He was too short, only about five six, and he had an annoying spray of freckles across his cheeks. He was average-looking, and his body was on the thin side. He had blue eyes and auburn hair. Sam looked a lot like he did, minus the blue eyes, so he was a little insulted.

"You're not ugly, okay?" he said awkwardly.

Sam pouted.

"Seriously." Jesse ruffled his brother's hair. "Besides, girls don't care about looks. They like guys who make them laugh. Or guys who aren't total jerks."

"Yeah, whatever." Sam batted his hand away. "I'm not even talking about girls."

Jesse laughed. "C'mon. We should at least try to clean this place up before school starts. I won't be able to find anything."

"Yeah, I guess."

*

The next day Monica enrolled Brian and Lissa in daycare. She assured the fussy toddler that it was very nice and full of fun toys and other kids to play with. Brian hated strange places and new people, and he wasn't having any of it. His first few days were going to be a nightmare. Monica needed to work though, and everyone else was starting school in the morning.

That night was hectic for everyone. Allison and Tyler didn't want to go to bed early, Brian was crying, Lissa was crying, Sam was pouting, and there wasn't much Monica or Jesse could do. Monica locked herself in the nursery with the baby, ignoring everyone else. The twins bounced off the walls in their room across the hall while Brian had a meltdown in the living room.

Jesse concentrated on Brian. He carried him up to his room and promised they'd sleep in his bed again.

Sam was depressed about school. He'd spent most of the evening sulking in bed, but he got up to handle the twins when they began shrieking with laughter. They got settled in their beds; the occasional sound of whispering and laughter gradually dying down.

Jesse gratefully fell asleep.

The chaos continued early the next morning. Getting ready for school was a familiar routine, but Jesse found himself annoyed and wishing for once he didn't have to take care of everyone else.

After he prodded Sam and Brian awake, he got everyone downstairs for breakfast, then cleaned Brian and the twins and helped them pick out some outfits. He chose a clean outfit for himself and then ran to the bathroom to brush his teeth.

When he heard the bus idling outside, he grabbed Sam and pulled him downstairs.

At least Monica was in a good mood. She sang a cheesy country song as she packed the twins' backpacks in the living room.

"See you boys tonight," she called.

Jesse waved goodbye and yanked Sam out the front door.

He was a little disappointed when he got on the bus and saw it was completely empty. Well, except for the driver. He smiled at the balding older man. "Good morning," he said pleasantly.

The bus driver nodded.

Jesse found a seat right in the middle. He was irritated when Sam sat beside him.

The bus ambled down the road a bit, and Jesse looked curiously out the window. He spotted the neighbor's house, and his spirits lifted when he saw there was another boy waiting in the driveway. He squirmed with impatience as they slowed to a halt in front of the house.

The neighbor boy briskly crossed the street. He pushed his way past the half-opened doors and onto the bus. He stormed all the way to the back. He didn't look at Sam and Jesse.

Immediately, the bus lurched into movement once more, and the boy threw his backpack violently into his seat. He slumped down after it and turned to stare out the window.

Jesse could barely contain himself. He had an odd feeling the boy wouldn't welcome company, but he climbed over his brother anyway and hurried to the back. He sat directly in front of the other boy, turned around, and smiled brightly. "Hi!"

The boy had been gazing listlessly out the window, but as Jesse continued to smile at him, the boy turned and leveled a spectacular glare his way. "Who are you?"

Jesse's smile faltered, but he didn't back down. "I'm Jesse. I'm new," he said.

The boy furrowed his thick eyebrows. He looked *deeply* unhappy.

"We live just down the road from you," Jesse said uneasily. "I guess that makes us neighbors."

"So what?" The boy grunted, looking even more hostile than before.

Jesse studied the other boy in confusion. *What's with this guy?* He looked to be about Jesse's age, possibly in the same grade as well. He had frizzy brown hair and squinty black eyes. He looked...*furious*, and his wide lips twisted into a snarl the longer Jesse stared.

He smelled strange too... Jesse tried not to wrinkle his nose. It was like cheese or something. Sweaty cheese and old stale smoke. "What's your name?" he asked.

"Why do you care?"

"I'm just trying to be nice," Jesse said. He received a scowl for his trouble.

Jesse and the boy stared at each other. The boy's dark eyes narrowed as he wordlessly refused to answer.

"Um...I'm sorry, I'll leave you alone now," Jesse said. He felt stupid. He wanted to hide.

"Shaun."

Jesse was already getting up, so he almost didn't hear the other boy speak. He turned back when he introduced himself though, a huge smile alighting his face.

The boy, Shaun, looked away quickly, trying to hide his momentary flash of interest. If it could be called that.

Either way, Jesse sat back down.

"What grade are you in?"

"Junior year," Shaun said gruffly. He looked boredly out the window.

"That's so cool!" Jesse said. "Me too."

Shaun grunted.

"I wonder if we have any classes together." Jesse hadn't received his schedule yet.

"Probably will. The classes are small."

"Oh." Jesse's eyes widened. "How many juniors are there?"

Shaun shrugged. "I don't know. Maybe thirty."

"That's all?" There'd been thirty people in every class in Jesse's last school. The high school had housed two thousand kids total.

The bus lurched to a stop and two girls got on. They were obviously middle schoolers, and they headed straight for Sam. Jesse's little brother sent him a panicked look, and Jesse grinned at him with encouragement.

"Who's that?"

"My little brother," Jesse said automatically. He was surprised to hear Shaun asking a question. He didn't seem very interested in conversation. In fact, once Jesse answered, Shaun pulled a battered CD player out of his backpack and hung the earphones around his neck.

"What're you listening to?" Jesse asked, hoping to stall the other boy. He didn't want to sit in silence.

"Pantera," Shaun said.

"I've heard some of their stuff," Jesse said easily. "They're pretty cool."

Shaun seemed surprised. "Really?"

"Sure," Jesse said, missing Shaun's look of disbelief. "I like all kinds of music."

Shaun frowned. "I like metal. I'm in a band. A metal band," he said dangerously.

"Awesome! What do you play?" Jesse asked. For all he knew, he could be talking to a metal god!

"I play the guitar," Shaun said as he fiddled with his CD player. "You wouldn't like us though. We're hardcore."

"You don't know what I like, dude," Jesse said with a laugh, refusing to be turned off by Shaun's rude behavior. "You should let me know when you're playing next. I didn't think there'd be any metal bands out here in the middle of nowhere."

"Yeah," Shaun said darkly. "People around here don't appreciate good music. It's all country shit or worse yet, that *fucking* rap."

Jesse laughed again. He liked both country and rap.

The bus stopped, and Jesse glanced toward the front. A few more people got on this time. Three girls and two more boys. They all seemed to be older, most likely high school at least. One of the boys, tall and athletic, smiled as soon as he saw Jesse. He headed to the back of the bus with his companions in tow.

"Speak of the devil," he said, sitting across from Jesse. "I was just telling everybody I heard there was a new kid in town and there you are!"

Jesse didn't know what to say, so he smiled at everyone. Two of the girls sat in front of Jesse, and they smiled back at him in a friendly manner. One was blonde, and the other had long, shiny black hair. They were both pretty.

The third girl was shockingly pregnant. It wasn't so much that she was pregnant that was shocking. He'd just never seen such a small girl with such a huge belly. It looked ridiculous on her. The other boy, the one who hadn't spoken, sat beside the pregnant girl. He took her hand possessively.

"I'm Emily," said the girl with long black hair. Jesse thought she had a nice smile. "And that's my dumb brother, Kenny," she continued, pointing to the athletic boy who'd started the conversation. "He's nicer than he looks."

Kenny stuck his tongue out, and everybody laughed.

Jesse turned back to Shaun, wanting to share the amusement with his new friend, but he stared intensely out the window. His face was red with anger. Jesse's eyes widened. Hadn't they just broken the ice? He was taken aback by the hostility wafting off Shaun in tsunami-sized waves.

Nobody else seemed to notice.

"I'm Sunny," the blonde said cheerfully, drawing Jesse's attention back to the new arrivals.

"And that's Lee and Rick." Kenny introduced the pregnant girl and her boyfriend. Lee smiled, but her boyfriend eyed Jesse with suspicion.

"Howdy," said Lee. "And this is little Ashley." She rubbed her enormous belly. "I didn't get that ultrasound yet, but I know it's a girl. I'm fixin' to name her Ashley. After my mama."

"Oh." Jesse scratched the back of his neck. He was having a hard time concentrating on the conversation with Shaun's glare burning into his back. He could see Shaun staring at him from the corner of his eye, but when he tried to catch him at it, Shaun switched to staring out the window.

Jesse wondered what he'd done wrong. "Ashley's a pretty name," he said distractedly.

"Thanks!" Lee said.

"So, where are you from, Jesse?" Emily asked.

"My family moves around a lot, so I wouldn't say we're *from* anywhere," he said, pulling up a typical answer to a typical question. "But we moved from Detroit."

"What year are you in?"

"Eleventh." Jesse got a smile from both Kenny and Emily. It seemed they were in the same grade.

"Do you like it here?" Sunny asked.

"I've only been here a few days, and I haven't gotten out much," Jesse said. "But it's okay, so far."

The questions continued in rapid succession. Jesse supplied information on the places he'd lived previously, his old school, his family. Emily and Sunny asked if he had a girlfriend.

"Nope," Jesse said, unable to admit he was single without blushing.

The girls giggled, and Emily gave him a flirtatious look.

They were all nice and extremely friendly. Even Rick managed to warm up a little before the bus ride was over. He asked if Jesse played any sports.

"Sure. I'm pretty good at football and baseball."

He received an approving nod from the boys.

But no matter how friendly they were, the entire conversation was spent ignoring Shaun's presence. Jesse didn't think he'd ever been in a more awkward position in his life. Everyone gave Shaun and his glowering looks the cold shoulder.

It was like he didn't exist.

If Jesse hadn't been able to smell Shaun's slightly rank scent, see his frizzy hair in the corner of his eye, hear the tinny sound of Pantera coming from his earphones, he would have had to conclude Shaun was just a figment of his imagination.

When they got to the high school, Shaun stood up the second the bus stopped. He purposefully shoved his bag into Kenny and then rudely pushed past Lee as the girl struggled to get out of her seat.

"Jerk," Kenny muttered under his breath.

"Is he...always like that?" Jesse asked curiously. He wasn't stupid. He got the feeling Shaun was a loner, but Jesse hadn't done anything to warrant his hatred. Yet that stare of his had been nothing but hate personified.

"Don't worry about him," Emily said before anyone else could respond. "I mean, it's best if you don't try to talk to him."

What kind of advice was that?

"I already talked to him. He wasn't so bad," Jesse said as he followed his new friends off the bus. He paused to hit his little brother on the back of the head. The middle school was the next building over, so he and his two new girlfriends were getting dropped off next.

Sam slapped his hand away. "Screw off, Jess," he muttered, sending the middle school girls into giggles.

Jesse smiled. He always felt better when he got to be a mean big brother.

"Shaun's strange. Sometimes...most of the time...he's okay. He's quiet and doesn't bother anyone," Sunny continued once they were off the bus.

"Yeah, but if you say the wrong thing, he'll go crazy," Lee chimed in. "He beat up my cousin a few years back. And my cousin's huge!"

"I remember that." Kenny frowned. "Didn't Shaun have a knife on him?"

"Oh my goodness, yes!" Lee cried, rubbing her stomach uncomfortably. "He was about to gut poor Georgie when the teachers came and pulled him off."

"He's a freak," Rick said viciously.

Jesse was surprised by the vehemence in Rick's declaration. He almost expected someone to refute his claim. To shake their heads and take everything back, but no one did.

"Stay away from him, if you can," Kenny said.

"And if you can't, then just ignore him. It's what we do," Emily said.

Jesse didn't know what to think about all that.

Sure, that stare Shaun had leveled at him had been strangely malevolent, but obviously, he was used to being hated. His new friends hated Shaun. They said mean things behind his back, purposefully excluded him, told scary—obviously exaggerated—stories about him, and spread rumors.

Jesse didn't know enough to pass any sort of judgment on anyone. His new friends seemed nice in every other way, so he decided to give them the benefit of the doubt. He assumed the only reason they were being so mean was that they honestly didn't know any better.

Jesse wasn't going to ignore Shaun, though. He was too curious to do that.

Shaun wasn't exactly pleasant, but that didn't bother Jesse much. There'd been something about him that he liked, oddly enough.

So, Jesse didn't promise anything. He simply followed his new friends into the smallest high school he'd ever had the dubious pleasure of entering. He had to get his class schedule.

Chapter Two

Shaun hit a freshman with his book bag on the way to his locker. The scrawny kid fell into his friend with an undignified squawk. It almost made Shaun feel better. Almost.

"Stupid kid..." he muttered under his breath. He tried to tell himself he was talking about the freshman and about what a goddamn brat he was for getting in the way, but it was the new kid on the bus that came to mind.

Jesse, or whatever his name was... He was an *asshole*. He'd started off all friendly and chatty, but the second someone else paid him a little attention, it was like Shaun didn't exist!

It was always the fucking same. People were always doing that. Either ignoring him or making fun of him. It had used to hurt his feelings—not that he would *ever* admit to that—but now it just pissed him off.

Shaun reached his locker. He opened it angrily as he thought about killing himself.

That'd make them fucking sorry, he thought bitterly.

But he wouldn't do that. Deep down, he knew suicide was *exactly* what his asshole classmates wanted from him. So, he'd stick around, fucking with them, and making them uncomfortable. It was the next best thing.

He gathered his books for first period and then slammed his locker shut.

"Watch it, loser!" yelled some jock a few lockers over.

"Fuck off," Shaun called over his shoulder and stormed off down the hall. He was pleased when the jock didn't come after him. The dumb meathead was too afraid to do anything.

He'd fought with the jocks a lot over the years. He didn't always win, but he always made sure his hits and kicks and bites were felt long after the fight was over. If the asshole could still feel your punches a week after the fight was over, it was just as good as a victory.

He made it to English without further incident. First period was Shaun's least favorite class. And that was saying something.

He despised every class he had.

His teacher, Miss Stevens, was *always* trying to get them to put more emotion into their writing. More *feeling*.

Shaun had seriously considered slitting his wrists and bleeding all over a piece of paper for the stupid bitch. "Here you go," he'd say. "This emotional enough for you?"

Emotions were fucking stupid and gay.

New kids trying to be friendly were stupid and gay, as well.

Thinking of Jesse once more—*little jerk*—he took his customary seat in the back of the room and stacked his books around the edges of the desk like a makeshift barrier.

Class started soon after. They were reading poetry again. Some fucked up faggy shit from the 1800s. Somehow, even a straight guy writing about a chick came off sounding incredibly gay when it was written in poetry.

"Shaun? Would you like to read for the class?"

Miss Stevens was a gorgeous woman, young, blonde, and straight out of college. The other boys fantasized about her, Shaun heard them talking sometimes, but he hated Miss Stevens. The bitch had gotten it into her head that he needed to be more active in class and had started forcing him to participate. On his last writing assignment, Miss Stevens had written that she thought Shaun was a great writer, but she knew he could do even better.

Shaun *hated* her.

Apparently, humiliating him and forcing him to read poetry was her great idea to help him improve.

"No," he said through his teeth.

The entire class turned around to stare at him. He could see that fucker Kenny, the jerk who had stolen Jesse's attention on the bus, looking at him and smirking.

"I'd appreciate it, Shaun," Miss Stevens said politely, but she wasn't backing down. Her stare was unwavering. There was no way out.

Clenching his hands into fists, Shaun forced himself to begin reading. Eric, another jock he had problems with, snickered from the front, but Shaun ignored him. He finished the fucked-up poem and then glared at his English teacher.

Miss Stevens smiled at him, totally immune to his death stare at this point. She moved on with the lecture about rhyme scheme and wrote something on the chalkboard.

Fuming, Shaun pulled a pen out of his pocket. He'd sharpened the plastic end to a point with his bowie knife, and now, he touched it gingerly with the tip of his finger. He looked up over the barrier of his textbooks, glaring bitterly across the room at Kenny and Eric.

Slowly, he pulled his shirt sleeve up to his elbow. The skin was pale and scarred. With a steady hand, he jammed the sharp end of his pen into his arm and dragged it across the brutalized flesh. It didn't break the skin, but it hurt.

Sometimes, Shaun liked being in pain.

Miss Stevens stopped blabbing. She called on another student to read the next literary example.

Shaun relaxed a bit. He dropped the pen harmlessly onto the desktop. He had a long, red furrow up his arm now, among the other, older self-inflicted scars. He dug a nail into the red irritated skin but soon grew tired of his self-torture. He felt weary for no reason, and he put his head down on the desk.

Shaun didn't sit up again until the bell rang. He got up quickly and started gathering his things when a hand fell on his shoulder. He whirled around. "What?" he growled.

Miss Stevens crossed her arms and said nothing. Shaun glared at her, and the two of them waited tensely as the room emptied.

"If you weren't such a great writer, Shaun, I'd give you a detention," she said as the last kid left the room. She was smiling though and seemed more amused than anything.

"Go ahead and give me one." It wasn't like it mattered anyway. "I don't care."

"Shaun..." Miss Stevens sighed, looking like she wanted to say something important. She opened her mouth, her eyes gleaming intently, but then she deflated and shook her head. "Never mind."

Shaun raised a bushy brow. "Yeah. Never mind." He grabbed up the last of his things and headed toward the door.

"Don't forget about the poem due at the end of the month," she called after him. "It's worth a lot of points, and I'm expecting something special from you."

Shaun turned back to see her grinning at him like a crazy person. She must really be getting a kick out of whatever it was she thought she was doing.

He sneered at her. "Whatever." He hated teachers who tried to be nice all the time. He'd much rather they be honest and hate him like everyone else did. He stepped out into the hall and ended the uncomfortable conversation.

He made it to second period a little later than usual. He walked into the science room to see everyone was already seated.

The lab tables held two people each. There was an odd number of students, and Shaun had sat alone in the back since the beginning of the year.

He liked it better that way. Alone. He was without distraction and stupid idiots making fun of him. He hated science, and his solo lab work sucked, but he didn't care about school anyway. It didn't matter if he failed.

Except, there was someone sitting at his table today...a very familiar someone.

"Hey." Jesse smiled at him as Shaun slid into his seat against the wall. "I guess we're lab partners now."

Shaun was a little stunned and thus resorted to his usual form of interaction. He scowled at the new boy and slumped further into his seat.

Jesse wasn't affected by the scowl. He continued to peer at Shaun with an intense level of interest, and Shaun glared harder at him. He folded his arms tightly across his chest and snapped, "What?"

"Y-you never finished telling me about your band."

Shaun blinked at him.

He was impressed.

Jesse was interested and still remembered their interrupted conversation.

His glare softened, and he looked Jesse over slowly, feeling a strange stirring of...*something* tickling in his belly.

He was embarrassed to even think it, but...Jesse was cute. Not that Shaun was gay or anything! It was nothing like that! It was just hard not to notice...

Jesse had a beautiful smile, and there was something incredibly...sweet about the way he kept trying to chat Shaun up. The messy auburn hair and sun-kissed freckles were nice, as well. Though Shaun, being completely straight and all, *didn't give a shit.*

"C'mon, dude, don't be so modest," Jesse said playfully. He elbowed Shaun in the side, leaning over much farther than was necessary to whisper in his ear. "It's so boring out here. If you don't tell me where your band plays next, I'll have to start stalking you."

Shaun pulled away immediately. He stared wide-eyed at Jesse, wondering wildly if he was being serious or not. Of course, when Jesse started laughing, Shaun figured he was only joking around.

Oddly, he was a tad disappointed.

Before either boy could say anything else, class started, and Mr. Barnes began the lecture on alkali metals.

Most people were taking notes.

Jesse hurried to pull out some paper and follow their example, but Shaun didn't bother. He watched Jesse from the corner of his eye as he jotted down some notes. His face was close to the page, and his freckled button-nose was wrinkled in thought.

Shaun *hated* him for being so endearing... He had an aching need to hurt himself again.

But he didn't. He couldn't.

Jesse would definitely see him, and there was no way Shaun was explaining his scars.

So, he resorted to drawing idle shapes on the inside cover of his textbook. He got so absorbed in his scribblings that when Jesse shoved a piece of paper at him, he was a little startled.

He glanced over at Jesse, scowling automatically at his cheerful expression. Jesse didn't react one way or the other though. He just went back to writing in his notebook.

Shaun glanced at Jesse's piece of paper.

It was a note.

Gimme your number so we can text.

Shaun huffed and jotted a reply. His writing was much messier than Jesse's. It was an ugly, childish sort of scrawl.

I don't have a phone.

Jesse stared at the piece of paper for a minute, squinting. But after a minute, he quickly wrote back.

That's kind of weird.

Whatever, Shaun wrote sullenly. He'd always thought passing notes was stupid. Not that anyone had ever passed him notes before. Jesse didn't seem to think so though. He changed the subject.

Do you understand any of this stuff? I suck at science. Underneath the message, Jesse drew a stick figure being blown up by a beaker full of chemicals.

Shaun couldn't help himself. He smirked.

Nope, he scrawled below Jesse's line of text. After a moment of consideration, he drew a picture next to Jesse's. A brutal fire monster coming out of a Bunsen burner.

Jesse studied Shaun's newest addition with a smile. *Guess I'm fucked then,* he wrote.

Shaun didn't respond. He took the note back and continued to doodle death and destruction under their lines of correspondence.

Jesse leaned over Shaun's shoulder with his pencil. He made Shaun's fire monster throw little fizzing beakers of deadly chemicals. Shaun vindictively added some dead classmates being burned by the acid.

Shaun grinned menacingly at their drawing. This was kind of fun.

I hope we don't end up like that, Jesse wrote. He drew an arrow to the burning stick figure wearing a Leatherman jacket.

Didn't you hear Mr. Barnes? Chemistry is dangerous, Shaun wrote with a smirk. Jesse added a smiley face next to his words in response.

Shaun gave the happy face evil-looking horns and vampire fangs, and Jesse drew in a hand making the peace sign. Shaun promptly leaned over him and erased the first finger, so it was flipping them the bird.

Jesse threw a hand over his mouth as he started to laugh in earnest. He looked up from their drawing to meet Shaun's cautious gaze, amusement shining in his blue eyes.

Shaun stared back at him in utter amazement. It was the first time he'd ever made someone laugh. But then he realized he was gawking, and he shut his slack jaw.

He glared down at the lab table, affixing his gaze on the black, lusterless surface. He kept his eyes down for the remainder of the lesson.

When the bell rang, Shaun snatched up the paper with their drawings. He folded it into a tiny square and stuffed it in his bag.

Jesse didn't notice. He slid his notebook into his bag and picked up his pencil. "What's your next class?" he asked.

"History," Shaun grunted. He hated history. Almost as much as he hated English and science.

"Oh! Me too," Jesse said. "Want to show me where it is?"

Shaun felt like he didn't have a choice. He was sure Jesse would easily follow him even if he said no. Not that he had a burning desire to refuse.

"I ah...sure." Shaun shouldered his bag and gestured for Jesse to follow him. He did and started up a bubbly conversation about something nonsensical. Shaun was still a little shell-shocked about the whole situation. He didn't catch much of what Jesse was saying unfortunately, and he wondered if maybe Jesse would give him some kind of *quiz* later on, on his memory. He kept waiting for Jesse to abandon him, but it seemed he was interested in Shaun now.

Most people weren't interested in getting past his rough exterior, to actually get to *know* him. Shaun wondered hesitantly if maybe that was Jesse's intention.

Whatever his intentions, Jesse and Shaun were separated in their next class together. The history teacher had strict seating arrangements, and Shaun had been stuck in the front row since the first day of class. He was irritated when Jesse was instructed to sit in the last row, right next to that goodie-two-shoes bitch, Emily Taylor.

"I'll see you after class, okay?" Jesse asked, but he couldn't even wait for a reply. Emily snagged him around the waist, whispering about class starting.

Shaun glared violently after the two of them, but Jesse didn't look his way. He started chatting with Emily, just like he had with Shaun.

He felt a horrible wave of jealousy tear through him as he watched Emily and Jesse together. His whole body vibrated with anger. Watching them felt like some sort of cruel and unusual punishment.

After class, Jesse left history without speaking to Shaun at all. He ran after Emily, and the two of them disappeared down the crowded hall.

There was another class before lunch, and Jesse wasn't in it. Shaun tried not to think about it. He was getting a headache, and the wound on his arm itched.

Lunch was more of the same though. Shaun took his usual table near the back of the room, eating his packed lunch alone with a grimace on his face.

There was no hope in forgetting about Jesse. He was the center of everyone's attention. Across the room, the entire eleventh grade mobbed his table. Shaun was feeling bitter, but he couldn't help watching Jesse laugh and talk excitedly with his classmates.

Jesse looked extremely happy as he joked around with Kenny and Eric and the other shit-head jocks. They were doubtlessly talking about sports or some other shit Shaun could never relate to. Shaun gave them a dirty look.

The two most popular girls in school, Sara and Alicia, watched Jesse with smiles on their faces. They giggled like idiots, and Emily, who sat directly to Jesse's right, kept giving the two girls territorial looks.

Shaun ate his lunch in a terrible mood. Jesse said he was single? Well, by Shaun's estimation, he wouldn't be for long...

He saw Jesse only one more time that day.

After lunch, half the eleventh graders had gym, so it wasn't a surprise when Jesse showed up in Shaun's class.

Shaun was already in the locker room when Jesse invaded the area.

Kenny and Eric followed him in like puppies. It seemed Jesse was telling one of his football stories, and the two jocks behind him listened raptly as they found spots to dress for class.

Nobody noticed Shaun changing in the corner.

Jesse threw his arms in the air as he made an impossible catch with an invisible ball. Everyone laughed at the stupid look of victory on his face directly after, and Jesse *glowed* with the acceptance.

Shaun jerked his hoodie over his head and hurriedly stuffed his arms through the holes. He stabbed his feet into his tennis shoes and then stormed from the room with a growl.

Today, they were playing kickball outside.

Shaun was grateful he wasn't put on the same team as Jesse. He honestly didn't think he could have played if he'd had to be teammates with that jerk. And Jesse was a *fucking jerk...*

During the first round, Shaun could feel Jesse's eyes on him. Kenny had forced him into the outfield with a single mean look. Shaun was used to it. He didn't argue or cause a fuss. He was still furious though, and Jesse's pretty blue eyes on him increased his anger exponentially.

Why couldn't Jesse make up his mind already? Why was he bothering to waste his time staring at Shaun when he was *oh-so-happy* with his new bullshit friends? Why couldn't he just leave well enough alone?!

Shaun didn't move from his spot in the outfield. He ground his teeth to dust as he watched Eric and Jesse run the bases.

Jesse kept sneaking looks at Shaun. He just couldn't seem to stop for some reason.

The teams switched positions after twenty minutes. Everyone was getting the chance to kick the ball.

Shaun was shoved to the back of the line; he was used to that too, but he waited patiently for his turn.

Jesse was on third base. Eric was pitching the ball. Shaun hated how well they played together. This game *sucked.*

When it was Shaun's turn to kick, Eric gave him a bored look. Shaun stood far behind the plate, but no one bothered to correct him.

Eric smirked meanly. He wound up his arm and threw the ball low and hard.

Shaun had been waiting for this. His eyes narrowed on the ball. He took a running leap, angled his foot, and kicked it as hard as he could back at the unsuspecting jock. Shaun had the pleasure of watching the smile slide from Eric's face seconds before the ball struck him square in the nose.

Everyone fell silent as Eric yelled in pain. He staggered and pressed his hands to his nose as it began to spurt blood. The coach sprinted from the dugout to help. As he passed, the coach banged his shoulder into Shaun's. The cold look he threw over his shoulder proved it had been on purpose.

Whatever. Eric deserved a broken nose. They *all* deserved to bleed and die.

Baring his teeth in a vicious smile, Shaun looked Jesse's way.

Jesse was still on third base. He seemed to be frozen in place. His face had paled and, his eyes were wide with fright.

Slowly, Shaun's smile grew wider and more terrifying. He felt he wouldn't have to worry about Jesse trying to be friendly anymore.

*

Shaun couldn't play anymore kickball that day. Like he cared.

After gym, he had math class by himself, just the way he liked it. Study hall was the last class of the day, but Shaun never stuck around. As usual, he skipped out early and walked home. It wasn't strictly allowed, but nobody really gave a crap either.

He spent the walk home listening to his CD player and compiling the day's many injustices. By the time he got to the house, only a few minutes before the bus would be driving past, he was angry again and decided he'd make a new cut on his arm. The last one he'd made was already scabbed over, and digging at a scab wasn't as satisfying as a bleeding wound.

Ruth, Shaun's grandma, was in the kitchen when Shaun walked through the door radiating gloom.

"Shaun?" she called from the back, her voice shrill and irritating.

Shaun didn't bother to answer. He trekked through the kitchen in silence. As soon as he entered the living room, Ruth poked her head out of the back room.

"What are you doing home so early?" she asked, narrowing her squinty eyes. She and Shaun looked a lot alike. They both had the same frizzy hair, though lately Ruth's was getting more gray than brown. They had the same scowl and the same narrow unpleasant eyes. Ruth did have about fifty pounds on Shaun, though, and had a hard time moving around the tiny, cluttered house. She was wearing a faded house dress and slippers.

"I'm home on time," Shaun sneered. He usually waited until the bus passed the house because Ruth was annoying enough to actually care if he skipped study hall.

To distract her, he stepped around the armchair and grabbed the TV remote. He turned it up as loud as it would go and pretended to watch the boring western program.

Ruth rolled her eyes and disappeared back into the other room. It took a few minutes, but he eventually saw the bus go past the front window. Ruth didn't hear it over the sound of the TV. Thinking himself rather clever, Shaun waited another minute, watching the lame movie on TV, before he shut it off and ventured down the hall to his bedroom.

"Shaun?" Ruth called from the master suite.

"What? I'm going to start on homework."

Ruth said nothing more, and Shaun shrugged his way into his messy bedroom.

It smelled musty, a mix of sweat, dried jizz, and pot. It didn't bother Shaun though; he barely even noticed. He threw his school shit down and picked his way over a pile of accumulated clothes, some dirty and some clean—not that he could tell them apart—and fucked around with his stereo system. He smiled grimly when Iron Maiden came on.

As the music filled the room, Shaun sat down on the edge of his bed. He opened his bedside table drawer and drew out his bowie knife.

It had been his father's hunting knife, but Shaun had owned it since he was six years old. It wasn't flashy or anything. It was a simple, curved blade with a dull, black grip. Shaun had sharpened the hell out of it though, and that's all that really mattered to him.

Shaun didn't cry or think about how horrified his stupid classmates would be if they could see him. Physically, he didn't even feel much as the knife pressed into the crook of his arm. It hurt, but the pain was a delicious feeling. He cut deeper, forcing the tip into his scarred flesh. He followed the line his pen had taken earlier that morning and opened his skin for real.

As dark-red blood welled from the wound and slid down into the palm of his hand, all the stupid thoughts about Jesse disappeared.

Later, Shaun cleaned his arm and bandaged it tightly to stop the bleeding. He put on a long-sleeved shirt to hide the evidence. He didn't own many short-sleeved tops.

He rolled a joint and smoked out his bedroom window. He clutched his wounded arm as he stared sightlessly at the unending landscape of fields and trees. He decided when he felt the pain the next day, it'd be his reminder not to get too close to anyone—specifically *Jesse*.

He reasoned that if he could hurt himself this much, Jesse would hurt him worse.

Shaun smoked for an hour. He always felt relaxed after he fucked himself up, but the pot made it even better. He was so calm that when Eli entered his room without knocking, he only gave the man a slightly offended look.

"Dinner's ready," Eli said. He snatched the joint from Shaun and took a hit.

"I'm not hungry." Shaun patiently waited until Eli gave him his pot back, absently digging his fingers into his new cut. It had a calming effect.

"Come tell your grandma that, son," Eli said, smiling.

Shaun sighed and took one last deep pull on the roach before he threw it into the dead bushes below his window. He wondered dreamily if all the joints he'd thrown down there had killed them.

Reluctantly, he followed Eli back to the kitchen. Ruth was just pulling a roast out of the oven.

"How was your day?" Eli asked as Shaun slid into his seat.

"Fucked up," Shaun said easily.

"Watch your language, young man," Ruth screeched. She hurried to set the roast on the table so she could hit Shaun upside the head. He scowled.

Ruth plopped into her seat across from Eli. The chair creaked ominously under her weight. "Who wants to say grace?" she asked loudly as she folded her pudgy fingers together.

"I will," Shaun sneered.

Ruth narrowed her eyes. "Do it right," she insisted. "Jesus is watching."

"Fine," Shaun sighed. He waited for his grandparents to bow their heads. He ducked his and began. "Bless this food, Lord, that my grandma made and that my grandpa paid for. We are helpless without your wonderful bounty. Jesus Christ, thank you. So, fucking much."

"Amen," Eli said, sounding amused.

Ruth smacked the back of Shaun's head again, but he was in way too good a mood to let that bother him.

Insulting Jesus always put him in a good mood.

Chapter Three

When Jesse came home, the house was blissfully empty. Well, except for Sam, but he didn't count. He was usually annoying, like he was currently, but Jesse was used to it.

Besides, Sam's whiny complaints were pretty funny today. He was super upset because those pretty little girls on the bus had followed him around the entire day, watching him.

"You're such a little kid," Jesse laughed as he ruffled Sam's hair. He remembered the days when all girls had cooties and females in general were a mysterious, otherworldly race.

"I am not!" Sam yelled, but Jesse ignored him. He sprawled out on the couch and put his feet up on one of the half-emptied boxes still stacked around the room. He turned the TV on to drown out the sound of Sam's wailing.

Eventually, the younger teenager grew tired of being ignored, and he stormed upstairs to be alone.

Jesse turned down the TV and sighed in the sudden quiet.

The lack of animosity was nice, but he still couldn't relax.

He couldn't stop thinking about the terrifying boy who lived down the road.

The gym teacher had called it an accident, and Shaun had been forced to sit in the dugout until the game ended, but Shaun hadn't looked very sorry.

The look on his face as he'd sat in the dugout, *fuck*...the expression he'd worn as he'd kicked the ball into Eric's face with a scary precision had been one filled with a slimy, smug satisfaction.

It was a frightening look, and he'd gazed at Jesse for the rest of gym class with the grim smile stuck on his lips.

Jesse wasn't paranoid, but he couldn't help but think Shaun had meant something with that creepy smile. Maybe people really didn't talk to him for a reason. Everyone had told him to stay away, but of course Jesse had ignored them, *like an idiot.*

In fact, Shaun had been acting "off" since they'd met just that morning. Gloomy, moody, glaring one minute and then being borderline friendly, or at least accommodating, the next. Jesse had been hoping Shaun would come and sit with him during lunch, but he had placed himself way across the room and had commenced yet another one-way staring match.

Jesse had tried not to stare back. He felt uncomfortable, and he involved himself with the other people around him instead to distract himself.

But Shaun hadn't let up.

He'd been completely unapproachable during gym too—even before the incident with the kickball.

Everyone had been giving Shaun extra space, like they'd known he was about to do something crazy. And then he'd exploded...

Jesse didn't know what to do. He sat with Shaun in chemistry for fuck's sake! They rode the same bus! Though Shaun had been mysteriously missing on the ride home.

Jesse felt like maybe he should back off and leave Shaun alone like he apparently preferred, but he didn't feel comfortable doing that either. After all, he couldn't very well sit next to him and never talk to him! It was impracticable! Plus, it would be really boring.

Jesse thought about the dilemma off and on all night.

Monica came home with a new job. She started training the next day and had brought home a bunch of fast food to celebrate.

Nobody was impressed though.

The twins were bouncing off the walls again and talking nonstop about their days. Both Melissa and Brian were crying, trying to outdo the other by raising their voices until Jesse would rather shove pencils, sharp points first, into his ears than listen to them anymore. Sam was still moping about the middle school girls, and he grabbed his fast food bag and took it upstairs.

Jesse wished he could escape the mayhem, but Monica needed him. They spent a good two hours coddling two five-year-olds, a toddler, and a screaming baby. The two of them ran themselves ragged.

Luckily, the screaming also wore out the two youngest members of the family. Brian and Melissa were in bed by ten.

Monica and Jesse got the twins ready for bed next and got them settled in their beds. Monica put switched the night light on, and Jesse found a CD with lullabies. They shut the door on them, and Monica let out a sigh of relief.

They called it a night. Monica disappeared into the bathroom to wash her face and brush her teeth. Jesse dragged himself to his room and up to his bed. Sam was texting someone down in the lower bunk. His screen was at max brightness. Jesse rolled over the face the wall, and it didn't bother him anymore. He fell asleep within minutes.

A good night's sleep did little to make up Jesse's mind, though, and he was still divided when he got on the bus the next morning.

He sat separate from his brother, and when Sam tried to sit next to him again, Jesse shoved his backpack into the empty space and didn't allow it. Sam sulked off toward the front of the bus, resigning himself to the middle schoolers.

Then the bus stopped in front of Shaun's house. Jesse's whole body stiffened to the point of discomfort.

Shaun got on the bus, a scowl already on his face. He wore a ripped, long-sleeved flannel over the same T-shirt he'd had on yesterday. His dark hair was a rat's nest. He smelled even worse too. Sweaty with a musky hint of smoke.

Jesse followed Shaun with his eyes. An extreme aura of hostility rolled off Shaun, and Jesse's belly filled with lead. Shaun slumped into the seat behind him and pulled his bag into his chest. He glared at Jesse hatefully.

"Hi," Jesse said cautiously.

Shaun was silent. He continued to glare.

Jesse felt itchy all over and highly unwelcomed. He waited tensely for Shaun to say something, anything, but after a few uneasy moments, he gave up and turned to face the front of the bus.

He couldn't think of one thing he'd done to make Shaun look at him like that. He thought they'd been getting along reasonably well the day before.

Soon enough, Kenny, Emily, and the rest of the gang got on the bus, and Jesse was bombarded by their friendly chattering. At least there was no mystery with these guys.

Second-period chemistry was even weirder.

Jesse didn't even attempt to talk to Shaun. He was already seated and scowling something fierce when Jesse came into the room.

Jesse took the hint and silently took his seat.

Class started, and Shaun began to glare hatefully at the teacher, the board, the backs of random kids' heads. Jesse watched him from the corner of his eye, deeply uncomfortable.

Every so often, Shaun took a break from the glaring to grab his left arm. His grip would slowly grow tighter until he was squeezing the shirt-covered flesh in what looked to be a painful grip.

While there wasn't anything especially strange about that, it was the look on Shaun's face when he did it that was disturbing. He got a weird, pained expression on his face, and all the color drained out of his cheeks. Then he'd smile. And it was the creepiest smile Jesse had ever seen. His lips pressed together until they were bloodless, and they turned upward at the corners, just barely.

After Shaun had done this a few times, he seemed to realize Jesse was watching him. He turned that creepy smile on Jesse, then, his eyes darkening.

Jesse looked away quickly as the hairs on the back of his neck stood up straight.

After that, he kept to himself. He stared down at his notebook and tried to jot down a few important facts.

"Are you okay?" Emily asked when Jesse arrived in history.

"Yeah...fine." Jesse's eyes followed Shaun's gloomy figure as he shuffled into the classroom. He tossed his bag onto his desk and then slumped into his seat. He hunched over the desk and built a shield between himself and his classmates with his stuff.

"Are you sure?" Emily leaned into Jesse's field of vision.

Jesse blinked. "Shaun's acting weird," he said sheepishly.

"When isn't he?" Emily flipped her hair over her shoulder and looked a lot less interested. "We told you to stay away from him. I don't have anything against him. It's just that…"

"Yeah?" Jesse wanted to know what it was about Shaun that made him seem so inherently dangerous. Maybe he was just imagining things. Maybe everyone disliked him because he smelled weird.

Emily shook her head. "This isn't the place to talk about that."

Jesse raised a brow, now intensely curious. He decided to whine and bitch until Emily told him everything she knew about the dark and sullen boy when the bell rang and class started. It seemed he had to wait.

But when class ended, Emily didn't bring up the topic again. Jesse wanted to ask but didn't want to mention Shaun a second time. He didn't want her to think he was obsessed or anything.

So, he stuck with studying Shaun from afar, pretending he wasn't somehow drawn to him despite his nastiness.

The day crawled by, but it ended in due time. Jesse and his new friends got on the bus home and found seats in the back.

For the second time, Shaun didn't show up for the trip.

Back home wasn't much better. The hospital had Monica on a weird schedule and promised it'd be temporary, but either way, tonight was Jesse's first night of what he suspected would be yet another long-term commitment to babysitting.

The twins got home an hour after Jesse and Sam did, and then Monica showed up around dinnertime to drop off Brian and Lissa. She had to use her "lunch" break to get them home. She was avoiding additional daycare costs, much to Jesse's annoyance. She wouldn't be home again until bedtime.

It was utter hell having to take care of five younger siblings every night on top of homework—not that he was especially worried about the homework part, to be honest.

Either way, Jesse was pulling his hair out long before Friday came around. The frustrations of constant responsibility were wearing him down.

That morning, when Jesse got on the bus, he knew better than to sit by Shaun, so he found a seat in the middle of the bus and waited for his friends to get on.

Kenny sat beside Jesse automatically. "Hey, man."

"Hi," Emily and Sunny said at the same time as they sat in front of them.

Lee waved as she waddled to her seat. Behind her, Rick had a hand on the small of her back, leading her protectively down the aisle. He was silent most of the time, but he was a good guy.

"What are you doing tonight?" Kenny asked when the bus started moving again.

Jesse wrinkled his nose. "Babysitting until my mom gets home."

Kenny gave him a sympathetic look. Jesse had complained once or twice about the unfairness of having so many brothers and sisters. He'd managed to make a joke out of it, making his rapt audience laugh, but he didn't really think it was funny.

"Until when?" Sunny butted in, her eyes hopeful as she peered over the back of her seat.

"I don't know, probably around eight."

"That's okay. We could pick you up around then." Kenny shrugged.

"Yeah, parties around here don't start until the sun goes down anyway," Emily added.

Jesse grinned. A party was just what he needed to unwind after a long first week. He didn't know what a party would be like out in the middle of nowhere, but it had to be better than babysitting and school.

"Sure. That'd be great!"

Thank God. Jesse's crappy week was finally looking up.

And then he remembered he had a chemistry lab with Shaun this morning.

Shit.

Squirming, Jesse sat through his first period math class. He and Kenny's friend, Jordan, had class together. Jesse kind of thought Jordan was an asshole, but they talked some. However, today, Jordan kept giving him dirty looks.

"Dude, stop kicking my seat," Jordon whispered over his shoulder.

Jesse forced himself to stop shifting in his seat. He studied Jordan's dreadlocks instead.

He was nervous though. It would be the first time he'd interacted with Shaun in days, and he didn't really know how he felt about that. Shaun had kept up the creepy act, going from completely ignoring Jesse to glaring at him bitterly. He kept doing that thing with his arm too, and once, during lunch, Jesse saw Shaun jab a pen into his hand!

Math ended, and Jesse leapt up and started to gather his things.

"What are you so excited about?" Jordan drawled. He followed Jesse's example, but at a much slower rate.

Jesse shrugged. "I have chemistry next." He finished packing and moved to exit the room.

"Oh." Much to Jesse's irritation, Jordan fell into step beside him with ease. "My brother had chemistry two years ago. He told me the whole 'exploding metals' thing is really lame."

"Hmm."

"I mean, can't these so-called *college-educated* teachers think of anything more interesting than alkali metals?"

"I don't know. It's better than worksheets and notes."

"You've got a point there. Honestly, the amount of busywork we get is unbelievable. Do you really think we need most of the math we learn in there?" Jordan pointed back the way they'd just came before answering his own question. "Math is mental masturbation, and people with no lives like to scribble equations down so everyone can see what great big cocks they have." Jordan laughed at his own joke. "I don't mean literally of course. That whole myth about 'if you don't use it, you lose it' is true, and everybody knows guys who make up equations for a living don't get any."

"Um..." Jesse didn't know how Jordan had gone from talking about the chemistry lab to making fun of mathematicians. "I think that's my class over there," he said.

"Yeah, I think it is too." Jordan mocked him. "See you in lunch."

"Okay, bye." Jesse attempted a smile, though he wasn't really feeling up for it. He tried though, and that's all that really mattered. Jordan was too busy being a jerk to notice anyway.

Jesse went inside, glad when he saw that he'd arrived before Shaun. He took his customary seat but didn't take anything out of his bag except his notebook. They'd have to take some notes on the reactions, but other than that, there wasn't much else they'd have to do today.

The moment Shaun came in the room, Jesse could feel it. He didn't even have to look up. He just *knew* he was nearby.

It was weird and Jesse was a little concerned he'd become so attuned to another boy that he could literally *feel* him from across a room, but he was perfectly happy explaining it away.

Shaun did have quite a presence.

"Are you ready for this?"

For a second, Jesse thought Shaun had spoken to him. But that was just wishful thinking. It was a girl's voice anyway.

It was Sara who had spoken up.

She was a gorgeous girl with blonde-streaked hair and a slim body. She was at the table next to theirs, and Jesse had started talking to her before class since Shaun had continued the silent treatment at every opportunity.

"Yes, I heard it's going to be really cool," Jesse said.

Sara laughed. "Who told you that?" She crossed her long, bare legs, smiling flirtatiously when she caught Jesse looking. "Mr. Barnes could make the Fourth of July boring."

Normally, Jesse wouldn't have had a chance with Sara, but since he was new and there was a limited supply of guys to choose from, he thought he might actually have a shot with her. Unless, of course, she wasn't already dating Eric.

Either way, Jesse was about to say something lame, like "You're the hottest firecracker I've ever seen," but luckily, class began before he could get it out. Sara smiled at him once more before she turned back to her seat and opened her notes.

Mr. Barnes started lecturing about chemical reactions—why they reacted, how they reacted, how much they reacted, before he went on to explain the safety measures and lab procedures. Class was almost over before everyone had their safety goggles on and their aprons tied.

Then it was time for Mr. Barnes to begin his demonstration. He started out with the more reactive metals, leaving the boring ones for the lab.

"Class, this is potassium," Barnes said as he sprinkled the substance into his bowl of water. The flakes broke into tiny pieces that caught fire and exploded with soft pops and fizzles.

It was pretty neat.

Beside him, Shaun leaned forward eagerly like he was trying to get a good look.

"And this is rubidium," Barnes continued, sprinkling a tiny amount into the bowl. It flared up the instant it hit the water, shooting out of the bowl like little neon fireworks.

"Fuck..." Shaun muttered, looking highly entertained. Jesse couldn't help being amused by his neighbor's reaction. He ducked his head and smiled softly.

"You'll be working with lithium and sodium, which are much less reactive, but I want you to describe what takes place anyway. When you're done with the reactions, complete the questions I've written on the board, and then turn in your lab before you go." Barnes waited for everyone to settle down before he asked for one person from each table to come up to the front of the room and take a small sample of both metals, and for the other group member to get the bowls and water.

Shaun got up and started to move toward the front of the room, but Jesse got a brilliant idea.

"Wait." He grabbed Shaun's shoulder.

Shaun whirled around, a fiery anger in his dark eyes.

"G-get the water, would you?" Jesse said in a rush before Shaun could bite his head off.

Shaun shrugged Jesse's hand off his shoulder. His nostrils flared. He looked highly offended. "You fucking do it," he said violently and started to move toward the front of the room again.

Knowing he should really give in and let Shaun do as he pleased, Jesse touched Shaun's left forearm, right where he was always squeezing and abusing himself.

Shaun froze.

"I promise it'll be worth it."

People were watching them as they wove around their table to prepare their labs. If Jesse couldn't convince Shaun to let him go up front very soon, then all this would be for nothing.

"Please?" he said, batting his eyelashes.

Shaun jerked his arm away, scowling darkly even as his cheeks flushed an ugly brick red. He didn't say anything, but he went toward the back of the room where the bowls and faucets were. Jesse smiled after him, amazed he'd been able to convince the wild beast.

But there was no time to pat himself on the back.

He rushed to the front of the room and eased his way through the disordered group of students gathering supplies.

It was way too easy. Really, *really*, easy to get a sample of rubidium into his petri dish.

He almost felt bad about it as he was doing it, which was just as well as he'd need to look awfully repentant to get out of this without a suspension or worse.

"Mr. Barnes?" he asked casually, sidling up next to the middle-aged science teacher.

"Ah...yes...Mr. Welch?" Jesse always thought it was funny when a teacher called him by his last name. He felt all formal and goofy as a "Mr." anybody.

"I just wanted to say how cool it is that we get to actually have a hands-on lab here. There were thirty kids in my last chemistry class. There was *no way* a single teacher could supervise an entire lab of us," he said dramatically. "You really make this an interesting class."

Barnes turned to Jesse, his eyebrows raised with incredulity. "Thank you, Mr. Welch, that's very nice of you to say. I'd like to try some new labs this year, as well. We got the levy passed a couple months ago, so we'll be improving the curriculum this year. You've come at a good time."

"Really? That's great. What sort of labs?"

It was then as Barnes blabbed on about all the boring things they'd be doing later in the year that Jesse reached out, trying to appear casual as he blindly searched for the small bottles of metals.

Nodding, he took a scoop of lithium in one dish and then reached for the rubidium when Barnes was busy scratching his head and trying to remember the exact specifics of a lab on covalent bonds.

"That sounds really cool, Mr. Barnes," Jesse said politely. "But I'd better get back to work. I don't want to turn in a bad first lab."

Barnes smiled pleasantly. "No, I suppose you don't."

"Thanks." Jesse hurried back to his seat and hunkered down beside Shaun.

"You done?" he sneered. "I thought you were going to suck him off."

Jesse shuddered. "You have a sick mind."

Shaun's face lost all expression at the mild insult, something Jesse recognized as a defensive mechanism. Hopefully, he could convince Shaun to drop all the wariness and hostility after this.

"Go on then." Shaun snapped as he watched Jesse fidget with indecision. He wondered if this poorly concocted plan was literally going to blow up in his face. "Do it already so we can finish."

"You first." Jesse nervously pushed the lithium across the table to Shaun.

The other boy snatched it up, sprinkling the powdery stuff all over the table. He held what was left over the water and scattered the small pile into the bowl. The lithium gathered into a little ball and skated across the water's surface, fizzing, and emitting the faintest hint of gas.

Shaun snatched up his notebook. He muttered to himself as he wrote in the reaction. "Fucking boring..." he bitched as he scribbled away.

Jesse wrote his reaction in, as well, and managed to finish first. He set his pencil aside and waited patiently for Shaun to look up again.

"Well, go on," Shaun said impatiently.

Jesse cracked a grin. "Ready?"

"For fuck's sake…" Shaun's cheeks flushed red again. It was a curious color on his normally pale face. Jesse's smile got wider.

"Seriously. Are you ready?" he prodded, grinning from ear to ear.

"Fuck you! I'm ready," Shaun hissed and glared daggers at Jesse. His cheeks were getting even redder, and his hair seemed to be getting frizzier and more unkempt with his foul mood.

"Trust me, you'll like this," Jesse said confidently. He moved the petri dish over the bowl of water, and with the other hand, he pushed firmly on Shaun's chest, steering him out of harm's way.

"What the—" Shaun's angry words were cut off as the rubidium hit the water and exploded brilliantly.

Jesse didn't even have to pretend when he jumped back, toppling his chair in surprise. That had been *way* better than Mr. Barnes' demonstration. Much closer anyway.

The entire lab erupted in chaos. People screamed and jumped. Chairs were overturned; someone splashed a bowl of water all over the floor. Everyone's eyes were instantly drawn to their little desk in the corner as Mr. Barnes, startled and horrified, came rushing down the aisle to assess the damage.

But it was totally worth it.

In the split second before the teacher was on them, questioning them sternly, Shaun looked at Jesse and actually smiled.

And that's what had gotten the two of them in so much trouble.

After separate trips to the office and one grim-faced lecture from the principal, Jesse and Shaun got the most devastating punishment of all, Friday after-school detention.

"Sorry about that," Jesse said sheepishly when they were alone. They'd been sent to their history class with late passes, but there was only five minutes left of class, so neither of them were hurrying.

"It's cool," Shaun said, and he really did seem cool with it. It almost seemed like he was having a good time. "That was fucking badass."

"Yeah. It was pretty sweet, huh?"

"Fuck yeah." Shaun smirked at him, and Jesse couldn't help but stare. He looked so normal when he smiled like that. In a flash, Jesse realized that part of what made Shaun so unattractive was his constant scowling and glaring. Well, he still had bad skin and hair and questionable hygiene, but he looked like a normal person when he smiled and not like such an unapproachable one.

"Well, I am sorry about the detention."

"Whatever. I get detention a lot." Shaun shrugged. "I'll walk home afterward."

"Yeah, I'll have to walk too. My mom's at work."

Jesse suddenly didn't mind that he'd have to stay after school. He'd have Shaun all to himself on the walk home, and they'd get an uninterrupted amount of time to talk.

Shaun stopped at a random locker and paused to enter the combination. Jesse hadn't realized they were walking anywhere specific until just then, and he watched Shaun sort through his things with curiosity. It looked normal enough. Books and notebooks were haphazardly crammed together among a pile of crumpled paper.

"What are those?"

Shaun slowly turned around, glaring at Jesse. He snatched several books from his locker and slammed it shut. "Nothing," he growled; then he stormed off.

What the fuck!

Jesse hurried after Shaun, wondering what he'd done now.

"Wait up," he called. He had to resist the urge to grab Shaun's shoulder again. He didn't think it'd go over well.

Shaun slowed to a reasonable pace. Jesse caught up on his shorter legs and searched desperately for a new topic of conversation. Somehow, he managed to make it worse. "What are you doing this weekend?" he blurted.

"I can tell you want I'm not doing," Shaun snapped. "Going to that *fucking* party."

"Why not?" Jesse felt like a complete ass for even asking. "Okay, dumb question," he said quickly, receiving a snort of amusement from Shaun. It was on the tip of his tongue to ask what it was exactly that made the other kids hate Shaun so much, but he stopped himself just in time.

"Yeah, fucking stupid question," Shaun said bitterly.

"Listen...I'm sorry. I just—" Jesse cut himself off, not exactly sure what he was going to say. "I just want to be your friend, okay?"

Shaun's eyes flashed. "Why?" he asked, sounding curious despite the unpleasant edge to his tone.

"Why?" Jesse repeated. "Well, why not? I think you're interesting. I like you—"

"Oh, you like me? What, do I make you happy? Do I entertain you?" Shaun whirled around, his voice wavering dangerously. "Are you fucking amused?!"

"No," Jesse said quickly. He lowered his eyes. "There's just something about you that..." He had no idea how to describe the strange pull Shaun had on him, and he didn't really want to either. He was afraid he'd only sound gay if he did. "Fuck, Shaun! What's so terrible about wanting to get to know you?" He blushed as he said it, embarrassed that he had to spell out something as simple as friendship.

"You want to get to know me? All right," Shaun said angrily. "I'll save you some fucking time." His voice rose sharply until he was shouting, and Jesse automatically shrank back. "I'm a white trash, son of a bitch who genuinely hates every last fucker in this damn town!" Shaun ranted. "I'm an ugly fucking asshole, a disgusting bastard, a motherfucking psychopath," he continued, his eyes blazing dangerously again. "I'm going to hell, and you know what, I don't fucking care!" He finished with a roar and glared at Jesse hatefully, breathing hard, his face red, before he turned on his heel and stalked off.

Stunned, Jesse stared after Shaun. It took him all of five seconds before he decided to go after him, but the moment he made a move to go after Shaun's retreating figure, the bell rang, and the halls began to flood with kids going to their next class.

"Hey." Emily emerged from the crowd. "I heard you blew up the science room." She stood in front of Jesse, trying to get him to look at her. Jesse was still staring after Shaun, however, lost in thought. "What?" she asked, following Jesse's gaze down the hall.

"Nothing," Jesse said after a moment. He turned blindly and started walking toward English, the next class on the schedule.

Luckily, Emily didn't pry. She did offer to pick Jesse up after his detention, though.

"It's my brother's truck, but I could come pick you up if you wanted. He'll probably offer actually," she said. The thought of Kenny picking Jesse up instead of her made a sour look flash across her face. Jesse wasn't paying attention, though. He missed the expression.

"No, I can walk," he said vaguely, thinking that Shaun would have to talk to him then. He'd have nowhere else to go.

"Why would you rather walk?" Emily asked in exasperation.

Jesse shrugged. He didn't want to tell Emily the real reason. She'd only try to dissuade him. "More time away from my brothers and sisters," he said coolly. He hadn't thought of it that way, but now that he did, it was a good idea. Maybe he should walk home every day.

"Well, I mean, I don't have to take you home right away," Emily said suggestively, but once again Jesse was oblivious.

"That's okay. I'll walk," he repeated, glad when they got to English and could drop the conversation.

Emily went sulkily to her seat, but he didn't really notice.

Jesse was practically famous by lunch time. Everyone had heard about chemistry and the huge explosion. He was sure it got bigger every single time someone asked him about it.

"It hit Shaun in the face, right?" Eric asked between massive bites of cafeteria sloppy joe.

"Yeah, I heard it blew a hole in the ceiling," Alicia said.

"No, someone told me it set half the room on fire," Kenny said as surely as if he'd been there himself.

But then again...

"Oh my God, you guys! I was there, and it was totally the size of the *freaking* atomic bomb! It was like mushrooming and everything!" Sara cried as she elbowed her way in front of Kenny.

Jesse laughed at the commotion. He didn't know what to say.

He got several offers for rides, but he awkwardly turned them all down. Nobody could understand why he would rather walk, and maybe he ought to give up his little mission to go home with Shaun. He seemed to be missing. Jesse had figured out that the reason Shaun was never on the bus after school was because he was skipping and walking home early. He wasn't at his lunch table, so it was a reasonable leap of logic to assume he'd gone home after their fight...if it could be called a fight.

People congratulated him on his stunt in chemistry all day long. Jesse smiled each time, but by his last class of the day he was getting tired of it. He still hadn't caught sight of Shaun, and now he was really starting to regret turning down all those ride offers.

He stuck with it though.

When class ended for the day, he went straight to the study hall room, where after-school detention was held. He gave the tired-looking woman in charge his name and sat down in the back of the room a few chairs away from a freshman boy he'd met briefly the other day in lunch and two girls who were surreptitiously texting each other under their desks.

The old gray-haired woman waited, watching the clock intently. Another two more boys came in, one after the other, and one more girl. They found seats and dutifully pulled out things to do. There was no sign of Shaun.

The woman waited for a few more minutes until it was three o'clock exactly. Then she strode over to the door and started to close it when a booted foot slotted through and blocked the jam.

"You're late," she said grumpily.

"Right on time," Shaun said as he shoved his way inside the room. He made his way to the back row and sat beside Jesse. He looked over at Jesse, taking in his pleased smile. He glared half-heartedly in response, took out his English book and a pad of paper, and started to write.

"Let's get busy, people. You've got an hour," the detention monitor barked from the front of the room. "No talking, no texting." She shot the two girls a look, and they sheepishly put their phones away. "No eating, sleeping, or staring at the walls."

Unable to keep from smiling completely, Jesse got out some of his math homework and got started. It was much easier to do when there weren't little kids running around all over the place; it was almost like Jordan had said, math was mental masturbation. Whenever he struggled with a problem and got it right, the warm happy feeling he got in the pit of his stomach was similar to rubbing one out onto his sheets. Not as good, mind, but almost as satisfying.

By the time the hour was up, Jesse had finished his homework and was doodling in the margins, trying to think of the best way to approach Shaun.

He didn't know why he was so obsessed with him, so it wasn't like he could justify himself to Shaun or give him a concrete answer as to why he wanted to be friends with him. Jesse hadn't been kidding or bullshitting around though when he'd said Shaun was interesting. In all the many places Jesse had lived, he'd never met anyone quite like him.

Plus, that quicksilver smile he'd shot Jesse right before they'd been hauled off to the principal's office had been strangely amazing. He wanted to see it again.

"All right, times up," the gray-haired woman announced, standing up from her desk. "Have a good weekend, folks. And stay out of trouble." Her gaze narrowed on Shaun specifically, though he didn't seem to notice or care. He forced his things into his bag, slung it over his shoulder, and stormed out of the room.

Jesse gathered his things up randomly. He tripped over himself as he ran to catch up with Shaun.

He was still shoving his things in his bag when he ran headfirst into Shaun's back.

"Jesus fucking Christ!" Shaun hissed, grabbing Jesse's shoulder to steady him. "What the fuck's your problem?"

"I'm trying to find you before you disappear again," Jesse accused with a glare. His glare wasn't as effective as Shaun's was, but he didn't care.

Shaun raised one of his bushy eyebrows. "I'm fucking waiting for you."

Jesse frowned, pouted more like, up at Shaun, unwilling to trust him on his word. "Sure, you were."

"Well, are you coming or not!" Shaun obviously wasn't about to convince him, so Jesse finished shoving his things into his bag and nodded curtly. He followed Shaun outside.

"I'm surprised your legion of friends didn't offer to pick you up," Shaun grunted. He looked critically around the empty parking lot before he started off toward the road.

Knowing Shaun reacted badly whenever the other kids were brought up, Jesse shrugged.

Shaun scoffed as if Jesse had just finished a speech on their innumerable good qualities, stalking down the road as he sought to put a considerable amount of distance between them. Jesse had to jog to keep up.

He didn't know where to go with this. All his plans had centered around him having to convince Shaun to even let him near enough to speak. But now that Shaun was here, and somewhat open to listening, he wasn't sure what he should say.

He decided to wing it. The first words out of his mouth were "Do you really believe you're going to hell?"

"Of course, I do," Shaun said flatly. "I wouldn't lie about something like that."

Jesse bit his lip. "I just thought you were exaggerating or something." He'd never met anyone who truly believed they were damned for hell. He'd met people who didn't believe in it, but never anyone who sounded like they expected it.

"My stupid grandma tells me enough." Shaun shrugged.

Well, they were further than they had been this afternoon, Jesse thought to himself. At least Shaun was talking.

"You live with your grandparents?"

"Yes." Jesse started to ask where Shaun's parents were, but Shaun cut him off with a severe look. "Don't ask," he said dangerously.

Jesse shut his mouth, embarrassed, though slightly grateful that Shaun was giving him some sort of clue as to what he couldn't talk about. There seemed to be a lot they couldn't talk about, but they were conversing, so Jesse refused to be discouraged.

"So, everyone thought our little science experiment was really cool."

Shaun grunted, sticking his hands into his pockets.

"I wish I had more of that stuff. Like a whole brick of it. I'd throw it in a lake or something," Jesse chattered. "Could you imagine? It'd be like...whoa!" He tried to convey the size of his imaginary explosion with his hands, bouncing in the air in his nervous excitement.

Jesse was relieved when Shaun smirked at him. "Yeah," he said.

They walked in silence for a few moments, Shaun smiling faintly and Jesse trying to think of something else to talk about. The weathered country road they walked along reflected a lot of heat and made the slight curve in the road about a half mile ahead appear like a wavy mirage. The wind through the corn fields was nice though. Almost musical. Certainly better than a household of kids.

"It's nice out here," Jesse said.

"I thought you were from the city," Shaun said.

"I've lived a lot of places."

"Oh yeah?" Shaun asked, obviously skeptical.

"Yeah. I've lived in California, Texas, Utah, Wisconsin." Jesse counted off on his fingers. "New York for a few months, Florida, Georgia..."

"No one likes it here," Shaun said as if denying Jesse's claim of being worldly. "I can't wait to get out of this place."

Jesse studied Shaun. Judging from the way other people acted around here, Jesse could see just how out of place Shaun was here. He was a pariah.

"Where would you go if you could go anywhere?" Jesse asked before Shaun could catch him staring.

"I dunno." Shaun rubbed the back of his neck, upsetting his wild curls. "California, I guess."

"Why there?"

Shaun sent him an impatient look. "So I can get in a real band and get signed," he said exasperatedly.

"You don't want to go there for that," Jesse said carefully. "I didn't like it there much. Too many fake people. Everyone's plastic."

Shaun grunted.

"Florida is more your thing," Jesse continued. "Tampa's the heavy metal capitol, ya know?"

"Anywhere's better than here," Shaun replied darkly.

Jesse shrugged.

He figured they were about ten minutes away from Shaun's house and another five from his. Jesse wished he could get Shaun to say something substantial, maybe actually involve him in a conversation. It was like trying to pull teeth with tweezers. Fortunately, Jesse liked a challenge, and something told him it'd be worth it.

"Well..." Jesse paused, fishing for a new topic of conversation. "Besides being in an awesome band—"

"Who said we were 'awesome'?" Shaun sneered the word, his upper lip twisting unpleasantly.

"Nobody." Jesse wanted to joke around but figured he'd better not. "I just assumed...you know...secret underground metal band? Too brutal for the likes of me? It must be pretty awesome." He grinned.

Shaun rolled his eyes. "Go on," he said, amusement in his voice.

Jesse laughed, hopping a little in place while Shaun watched him warily. "So, you're in this awesome band, right? What does a badass guitarist like you do for fun?" Jesse bounced closer to Shaun, waving a hand in his face. "I mean besides hanging out and being ultra-brutal and shit."

Shaun smirked. "I like shooting things."

"You have a gun?" Jesse's blue eyes widened despite his best effort to appear casual. "I've never seen one in real life."

"Sure," Shaun said, seemingly pleased with Jesse's reaction. "I'm pretty good at throwing knives too."

"Dude! Seriously?" Jesse could picture Shaun throwing knives in such a way that they would sever someone's jugular vein, like in a movie.

"I collect weapons. I'm pretty decent with them."

"Oh man, you've gotta show me some time."

"Hmm."

"*And* you play guitar," Jesse gushed, realizing that flattering the other boy seemed to be working in his favor. "I always wanted to take guitar lessons, but I never had the time because I'm always babysitting." Unconsciously, Jesse made eyes at Shaun. "Have you ever taught anyone?" he asked sweetly.

"Ah...no." Shaun blushed as their gazes met. He looked resolutely away, off toward the dusty fields. "I think I'd be a shitty teacher."

They walked along in silence for a few moments, though for once it wasn't awkward. It was quite nice actually. Shaun wasn't as talkative as the other kids at school, but Jesse didn't mind. When he wasn't glaring daggers, Shaun had a calming presence, go figure.

Jesse could see Shaun's house coming up on the horizon. Time was almost up. He felt a curious tendril of disappointment blossom in his belly.

"You're not going to be weird again on Monday, are you?" he asked out of the blue.

"How do you mean?" Shaun asked cautiously, as if he were waiting to get pissed off.

"Like all hostile and stuff," Jesse said lamely. "You'll talk to me in class, right?"

Shaun was quiet for much longer than Jesse felt comfortable with, but he eventually nodded. Slowly.

"If you want, I guess."

"I do. I think you're cool."

"Fuck you," Shaun muttered, sounding slightly amused again.

"And you can sit by me at lunch, you know. And we can talk during gym. You don't have to be so shy."

"I don't want to be anywhere near your fucking friends," Shaun said angrily. "I hate them all."

Jesse bit his tongue. "Okay, fine. But we're still friends, right?"

"I guess." Shaun kicked a rock off the side of the road, clumsily avoiding Jesse's gaze.

"Good." And weirdly enough, it was. Shaun went home, muttering a half-hearted goodbye, and Jesse smiled sweetly after him, walking to his house with a vague feeling of success.

"Hey. Sorry I'm late. I got—"

"Detention. I know." Sam finished for his older brother. "Your *girlfriend* Emily told me," he taunted in that way only a preteen could.

Sam sat on the couch between the twins. They were watching TV, some violent cartoon. Allison doodled on her jeans with a magic marker while she watched. Tyler kicked a box full of Monica's framed pictures and picked his nose.

Sighing, Jesse took the marker away from Allison before she started drawing on the couch. Then he eased Monica's pictures out of harm's way. "Give me that," he demanded, snatching the remote out of Sam's lap. He switched the TV to the Disney Channel.

"Go back!" Tyler yelled, making a grab for the remote. Jesse held it out of reach.

"Stop yelling or you're going into time-out," Jesse said calmly.

Tyler didn't want to hear that. He immediately began throwing a tantrum.

"You're not the boss of me!" Tyler screamed at the top of his lungs. "I hate you!"

Jesse rubbed a hand over his face. He was suddenly drained. Just seconds ago, he'd been happy about how the day had gone. Now he couldn't wait to lay down.

"Watch them. I'm going upstairs," he said, already tired of his family.

"I was!" Sam yelled after him. "And I was doing a good job too until you had to come home."

Jesse ignored him and trekked upstairs to his room, climbing onto the top bunk and falling asleep within minutes.

He had a weird dream. Shaun was trying to teach him how to play the guitar. He had his arms around him from behind, his larger body curling perfectly around Jesse's smaller one.

"There...just like that..." Dream Shaun whispered in his ear as he manipulated Jesse's fingers on the fret board. He didn't stop until Jesse curled his fingers perfectly around the fingerboard. "Now play," he ordered, his voice sounding distant, and it felt as if it came from deep within Jesse's head.

Jesse's fingers moved effortlessly as he started to play. It was a song, though Jesse couldn't make out which one.

"Good," Shaun said, his voice getting softer, farther away. The warmth of his body disappeared.

"Shaun?" Jesse called. He stopped playing.

"You're so *fucking* good," Shaun hissed. In a flash he was right behind him again, his mouth hot at Jesse's ear. His tongue snaked out and wet Jesse's earlobe.

Jesse gasped in surprise. He arched his back and moaned.

"So *good*," Shaun whispered into his ear, and goose bumps erupted along Jesse's soft skin. Shaun wrapped an arm around his midsection and held him tight. The air was forced from Jesse's lungs. "Jesse..." Shaun pressed a long, thin blade to his throat, and Jesse began to panic. *"So fucking—"*

"Hey!"

Jesse jumped, the dream forgotten as he was yanked out of sleep by the sound of his brother's voice. He jerked into an upright position and nearly toppled out of bed. There was a strangled yelp beside him, and when he looked down, he realized Brian was napping in his bunk again. The little blond woke with a muffled cry.

"What the hell?" Jesse peered down from the top bunk, rubbing a hand through his hair. Sam was looking up at him through narrowed eyes.

"Your stupid friends are here."

"Oh." That's right; he was supposed to go to a party tonight. "Shit!"

"Nobody invites me to parties," Sam said sourly.

"That's because you're thirteen. What sort of parties do thirteen-year-olds have?" Jesse scooped Brian up and carried him down the ladder. He handed him off to Sam after giving the sleepy toddler a kiss on the forehead. Sam sighed, but moved Brian to a comfortable position on his hip.

"I want to come with you."

"No," Jesse said.

"Why not?!" Sam whined. "I'm tired of being cooped up here all week!"

"Go hang out with those girls you're always chatting up on the bus," Jesse suggested. He stripped out of his clothes and then rifled through his side of the dresser, picking something clean to wear.

"You're a fucking asshole, you know that?" Sam cried. He stormed out of the room and slammed the door behind him.

Jesse concentrated on getting dressed. He could hear Sam complaining to Monica downstairs, but he wasn't concerned.

He spent a minute checking himself over in the mirror. He ran a hand through his shaggy hair and checked his teeth.

"Jesse!" Monica yelled from downstairs.

"Coming!" Jesse yelled back. He gave his reflection an impish smile and then turned to go downstairs.

Kenny and Emily waited in the living room. Monica chatted amicably with Kenny. She had one arm around Sam while Lissa sat on her hip. The baby looked around.

Allison and Tyler had Emily's attention. She cooed over them. They milked it for everything they could.

"You shouldn't be friends with my brother. He's a butthead," Tyler was saying.

"Yeah, you should be our friend," Allison added. "Jesse's boring lately."

"Oh, Jesse isn't so bad," Emily laughed. She glanced up then, shyly meeting Jesse's eyes.

The twins started to protest again, but Jesse moved to intervene. Kenny noticed Jesse standing in the threshold.

"Hey, man!" he called out. He threw an arm over Jesse's shoulders. "Have a good nap?" He laughed.

"Shut up." Jesse playfully punched Kenny in the arm. Kenny punched him back.

"Well, you ready to go?"

"Yep." Jesse glanced at Monica, hoping she wouldn't make a big deal out of him going out. She gave him a stern look but said nothing.

"This is so unfair," Sam bitched from Monica's other side. He put Brian down. "I never get to go anywhere."

"You have nowhere to go," Monica pointed out. She stroked Sam's hair in a motherly fashion.

"I wanna come, Jesse," Brian said. He hurried to Jesse's side and clutched his jeans.

"No, not this time Brian." Jesse cupped the toddler's cheek. The little boy's lower lip started to tremble in preparation for one of his epic pouts. "We'll do something fun tomorrow, all right?"

"Okay." Brian looked like he was going to cry, but he let go of Jesse's pants.

Emily watched the exchange with wide, glittering eyes, obviously just barely containing herself. When they all went out to Kenny's truck, however, she exploded.

"You're really sweet with him," she cooed as she got in the front seat. She patted the place beside her, and Jesse climbed in. Once they were settled, she turned her starry-eyed look back at Jesse. "You're a good big brother."

"Jesus, Emily." Kenny snorted as he started the truck. Loud country music blasted from the radio, but he didn't turn it down. "Let's get outta here! Party's already started!" he yelled over the music.

Emily smiled at Jesse but was silent afterward.

They peeled out of the driveway and started down the road. Jesse was a little surprised when they passed Kenny's house a couple minutes later. He'd assumed Kenny was hosting the party, as he was the one who had invited him. But then again, maybe it was at someone else's house. Maybe at Jordan's or Eric's place.

After a while, they pulled off the road and onto a dirt trail leading through the corn fields.

"Where are we going?" Jesse yelled to be heard over the music and now the sound of the truck as it bumped roughly along the uneven path.

"You'll see," Kenny said.

Jesse gave him a bemused look but waited patiently for the surprise.

It was completely dark. The stalks of corn were lit a cool-blue and silver by the moon. They swayed gently in the breeze. It was pretty.

It took another two minutes before Kenny slowed down. The path dead-ended alongside the crops, and the woods formed a natural border. In a small clearing between the corn and the trees, there were six vehicles parked in a rough circle. Some of the stalks had been flattened to make room. Kenny drove over the flattened stalks and parked in an empty space. There was a bonfire erected between the cars, and Jesse spotted people from school standing around it.

"Whoa." He was impressed, especially when he saw the keg in the back of someone's truck.

"Let's party," Kenny said with a grin. He killed the engine and hopped out to join the others. Emily and Jesse were eager to follow.

It was a normal party, as far as Jesse was concerned. A bunch of friends hanging out, shooting the shit, and getting spectacularly drunk.

Eric and Jordan greeted them warmly. They had cups of beer, and Kenny and Jesse went to get some for themselves. Emily split off to be with Sunny and a couple of the other girls by the fire.

Sara, the cute blonde from science, had her car radio playing through the window. Both she and Alicia danced together in front of the fire. Their slender bodies cast alluring shadows across the grass. They had their arms around each other, and their bodies moved in perfect sync. They were entertaining to watch. Eric whistled in appreciation.

Sunny and Emily watched them too. They glanced critically from the dancing girls back to Jesse.

And Jesse wasn't stupid. He knew Emily had a thing for him. He liked Emily too. But that didn't mean he wasn't going to watch Sara and Alicia grind against each other. At least he wasn't catcalling them like Eric was.

Jesse put the jealous girls from his mind and followed Kenny's, Eric's, and Jordan's example. They climbed into the back of Kenny's truck, beer in hand, and began chatting rather candidly about the qualities of the females.

"Dude, you're so lucky you're with Sara," Jesse told Eric after a few beers. "She's the best-looking girl here."

"Fuck you, man," Eric said, trying to be angry, but fighting a grin. "Oww." He touched the splint over his nose. It looked brutal. There was still some swelling under his eyes. "That's...that's my girlfriend," he said.

"We're just admiring her," Kenny said, watching Alicia spin Sara in a circle. Sara laughed and tossed her head back. Her blonde hair spilled over her shoulders. "It's a compliment."

"Alicia isn't bad either," Jesse said. She wasn't quite as pretty, but she did have a nice rack. It was one of the reasons she was so popular. She was wearing skimpy shorts, cowboy boots, and a matching hat. Jesse would *definitely* do her.

"I've done 'em both," Jordan said with a lecherous grin. Eric flicked him off aggressively while Kenny howled with laugher.

"Seriously? Which was better?" Jesse asked, totally missing the glare Eric shot in his direction. He was curious.

"Eh." Jordan shrugged. "I don't live in the past, man. I look forward."

"Screw you," Jesse said with an eye roll. Jordan was always so damned lofty. It was fucking irritating.

"The only girl I'd fuck right now is Emily."

Jesse wasn't so smashed yet that he didn't pause at Jordan's bold announcement. After all, Emily's twin brother sat right beside him. He expected some sort of blowout, but there was almost no reaction from Kenny. He rolled his eyes, in fact.

"I thank God every day my sister isn't dumb enough to date you," he said in amusement.

"It isn't right for a girl as pretty as Emily to be single," Jordan complained.

"Yeah, she is pretty," Eric agreed. They all glanced at the dark-haired girl talking quietly with Sunny.

"I think she likes me," Jesse confided in the other three boys. He looked cautiously at Kenny.

"Yeah, she told me she did." Startled, Jesse smiled, but Kenny cut him off. "Don't even think about it though."

"Aw, shit. Don't be that way," Jesse whined, pausing to finish his fourth beer before he bothered to continue with his argument. "You don't have to be all protective. I'm not like Jordan. Girls like me for a reason; I'm a nice guy."

"Girls don't like nice guys," Jordan said bitterly, but nobody acknowledged that he'd spoken.

"We'll see," Kenny said.

The seriousness did not fit Jesse's mood at all. He quickly changed the subject. He brought up a mostly fabricated story about his ex-girlfriend in Detroit. At least it got everyone laughing again.

As his friends laughed at his story, Jesse noticed a faint red light between two trees at the edge of the forest. It was shadowy, and the trees had to be ten or so yards away, so Jesse couldn't be sure, but he thought he saw a figure.

It wasn't especially weird. It wasn't like they were alone or anything. It might be one of the partygoers fucking around. Anyway, the red light looked like a cigarette or a joint.

"Oh man...that reminds me of this one time..." Eric said, starting in on a story of his own. Jesse tried to listen, but he couldn't help but keep an eye on the figure. He could almost make it out now as it stood there in the dark. He hoped it wasn't a cop or someone who was going to get them in trouble.

The other guys laughed, and Jesse grinned automatically even though he'd missed the punchline. He tried to ignore the mysterious person. If they wanted to be acknowledged, all they had to do was come closer to the fire or step out into open so the moonlight would illuminate their features.

"Hey!"

Startled from his thoughts, Jesse jumped.

Kenny laughed at Jesse, nudging him playfully. "What're ya thinking so hard about over there, Jess? My sister?"

"Ah…" Jesse scrambled to find a suitable answer, but he was interrupted.

"So, you're Jesse?" A stranger climbed into the back of Kenny's truck. Another boy. The other guys shifted to make room, so Jesse figured he was cool.

"Yeah?"

"I heard about that explosion in Mr. Barnes' room today. Nice job!" the boy complimented, smiling cheerfully.

"Oh, thanks." Jesse smiled back.

"I'm Kyle." He held out a hand, and Jesse awkwardly shook it. He didn't get introduced to people with handshakes very often, but this boy seemed kind of…different. He was pretty well-dressed for the occasion. Jesse, Eric, Kenny, and Jordan had all dressed similarly, jeans, T-shirts, and both Jordan and Jesse had tennis shoes on, though the other two had boots. Kyle, on the other hand, had on very neat khaki pants and a sweater. His dark hair was styled impeccably, and his hand was incredibly soft. As Jesse looked at him curiously, Kyle stared straight back at him, smiling coyly.

"Well? Did you bring the stuff?" Jordan prodded in that arrogant way he had that so irritated Jesse.

"Of course, I did," Kyle said. He shared one last, oddly intense look with Jesse before he pulled a heavy-duty Ziploc bag out of his back pocket. It was full of weed.

There was a practiced exchange of money. Jordan slid four twenties into Kyle's palm before he handed over the pot. Jordan started to roll a joint.

"Fuck," Jesse said after a minute of watching Jordan doing his thing. The others seemed similarly involved. "If I would have known you guys were buying stuff, I would have brought my money."

"I'm paying tonight," Jordan said absently. He twisted the ends of a fat joint and then handed it off to Eric. He started on a second.

"Awesome!" Jesse grinned. He was already enjoying a buzz. Soon, it would get even stronger.

He was so distracted; he completely forgot the weird figure in the trees.

Chapter Four

When Shaun got home, Ruth was up in arms.

"Detention?" she yelled at the top of her considerable lungs. "Exploding things in science class?! You little delinquent!"

He didn't feel the need to defend himself. Even though, technically, he'd had no part in the mishap in chemistry, not once had it crossed Shaun's mind to rat Jesse out. He just wasn't the sort to fucking tattle.

"It was an accident," Shaun said. He forced his way around Ruth and made his way toward his room in the back of the house.

Ruth followed him down the hall.

"I know damn well nothings ever an accident with you," she hissed. "You're just like your father."

That was fucking low.

Shaun paused on the threshold to his bedroom, his back to Ruth as he shook with the force of his restrained anger.

Normally, he would have swung his fists first and waited to regret it later, but this was his grandma. He couldn't very well kill his own grandma, no matter how tempting it was. People were expecting it after all, and Shaun didn't live up to anyone's expectations.

"Leave me the fuck alone," Shaun said quietly, his voice wavering. He didn't turn around, but he could feel Ruth's dark gaze drilling into the back of his head.

"You're worthless," Ruth sneered, before she backed off, leaving Shaun alone in the hall. He wanted to do something childish, like punch a hole in the wall or at least slam his bedroom door behind him loud enough for Ruth to hear it and know how angry he was, but he didn't.

He went into his room and turned his music on loud. He thought about cutting himself again, a nice new line beside the one from Monday, but he didn't feel like it.

Sure, Ruth was a mean bitch, but she'd always been and always would be. She didn't bother him all that much.

And besides, he still felt strange from that unexpected walk home with Jesse.

"We're still friends, right?" Jesse had asked, all too innocently. Shaun kept thinking Jesse was going to start laughing at him, call him a "pathetic loser" or maybe a "goddamn freak" before he left to go and laugh with his friends.

Nobody had ever wanted to be his friend. Ever! And it was ridiculous to think Jesse, a completely normal, reasonably popular boy, wanted to be his.

There had to be some fucking catch, because if someone really wanted to be a part of Shaun's life, it could never be for real.

Instead of sitting in his room and cutting his arms up, Shaun climbed out his bedroom window and went around the house to the garage.

His gun was hanging up in the back, next to two of Eli's. He borrowed an old coat he found draped over the workbench, pleased to find two worn cigarettes and a lighter with the American flag on it in the pocket.

As he'd already told Jesse, he liked to shoot things.

The woods behind his house were full of things to kill. Little stupid animals, squirrels and rabbits, sometimes even a stray cat or a deer or two, but he wasn't looking for anything that big today.

He just needed to relieve some fucking stress.

Shaun walked for a while. He stopped in one of his favorite places about a mile from home and hunkered down to wait.

Generally, Shaun was pretty patient. He could wait for long periods of time, especially if it was something worth waiting for. And usually waiting for a kill was worth it. But today he was distracted.

All he could think about was Jesse, and that kind of pissed him off.

Jesse had gotten in trouble in Mr. Barnes' class, just for him. And he hadn't whined or complained once about it; he'd even smiled when Shaun had shown up in detention. Jesse was impressed by Shaun, interested in him. It also seemed as if Jesse were becoming somewhat resilient to Shaun's bad moods. Or at least he was trying.

Shaun didn't exactly know what to do about it either.

But just then, Shaun saw a squirrel scrambling down from a nearby tree. Shaun took careful aim, following the tiny gray animal in his sight, waiting for it to pause. There was a split second when it seemed to hesitate, and Shaun squeezed the trigger.

The squirrel's head exploded in a messy and somewhat disgusting display. It wasn't very sporting of Shaun to be hunting tiny animals with his rifle, but he didn't feel like being fair at the moment.

And what did it matter anyway? He would have killed it either way.

This way, the stupid little thing was sent to hell just a little sooner.

Shaun spent the rest of the afternoon in a similar manner. Usually, he would have taken his best kills home with him so Ruth could cook them up, but he didn't feel like going back home.

As the sun began to set and Shaun grew hungrier and more tired, he realized with resentment that he was heading in a very familiar direction, almost without thought. Though it couldn't have been without at least some subconscious decision, because Shaun was heading toward an area he knew very well didn't have a lot of game and the very reason there wasn't was because it was so often populated with humans.

The clearing behind Mr. Jay's farm was the local teenage hangout. There were always parties going on there, as long as the weather permitted, and sometimes even when it didn't.

Shaun had never been invited to one of the parties there, but he watched them sometimes, just to see what all the fuss was about.

It was pretty run-of-the-mill stuff, drinking, smoking, girls socializing, boys fighting, couples making out.

By the time Shaun arrived it was getting late. He was starting to shiver from the cold, exhaustion, and hunger, but he'd already spotted Jesse and there was no way he was leaving without getting a good look.

Lighting a cigarette in an attempt to warm up, Shaun watched Jesse talk with his friends.

Shaun had spent the last few hours trying not to think about him, but he had been anyway.

He'd sort of pictured Jesse sitting, bored and glum faced at the stupid party. He'd imagined Jesse wishing Shaun was there with him, the two of them having some stupid inane conversation.

But of course, this was real life and Jesse didn't look bored. On the contrary, he looked like he was having a great time. Shaun couldn't hear what was being said, but he felt stupidly self-conscious. Jesse looked like he was telling everyone a story or something, and when they started laughing, Shaun got the distinct feeling Jesse had been talking about him.

He glared at Jesse, trying to imagine what stupid and embarrassing things he could be telling his little friends about him.

And then Jesse looked at him...*right* at him. Shaun stood his ground. He raised his chin and determinedly stared him down, but Jesse only stared blankly back.

Maybe Jesse couldn't see him after all. Shaun considered moving into the light, so he could, but he didn't want everyone's attention on him. Just Jesse's, he thought bitterly.

After a few moments of Shaun staring at Jesse and Jesse focusing on apparently nothing, Kyle, a fag who just so happened to be the little brother of the town's only drug dealer, appeared, startling Jesse and drawing his attention away. Shaun stayed just long enough to watch Jesse start smoking before he turned and headed home.

Shaun woke up the next morning, sprawled across his bed. He'd opened a fresh new cut on his thigh the night before and was displeased to find he'd bled through the rag he'd tied around it.

Already in a horrible mood, Shaun tore the sheet off his bed, crumpled it up, and threw it in his closet. He'd try to wash the blood out later. Hopefully tomorrow, when Ruth and Eli went to church. If he was home by tomorrow morning.

Shaun got dressed, taking a few minutes to crudely wrap some gauze around his leg. It was already three, and Shaun had stuff to do today.

He got some cereal from the kitchen and ate it in the living room, enjoying the relative silence of the house. He turned on the TV, watching some old black-and-white with disinterest.

"Morning, son." Eli appeared. He sat on the couch beside Shaun.

Shaun grunted an unfriendly greeting.

"You were out pretty late last night," Shaun's grandfather said, watching him eat with half-lidded eyes.

"So?"

"Your grandmother was upset."

"I can't help that," Shaun said, shrugging off any blame or guilt.

"She said the school called her. Told her about that stunt you pulled in chemistry."

"For fuck's sake..." Shaun muttered, shoving a spoonful of cereal into his mouth. He considered getting up and leaving the room, but he tended to at least listen to what Eli had to say. He was one of the only people who seemed to care about him, even though Ruth must have as well. Most people didn't bitch at you unless they gave a shit.

"I won't lecture you," Eli said, which was practically music to Shaun's ears, but then he had to go and ruin it by doing just that. "But you've got to clean up your act, Shaun. It tears Ruthie up every time she hears about you getting into trouble. You know what it reminds her of."

"That's not my fault!" Shaun cried. He almost threw his cereal at the damned TV. "Tell her to fucking forget about him if it bothers her so much. I fucking have."

"Shaun…"

"Fuck you. I don't have to listen to this." Shaun stood up and stomped to the kitchen. He dumped his breakfast into the sink. "I'm going out!" he yelled before he escaped out the front door.

His guitar was in the garage. It was the only place Ruth allowed him to play. Shaun grabbed the case and amp and dragged the whole lot of it to Eli's beat-up Ford. He shoved everything in the back and climbed in. As always, the keys were in the ignition. Shaun started the shitty car, backed out onto the road, slammed the car into drive, and gunned it to sixty.

It was quite a drive to Will's house, almost forty-five minutes away in the next town. Will was the lead singer of Execute Invasion, Shaun's band. They normally practiced every Saturday, unless they had a gig, then they'd find other days of the week to practice. Technically, practice didn't start until sometime after six since Will tended to get drunk Friday nights. Danny had a kid to take care of, and Ben had a girlfriend to please. Shaun hated his bandmates with varying degrees of intensity but would have rather been there practicing with them than at school or at home with his grandparents.

He loved music. More than anything. It was the one thing that never disappointed or let him down. It was brutal and awesome, and he felt untouchable when he was playing.

That effect was multiplied when he had someone decent to play with. The band, for example, were all pretty good. He was the best skill wise, or at least he liked to think so. The others were all getting up there in age. They had day jobs.

Will, the second youngest at twenty-nine, was the only one who'd had some sort of success. He'd been a lead singer in another band about five years ago. They'd gotten signed to a small but respectable label, and they'd toured around the country for a few years. Eventually, the constant touring got to the young band. Will overdosed on a cocktail of drugs and had spent half a year in rehab. As they grew more and more out of control, they started to lose money, gigs, fans, left and right. Before long, the label dropped them and the whole thing just fell apart.

When he was really drunk, Will sometimes talked about how good the old days were. It was pretty sad, and Shaun had definitely had his doubts about hooking up with the washed-up singer, but like Shaun had told Jesse, there really weren't a lot of death metal bands around. And most of them weren't hiring anyway.

So, he stuck with the washed-up has-beens, because getting paid to play guitar was a pretty sweet deal and he liked playing either way, so why not.

Will's front door was open, so Shaun went right in.

He'd cooled down on the ride over, but he thought a beer or maybe something a little stronger would mellow him out a bit more.

"Hey," Shaun said as he passed Will on his way into the kitchen. Will had a shitty house, a little one-bedroom deal with an attached heated garage that they used as a practice space. He was slumped on the couch, half-awake, watching porn.

"What are you doing here?" Will asked groggily. He was half naked, only a stained pair of briefs covering him. He scratched his hairy stomach. "Practice isn't for like... two hours."

"I had to get out of there," Shaun grunted in reply. He returned to the living room with a can of beer he'd swiped from the refrigerator.

Will huffed. He knew just enough about Shaun's home life to know it was better not to ask questions. He reluctantly moved over, making room for Shaun to sit on the sagging couch.

There were two girls on the TV, both blondes, getting fucked up the ass by an enormous black cock.

"I fucked a groupie like that once," Will said after several minutes of silence, interrupted only by the sounds of sex. "Not the one with the little tits...that one." The older man pointed to the blonde with slightly larger breasts and smiled, slow and sleazy like. "Yeah...her."

"Oh yeah?" Shaun wasn't all that interested. He'd heard numerous stories of Will's past lays and had never cared to begin with.

"Yeah. Just wait until we're big enough to have groupies... Maybe we can get you laid." Will sniggered at his own joke while Shaun continued to glare at the TV. He drained his beer in a single gulp and got up for another.

"Tsk, don't drink it all, kid. Unless you wanna pay for some for once."

"Whatever." Shaun huffed. He got another drink.

Hanging out with Will wasn't exactly a fun experience. He either insisted on talking about himself or making lame jokes at Shaun's expense.

At first it pissed Shaun off royally and he was itching to hit the smug asshole in the face, but after a couple beers, he didn't care anymore.

Luckily, before too long, Will disappeared into the back to take a shower and get dressed. Shaun took the opportunity to raid Will's pantry for food.

Eventually, the other guys showed up.

"What's up, man," Ben greeted as he came in. He glanced around the dim living room, then took a seat next to Shaun on the couch. He thumped him on the back in a friendly way.

"Same old shit," Shaun said back, smiling slightly. Ben was his favorite band member and the only person he could really call a friend. They didn't have much in common besides the band and similar tastes in music, and the only time they ever hung out was during practice and when the band went out together, but he was a nice guy.

"Tell me about it. At least you don't have a girlfriend nagging your ear off," Ben said before launching into another horror story involving his girlfriend, her parents, and the approaching wedding. That's right. Shaun kept forgetting he was engaged now.

"Don't get married," Will said, as he reappeared from the other room. "Women are nothing but trouble."

"They fuck with the music," Shaun added.

"Damn right they do," Will said enthusiastically. "That's why I let young Shaun here play instead of that other fuck head, Hank. Shaun won't be getting a girl anytime soon." He laughed, once again making fun of Shaun and his limited prowess with the ladies.

"Dude, lay off, okay," Ben said, sending Shaun an apologetic look.

"Fuck you," Shaun said absently. He fucked girls. Maybe not as many as Will had—the man had been in a headlining band, for fucks sake! And maybe not as much as Ben...or Danny...but that didn't mean he hadn't been with any girls. He'd had sex before, he reassured himself.

"Hiya, douchebags." Danny strolled in, late as usual. "We gonna practice or what?"

As they set up in the garage, Will told them about their gig next Saturday. They were playing another crappy bar and were being paid very little, but apparently Will had a deal with the owner, and they could have as many drinks as they liked afterward. The owner must not know how much they could put away. Will alone could outdrink the rest of the band, and they were no slouches when it came to alcohol.

"We'll practice on Friday then," Will said decisively. He'd put a shirt on and ran his fingers through his longish brown hair. He was attractive when he tried, which always got them a few pleased looks from the girls in the audience. But usually when they started playing it was a different story. Will didn't have the best voice for death metal; it was definitely loud, but it was a little too screechy to do anything but clash disharmoniously with the music.

"Shit, man. I'm supposed to have Connor Friday night," Danny said from behind his drum kit. "Can we practice earlier?"

"Fuck you and your fucking kid," Will groused, receiving a raised eyebrow from Danny. Will sighed. "How early?"

"I don't know. Before he gets out of school."

"I've got school," Shaun reminded them, pissed they never seemed to remember he was still in high school.

"Give it up, dude. You're never gonna get out of that place." Danny poked his drumstick in Shaun's direction. "You should drop out already. I could get you a job at Walmart."

Ben rolled his eyes at the old conversation but didn't butt in. His long fingers plucked restlessly at the strings of his bass.

"I can be here early," Shaun grunted just to get Danny to shut up.

"Fine. Now let's get to it." Will glared at the other band members, and all talk stopped. They began to play.

The band went through the entire set list three times. It felt good to be playing again. They all sounded reasonably good for a band playing in a garage, but the normal level of calm didn't come to him today. For some reason when Shaun threw his head back, eyes closed, nimble fingers dancing along the fretboard, his mind wasn't as blissfully clear as it usually was when he was immersed in his music.

Jesse's round, freckled face appeared in his mind's eye. Full pink lips curving around a smile, that ridiculous red hair of his mussed and sticking up in the back, his blue eyes warm.

For once, Shaun was glad when practice was over, and when Will offered to take everyone out to the bar a few blocks away, he eagerly agreed.

They all got a booth in the back of the perpetually dark bar. The seats were made of cheap plastic, and the table was sticky with old beer. Will ordered several rounds in quick succession, and Shaun allowed himself to get completely wasted within the hour.

Something was wrong with him. Why couldn't he get Jesse out of his head? Maybe he needed to bleed some more to force him out. It had worked last night. His sleep had been deep and without the pesky interruption of dreams.

At least he was a quiet drunk, and he was able to keep his troubles to himself. Most of them.

"You okay?" Ben asked once Will and Danny had gone to the bar. They were chatting up some slutty-looking girls. "You're acting...different," Ben said.

"What?" He was acting different? How was he acting different? Shaun looked around as if there would be a precise list somewhere. Besides the whole constantly thinking and obsessing over a random red-haired boy, he didn't think he was acting any differently.

Ben didn't seem to know what it was about Shaun that was different either, because he only shrugged. "You're not letting Will get to you again, are you?" Shaun sneered at the mention of the lead singer even though he'd been sitting amicably next to him for the past two hours. "Don't fuck him up again, dude. I really need the money from this next gig. It's not much, but weddings are expensive."

"I'm not gonna beat 'im up," Shaun growled.

Surprisingly, that didn't seem to make Ben feel any better. "Maybe you shouldn't drink so much," he pointed out.

"Fuck...you."

Ben sighed. "Just trying to help." This wasn't the first time Shaun had insisted on being stubborn. They'd all learned early on not to push the sullen teenager's buttons when he didn't want to be bothered. It never ended well for anyone. So, Shaun watched bleary-eyed as Ben gave up on him and leaned back in the booth with his arms crossed.

Unfortunately for Danny and Will, they were both too drunk to be picking up girls, and after multiple rejections they were thrown out of the bar. The four of them stumbled back to Will's house for lack of anything better to do.

The rest of the night was a blur. Shaun remembered watching more porn with the guys before Angela, Ben's girlfriend, showed up and dragged the bassist out of the house. She was yelling up a storm and threatened to call off the wedding.

He remembered Will telling the story about the time he got busted for sneaking cocaine over the border. He and Danny laughed and laughed.

Danny whipped out a joint after that. He promised it was "just" weed, but it made Shaun's head spin. He ended up puking all over the floor twenty minutes after smoking.

The last thing he remembered was Will and Danny arguing drunkenly over who was going to clean it up. He passed out on the couch before they could decide.

There was still puke on the floor when Shaun woke up the next day. He narrowly avoided stepping in it on his way to the bathroom.

About 50 percent of the time he ended up crashing at Will's place Saturday night. The only time he didn't stay was when Will and Danny found girls for the night. It was always awkward sitting around and waiting for them to finish fucking some random chick.

Once, Will had convinced a random pickup to fuck him, and knowing he'd be teased mercilessly if he didn't, Shaun had agreed. Having two other guys watch him lose his virginity with a girl so drunk she had passed out right in the middle had been humiliating. It hadn't even felt good. He tried to avoid a repeat performance ever since it had happened.

Shaun threw up in the toilet. His head ached and his mouth was dry and scratchy. He felt miserably sick inside. He needed beer. Hair of the dog and all that. So, after he grabbed a few towels to throw over the mess he'd made on the floor, he went into the kitchen to get more alcohol. It was the only way he knew of to get rid of hangovers.

Danny was gone, and Will was asleep in his bedroom. Shaun hung out for a while, watching TV and drinking. Eventually Will stumbled out of his room. He looked surprised to see Shaun sprawled out in his living room.

"Don't you have somewhere else to be, man?" Will prodded.

Shaun shrugged.

"Well, if you're going to hang around, at least clean this shit up." Will nodded toward the towel-covered vomit on the floor. Then he slipped into the bathroom. Realizing now was probably the best time to leave, Shaun mustered up the energy to drive the forty-five minutes back to his house.

By the time he got home, it was dinnertime. Eli and Ruth sat at the table, in the midst of another roast. Shaun had grabbed something to eat at the drive-through on the way back, so he wasn't hungry. He stalked past his grandparents.

"So nice of you to drop in," Ruth bitched.

Shaun totally ignored her. He stomped to his room and slammed the door behind him. He turned on his music and cranked it up loud. He had sulking down to an art. Brooding, slamming doors, and playing obnoxiously loud music was his forte.

Doubly irritated, he noticed signs Ruth had been poking around in his room again. That awful flowery smell she liked to spray around the house permeated the air. The bed was freshly made, and the piles of clothes on the floor had been washed and put away. The bloody sheet was gone.

Shaun sat on the edge of his bed. He suddenly felt exhausted. He'd been lying around all day, but he'd never felt more tired.

There was a knock on his door.

"Shaun?" Eli's voice drifted from the hall. "Aren't you hungry?"

He didn't answer. He stared blankly at the wall.

Now that he was back home, he realized how stupid he was being. He'd spent the entire weekend trying to forget about Jesse, to drown his sunny face from his thoughts with alcohol and various illegal substances. Even worse, Shaun knew Jesse hadn't thought about him once the entire weekend. He knew with a bone-deep certainty Jesse had spent time with his new friends and had enjoyed it immensely.

"Shaun, can I come in?" Eli asked. He jiggled the door handle.

"Leave me alone," Shaun snapped. He wasn't in the mood for company. His thoughts hovered around him in a dark and dismal cloud. The alcohol he'd previously consumed was making everything worse. Nausea overtook him. He felt like throwing up again.

"You know I can't do that Shaun. We...we all need to sit down and have a talk," Eli said through the door. "I'm coming in—"

Feeling a spike of white-hot anger erupt from deep inside him, Shaun leapt to his feet. He crossed the room in two steps and jerked the door open.

Eli stood in the hall, his arm outstretched.

Shaun got in his face. "If you don't leave me the *fuck* alone, I swear to god I'll *murder you!*" he yelled, a bit of spittle landing on his bottom lip.

Eli shrunk back. "Son—"

"I'm not your fucking son!" Shaun screamed. His nostrils flared; his eyes burned with fury. He kicked the door shut in Eli's face, stormed over to the stereo, and turned the music all the way up.

The music tore through Shaun's body like a knife through tissue paper. For once, he wasn't enjoying the riffs of the guitar and the pounding beat of the drum. He wasn't about to turn it down though. He shuffled to the bed and fell across the mattress, limp, totally zapped of energy. He curled up on the bed and let himself wallow in his misery.

He was pathetic. A disgusting freak who had no business being alive. He hated himself. He wished for the umpteenth time that he was dead.

That'd show all those stuck-up pussies at school.

Instead of slitting his wrists and letting himself bleed to death like he so often thought about, he pulled out his stash of weed and smoked the last it. He made a mental note to talk to Kyle tomorrow.

Eventually, he fell asleep.

"It's time for school."

Shaun was roused from a deep sleep by the sound of Ruth's voice. He was facedown in bed, drooling slightly, one leg hanging off the mattress. He rolled to his side and peered up at his grandma. She stood at the foot of the bed, her arms folded sternly.

"I know what you've been up to," she hissed. "You need to pray for forgiveness."

Shaun grunted and rubbed his face against the bedsheet. It was too early for this shit.

"I won't let you turn out like your father," Ruth continued in her doom and gloom voice. "You're going to school today. And you're coming to church with me Wednesday. You won't turn into a delinquent...at least not while I'm around."

"Grandma—"

"Take a shower, put some clean clothes on, and comb your hair, Shaun. I have breakfast ready for you." Ruth threw her grandson a heated look; then she left the room.

Rolling his eyes, Shaun got up and went to the bathroom to piss. He had another hangover, but it wasn't as bad as it had been the day before. He sniffed under his arms as he stood in front of the toilet. He didn't smell too bad, so he skipped the shower. He scratched his fingers through his tangled, frizzy hair, but that only made it worse. He didn't bother changing his clothes. They were basically clean.

Ruth didn't comment when he came into the kitchen looking exactly the same. She set a glass of orange juice on the table next to a plate of scrambled eggs and toast.

"Not hungry," he said simply, though he did grab the juice. It tasted better than morning breath anyway.

Looking displeased, Ruth handed Shaun his lunch and his bag. "I'd better not get another call from the school," she said.

Shaun grit his teeth. He snatched his bag from Ruth and stuffed the lunch inside. He finished the juice, got up, and stormed out of the house.

"Fucking bullshit," he cursed under his breath. Outside, he paced the length of the driveway, anxious to get the day started. He didn't look toward Jesse's house. The thought of what he might see sent his nerves into overdrive.

He had to wait about five minutes, but finally, the bus arrived.

His stomach clenched into a knot. His heart hammered in his chest. He crossed the street and shouldered his way onto the bus.

At the top of the stairs, he looked down the aisle.

Jesse waited for him. He smiled and waved enthusiastically.

There was an instant lessening of tension in his gut, but Shaun couldn't stop his heart from beating like a drum. He edged down the aisle as the bus took off. He was fighting a smile. He bit down on his tongue as hard as he could to stop it.

"Hey!" Jesse chirped, way too fucking excited for a Monday. "Oh…you okay? Your eyes are red."

Shaun sat in his customary seat at the back of the bus. He shrugged. "Hangover," he muttered.

"Wow." Jesse looked impressed. He leapt up, abandoning his bag. Shaun watched him warily as he slid into the seat beside him. "You were drinking on a school night?" Jesse asked.

Shaun blinked. "You're in my seat."

"C'mon, let me see," Jesse said and grudgingly, Shaun turned to face him fully. Jesse touched Shaun's cheek with the tips of his fingers. He looked deeply into his eyes. Slowly, his lips curved into a devastating smile. "Jeez…how much did you drink last night?"

Shaun knocked Jesse's hand away, fighting a blush. What was wrong with Jesse anyway? Why did he always insist on looking at him and touching him?

"It was a long weekend," he said casually, but his heart was all aflutter. He grabbed his thigh over the deep cut and squeezed as hard as he could.

"Really? Mine was boring," Jesse pouted.

"Liar. You went to a party," Shaun said.

"Yeah, I did." Jesse's hand fell away. He shifted so his shoulder rested against Shaun's.

Shaun's instincts told him to shove Jesse away and send him back to his own seat, but Jesse didn't even notice the small contact. It was like this was a normal occurrence with him. And it really wasn't such a big deal, Shaun admitted grudgingly. Nobody could see them. Still, he concentrated a little more than was healthy on the feel of Jesse's arm pressed against his.

"I had to babysit all day Saturday though," Jesse said glumly. "My mom was pissed I stayed out so late Friday. I think she was punishing me. I mean, there was no reason for her to be out all day long," he said with an eye roll. "Then I went to church with Emily and Kenny on Sunday. It was boring, but I guess Kenny's an asshole when it comes to Emily dating. I wanted to get some face time with him, so he'll see what a totally nice guy I am."

"What?" Jesse went to church? And he was already planning to ask Emily out? How much worse could things get?!

"You don't think I should go out with Emily?" Jesse asked. "I think she's cute."

"She's a fucking bitch," Shaun growled.

Unexpectedly, Jesse laughed. "She's not so bad."

Shaun turned to the window with a huff. Stupid Jesse, ignoring Shaun's sagely advice. Emily was a preppy whore. Jesse could do better.

"So, are you going to tell me about your weekend now that you've gotten to critique mine?" Jesse asked in amusement. He poked Shaun in the ribs to get his attention. It tickled.

Shaun did push him away this time. His nostrils flared with rage. "Why are you so obsessed with what I'm doing all the time?" he asked sharply. He purposefully didn't think about the weekend he'd spent obsessing over Jesse.

"I already told you. We're friends." Jesse poked Shaun again. He grinned when Shaun flinched and tried to stifle a smile. "Does that tickle?"

Shaun slapped his hand away, highly offended. "Quit it," he hissed. "And we never agreed to be friends."

"Yes, we did. We said…well, you said you 'guessed' we could be friends," Jesse reminded him. "That's practically an iron clad agreement."

Shaun sneered. *Friends?* What a load of shit. He wanted to say it out loud, but when he caught sight of Jesse's warm blue eyes, his eager smile, he caved.

"If it's so important to you, I went hunting on Friday, practiced with my band Saturday, and spent Sunday drinking and smoking so I wouldn't have to deal with the hangover from the night before."

Jesse perked up. "Band practice? That's awesome. I bet you guys are really good."

"What the fuck…how do you figure that?" Shaun was flattered, but he had an irrational fear Jesse was only pulling his leg.

"I don't know. I can't imagine you sucking at anything you do."

"Fuck you." Again, with the flattery. Jesse was treating him like a girl, someone who constantly needed to be fawned over. As revenge, Shaun poked Jesse back. He did it meanly and as roughly as possible, right in the middle of his stomach.

Jesse laughed. "I'm ticklish!" He giggled and flailed around as Shaun poked him several times in rapid succession. Shaun was quickly on the verge of laughter as well. Jesse giggled like a madman, and his face was red with exertion. When Jesse threw himself in Shaun's lap, doubling over with laughter, Shaun withdrew his hand.

He glanced around to see if anyone else had noticed their strange behavior, but they were still alone, minus Jesse's little brother.

The middle schooler watched them over his shoulder with an eyebrow raised.

Shaun shoved Jesse back to his side of the seat.

"You're so mean," Jesse whined, but he seemed to be joking. In fact, when he got his breathing under control, he flashed a brilliant grin in Shaun's direction. His eyes sparkled with mirth.

"Jesus Christ," Shaun muttered. He turned toward the window to hide his reddening cheeks.

Jesse leaned his head on Shaun's shoulder. His fucking *shoulder*! Like some girl cuddling up to her boyfriend!

"Let's do something after school, okay?" Jesse said with a dreamy sigh. "If you don't mind kids, maybe you can come help me babysit."

"I'm not fucking gay, all right?" Shaun sputtered. Fuck, Jesse was coming onto him, wasn't he!

"Ah... Okay. Who said you were?"

Shaun glared at him. "You're all fucking over me!" He was embarrassed he had to point it out.

"Oh." Jesse blinked. He sat up slowly until they were no longer touching.

Shaun scowled and looked away. He could feel his cheeks getting hot again. He regretted saying anything, and he didn't know why. He *wasn't* gay. He was straight! He didn't need some redheaded boy laying all over him.

"Sorry," Jesse muttered. "I'm used to hanging out with my little brother. He's always climbing in your lap and shit."

A little weirded out by that comment, Shaun glanced up toward the front of the bus where Jesse's little brother was talking with two little middle school girls, Natasha and Maggie. The kid didn't look young enough to be climbing in anyone's lap. As he was surveying Jesse's little brother, whose name he'd forgotten, he noticed Kenny and Emily and their little gang sitting in their usual seats near the front. Sometime during Shaun's and Jesse's rousing conversation, they'd gotten on the bus.

Kenny and Rick glared daggers at Shaun. Emily watched her precious little Jesse with an unhealthy longing. None of them looked happy.

Shaun leered at them. For once, he'd beaten those stuck-up brats, and he hadn't even been trying.

"So...do you want to come over tonight?"

"What?" Shaun was pulled back to the conversation with a jolt.

"Do you wanna hang out after school?" Jesse asked.

"I ah..." Shaun stalled. He didn't know what to say. Jesse was still acting like a fag and Shaun definitely wasn't into that, but he also wanted very much to hang out with him, if he was being completely honest with himself. Nobody bothered to try to get close to him. Even his bandmates only did it out of familiarity and necessity. Jesse had no such obligations, but he still wanted to be Shaun's friend. Shaun was still aware it wasn't healthy to be sneaking around, spying on Jesse and then spending an entire weekend, drunk, trying to keep his thoughts from running over him again and again. But something clicked into place. For once, Shaun would take a chance.

"I mean," Jesse hedged. "I can't imagine watching me babysit sounds fun—"

"I'll come over, I guess."

Jesse grinned. "Really?"

"Yeah," Shaun said with a shrug.

"Great! We could...we could play Xbox or watch TV or—"

"Or whatever." Shaun was a little disturbed by Jesse's eagerness, but he was pleased as well. He couldn't remember a time when someone had been excited to be with him.

"Yeah or whatever." Jesse bounced with excitement. He grinned, and Shaun couldn't help it; he cracked a smile too.

The anguish Shaun had put himself through over the weekend melted away. All that was left was an unbearable longing for the day to hurry up and be over with. He wanted to hang out with his stupid, stubbornly attached new friend.

Shaun's first class was largely uneventful. He sat through English, pleased with the hateful looks he got from Kenny. The jock seemed to be under the impression that Jesse had abandoned him in favor of Shaun.

Shaun wished that was the case, but Jesse had mentioned the party he'd gone to with Kenny and Emily when he and Shaun stopped at their lockers before first period. He'd also brought up Kyle and his dank weed, which reminded Shaun about his dwindled pot supplies. He decided he'd need to talk to Kyle before he went to Jesse's house that night.

Miss Stevens was harping on about poetry again, and Shaun, bored by her speech, carved the word *bitch* onto his desktop for lack of anything better to do.

Science class brought a marked improvement. Jesse's eyes lit up when he walked in and spotted Shaun at their usual table. Shaun didn't let it show, but he was pleased to see him, too. He almost did something stupid, like smile.

"Hey there." Jesse sat beside him.

Shaun grunted a greeting.

When class started, Mr. Barnes began his lecture without preamble. Jesse immediately passed Shaun a note.

It wasn't anything significant, just some silly ramblings about math class and how Jesse didn't like that snob Jordan. Shaun read the note, pleased with himself. Jesse had spent their hour apart storing up things to tell him. He took out a pencil and added a couple lines about his English class.

Mr. Barnes looked their way a few times, but he never caught them passing notes.

When class ended, Jesse put his book away in slow motion. "So... Are you sure you don't want to sit at my table during lunch?" He seemed to be stalling for time. He closed his notebook and held it to his chest, watching Shaun intently.

"Fuck no," Shaun spat. He couldn't believe Jesse would even ask.

"I just..." Jesse said. He put his notebook away and zipped his bag up. "Never mind." He shook his head, and Shaun scowled at him.

Great. Jesse was already tired of choosing between Shaun and his other friends.

How long would it take before Jesse got it through his head Shaun and the other kids just didn't mix? How long before he gave up and Shaun was alone again?

Shaun swung his bag over his shoulder and stormed out of the room. He was pissed off and irritated. He was always alone. He didn't have friends. He should have known Jesse would get tired of him. He elbowed his way through the crowded hallway, eager to start the inevitable demise of his only friendship.

A hand wrapped around his forearm.

"Hey, wait up," Jesse called.

Shaun stopped in the middle of the hall. Jesse stood behind him, his eyes brimming with concern. Shaun sneered and tore his arm out of Jesse's grip. "What?"

Jesse pressed his hand to his chest as if he'd been wounded. "I'll see you later, right?" he asked softly.

Shaun huffed. He was overreacting, and people were watching them. "I said I'd come over, didn't I?" he snapped. He gestured for Jesse to follow him.

"Well... I'm just making sure," Jesse said in exasperation. "I mean, I won't get to talk to you for the rest of the day, right?"

"Fuck off," Shaun said half-heartedly.

Jesse had been right, of course. Shaun kept his distance once Jesse rejoined his friends. When history ended, Jesse left with Emily. He met Shaun's eyes from across the room, but he didn't try to approach him.

But Shaun wasn't upset.

When lunch rolled around, he watched Jesse and his admirers with a numb acceptance. He ignored Kenny's triumphant look. He obviously had no idea Jesse had invited Shaun to his house after school. Shaun was invited...not Kenny, and that utterly nullified the jock's smug self-assurance.

Gym was more of the same. Shaun could tell Jesse wanted to talk to him, but he was easily distracted by Eric and Kenny and another round of kickball, which Shaun wasn't allowed to participate in.

When Shaun finished his classes for the day, he stopped by Kyle's locker.

He was alone, rummaging through some papers.

"Hey."

Kyle turned. His lips curved into lusty smile. "Hey, sugar. Is there something I can do for you?"

He always asked that. And he always smiled in that sly and disgusting way Shaun had long ago realized was supposed to be flirty. If Shaun didn't like Kyle's weed so much, he would have castrated the sick fuck years ago.

"You know what I want." Shaun crossed his arms.

"Well, you know I don't have it here," Kyle said with amusement. "I'll bring you some after school, okay, big boy?"

Shaun grunted.

Kyle was an interesting breed. Not only was he a closet gay and a drug dealer, he was also a conniving snake.

Their mutual history started in middle school when Shaun had first bought some green. After a few successful transactions, Kyle had struck up a cautious friendship between them.

Shaun had been naïve. He'd been glad to meet someone who didn't regard him with fear and disgust. He'd welcomed Kyle's friendship with...well...a little less hostility than he had Jesse's. Honestly, he may have been naïve, but he'd never been trusting.

While they were friends, they didn't talk much outside school.

They met on the bleachers after school once, maybe twice a week to talk and smoke. It wasn't a big deal. Before too long, however, Kyle confined some heavy secrets about his home life. And all at once, the meetups after school weren't so casual.

Kyle told Shaun he and his stepdad had sex whenever his mom wasn't home. He told Shaun how he liked to get high and have several of his stepdad's such-inclined friends gang bang him. Kyle told him he loved cock and that he was a raving homosexual.

Shaun had been totally disgusted by the things Kyle told him. Who wouldn't have been? But Shaun hadn't had the best childhood himself, so he tried not to judge.

Like a good friend, Shaun had kept Kyle's secret.

They continued to meet after school, though Kyle was busy at home most the time, doing things Shaun was happy not to know about.

Shaun kept waiting for Kyle to ask him about his secrets, the ones all the kids, even the adults, whispered about behind his back, but he never did.

And soon Shaun realized that it was because Kyle wasn't interested in what Shaun had to say. In fact, it was what Shaun wasn't interested in saying that had caught Kyle's attention.

One day, Kyle had asked Shaun to fuck him.

Shaun had been embarrassed and frankly *disgusted* by his so-called friend's casual offer of sex. Especially after all the things Kyle had told him, Shaun would never his dick anywhere near the other boy.

Shaun had vehemently refused, thinking that'd be the end of it, but Kyle had become enraged.

"Nobody likes you," Kyle had told him outright. "You should be grateful I'd even want to touch you."

He'd threatened to tell everybody Shaun was a faggot and that he'd tried to rape him, which was ironic as that was basically what Kyle was trying to do to Shaun.

Kyle had friends. He was popular—well, more popular than Shaun—and his dealer brother protected him.

People liked Kyle.

And he was right. Nobody liked Shaun. No one was going to believe him if he told the truth.

Finding out that the only reason anyone had ever wanted him, in any capacity, was because he couldn't tell was humbling. Shaun didn't want to be known as a faggot, but he'd still refused. He chose to be known as the town faggot rather than be Kyle's secret sex toy. But Kyle had never followed through with his threat.

Shaun was hurt. He'd become embittered by the whole thing. He'd tried to stay far away from Kyle, but after a few months of not speaking, Shaun had crawled back to him, looking to buy.

Thus, the mocking flirtation and the silly name calling had started. It grated on Shaun's nerves, but he put up with it. It was that or live a sober life.

The memory pissed Shaun off. He was almost glad for the long walk home. Shaun listened to his music and distracted himself by wondering what Jesse had planned for the night.

Whatever they did, at least he knew Jesse would appreciate the pot.

Shaun got home before the bus went past. He'd walked faster than usual, eager to get home so he could go to Jesse's house. He had to wait in the garage until it was safe.

"Shaun?"

Ruth's voice came from the back of the house.

"Yeah, it's me." Shaun tracked his grandma to the master bedroom. She sat on the bed, patching a hole on a pair of Eli's work pants.

"How was your day?"

Shaun shrugged. "Wonderful."

"No trouble?"

"None."

"Good." Ruth peered at him. "You're to stay inside today. I don't want you out there doing God knows what."

"I'm going to my friend's house today," Shaun said, his eyes narrowing to slits.

Ruth responded in kind. "Is that so?"

"Yeah."

"Don't make me ground you, young man," Ruth said. The two of them glared at each other.

"Fuck off," Shaun sneered. He turned on his heel and darted across the hall to his room.

"You come back here, you little shit!" Ruth yelled after him, but they both knew he wouldn't. She didn't even come after him.

Shaun dumped his bag in the corner and went to crouch next to his bed. He felt around underneath it, looking for his box.

Feeling the hard edge of the metal, Shaun yanked it out and flipped the lid.

Every cent he owned resided in the box. Money from playing gigs and from doing some odds and ends around the house. There was even a little left over from his parents. A meager inheritance his grandparents had been kind enough to hand his way.

He pulled out sixty.

"Shaun?" Ruth knocked sharply on the door. "I don't want you going out!"

But Shaun ignored her. He shoved the box back under his bed, then rushed to the window. He twisted the latch and pushed it open.

"Shaun!"

"Leave me alone!" Shaun yelled after his grandmother. He vaulted out the window and down into the bushes below.

Ruth didn't follow him despite her determination to keep him inside. Shaun snuck around the house to wait by the road. He sat in the grass beside the dusty road.

It took a while for Kyle to show up. He got to watch the elementary school bus go past. But eventually Kyle's old Cadillac came rumbling down the road, pulling partway into Shaun's driveway.

"What are you doing out here?" Kyle got out of his car. He peered at Shaun over the hood.

"Waiting." Shaun stood and up and dusted his jeans off. "Give me the usual."

"Well, right to business then," Kyle said with a smirk. He leaned across the seat to access the glove box. When he returned, he had a baggie of merchandise.

"Do you have some papers too?"

Kyle raised an eyebrow, but pulled some rolling papers off the dash. Once Kyle had everything on the hood of the car, Shaun snatched it up and left the money behind.

"Always nice doing business with you, sweetie." Kyle batted his eyes. He smoothly pocketed the cash.

"Yeah," Shaun grunted. He rolled the baggie up and shoved it in his back pocket. He nodded wordlessly then started the trek to Jesse's.

"Where are you going?" Kyle called after him. "Need a ride?"

"No," Shaun said easily, continuing down the road. He thought he was off the hook when he heard Kyle get back into his car and back up, but when the Cadillac pulled up beside him and Kyle rolled down the window, grinning across the empty passenger seat at him, Shaun scowled.

"I know where you're going," Kyle said, sounding smug. "You're going to the new kid's house. Aren't you?"

"So, what if I am?"

Kyle smiled. "Get in, honey."

"For fuck's sake..." Shaun got in the car. He slammed the door as hard as he possibly could. "Happy now?!" He crossed his arms tightly across his chest.

"Very." Kyle grinned. His eyes were half lidded and full of something that made Shaun distinctly uncomfortable.

It was a short ride to Jesse's house. It was barely a mile away. But Kyle drove under the speed limit, irritating Shaun with how obviously he was stretching out their shared time together. He kept quiet, though he wanted to reach across the seat and strangle the conniving little faggot. He sat stiffly in his seat. His hands wedged under his arms.

"So, you've got a new friend?" Kyle asked at last. They were almost there. Shaun could see Jesse's house several yards ahead. He could have gotten out of the car and walked, ran maybe, but now he had to answer Kyle. He didn't want him thinking he was afraid.

"What's it to you?" Shaun snarled.

Kyle shrugged. "Nothing. You're a likeable guy," he said sweetly. "I mean, I like you."

"Whatever," Shaun sneered.

"I'm just wondering why it's okay for him to like you but it's not okay if I do."

Shaun laughed harshly. "Well, you're a gay whore and Jesse isn't—"

"That's not fair. You don't know anything about Jesse. He could be trying to lure you in before he makes his move."

Shaun felt this was highly unlikely. Nobody liked him. Not even Kyle liked him. He was just desperate for someone to treat him like a whore.

"Fuck you. He's into Emily." It made him sick to bring it up, but it was true. The very thought of Jesse and Emily becoming one of those nauseating couples he saw kissing in the halls infuriated him.

"I didn't think you were so gullible," Kyle drawled. "You believed that?"

Shaun lunged across the seat and grabbed a fistful of Kyle's shirt. The car jerked sharply to the right and tore through a patch of gravel and grass. Kyle eyes bugged out of his stupid face. He slammed on the brakes before they went into the ditch.

"Stay out of my business," Shaun spat in his face. "The only reason I haven't slit your throat is because you have good weed. Don't make me change my fucking mind."

Kyle swallowed. He jerked his head up and down mechanically. Shaun let him go, gave him one last piercing look, then got out of the car. Kyle didn't waste any time. He backed up in the middle of the road and drove off.

As Shaun crept up Jesse's front walk, he started to have second thoughts. Maybe this wasn't such a good idea. Maybe he should go home, make up an excuse, and apologize. But no.

He remembered how good it had felt that morning to have all of Jesse's attention on him. He hated himself but he wanted to feel that again. He just hoped he'd be able to handle all the undivided attention.

Still feeling uncertain, Shaun knocked on the door.

After a long minute of waiting, Shaun raised his fist to knock again. He was already having second, second thoughts and was wondering how long he should wait for a reply when the door opened.

A little red-haired boy stood in the doorway. Shaun blinked in surprise. He looked so much like Jesse he thought for one crazy moment Jesse must have magically shrunk himself.

"Who are you?" the boy asked, looking up at Shaun with open curiosity. Well, that solved that then. The little boy wasn't Jesse after all.

"Shaun," he said curtly.

He was deeply uncomfortable. He'd never been around a little kid before. He had no idea how to act. He hadn't realized Jesse had any other siblings besides the one he saw every day on the bus. Though he supposed it made sense Jesse had another little brother. The one on the bus had to be at least twelve years old, surely old enough to look out for himself for a few hours after school.

"Oh hey!" Jesse swept into the living room, grinning from ear to ear. "Sorry, I didn't hear you knocking." He nudged the little boy out of the way and ushered Shaun inside.

"It's okay," Shaun said. He made a furtive attempt to scan the room. Jesse's house was nicer than his, though most of the general furnishings were only of moderate quality. It kind of bothered him that Jesse's family had more money than his.

"Who's he?" Another voice spoke up. Shaun whirled around and spotted another little redheaded kid hopping down the stairs. The girl was the same age as the boy. In fact, they might have been twins. Jesus! How many kids did Jesse's parents have?

Jesse drummed his fingertips together, looking somewhat lost. When he caught the questioning look on Shaun's face, he relaxed and launched into introductions.

"These are the twins, Allison and Tyler." Both already looked bored with the proceedings. Allison waved half-heartedly. Tyler rounded the couch and took threw himself into the cushions. "And that's Sam." Jesse pointed at the other end of the couch. The very top of a red head could be seen peeking over the back. "Say 'hi,' you guys!" he ordered.

There was a chorus of hellos. Shaun fidgeted with his shirt sleeves. He didn't want anyone to look at him.

Jesse chewed lip. He had a moment of indecision, but then his face brightened considerably.

"We should play *Guitar Hero.*"

"Not again," Sam cried from the couch. He didn't bother to look away from the violent cartoon on the TV.

"I want to play!" Allison rushed to the entertainment center. She changed the TV into video mode, much to Sam's annoyance, and got the Xbox up and running.

Jesse smiled at his little sister. He collected guitar controllers from a moving box.

"Here." He gave one to Shaun and took the other, sliding the strap over his shoulder and standing in front of the TV as the game's screen came up.

"I've never played this before," Shaun said sourly as he followed Jesse's example.

"Well, you should be awesome at it, right? It's a guitar."

Shaun shrugged. If that's all it was, he shouldn't have any problems. But then again, there weren't any strings on the plastic guitar. There were colored buttons and a flip switch.

"What the fuck—" Shaun muttered, wrenching an obnoxious laugh from Tyler.

"Fuck!" he giggled.

"Shut up, little baby," Sam snapped at the younger boy.

Jesse hit Shaun in the arm with his controller. "You gotta watch what you say in front of the kids," he hissed, like Shaun should have already known that.

"Sorry," Shaun grunted. He wished the kids would go away already.

"Wanna pick a song?" Jesse asked. He scrolled through a list of lame songs.

Shaun made a face.

"Play Ed Sheeran," Allison cried from her place on the couch.

"I hate that song," Tyler whined. "Do Rage Against the Machine."

"Naw, we're going to play Pantera."

"They suck," Sam said, but Jesse picked it anyway. Shaun was surprised Jesse had remembered he listened to Pantera, but the surprise vanished as soon as the song came on and "notes" started flying past.

Shaun tried. He did! It wasn't like he'd never played a video game before, but he preferred real life, as shitty as it was, to some fantasy made-up crap. And this was fucking crap.

"You have to press the buttons and the strummer at the same time to play a note," Jesse said over the sound of Shaun fucking up the song.

Shaun scowled. "Fuck you." He looked down at his hands, playing with the buttons. By this point, he'd completely forgot about the kids copying his crude language with gusto. "This isn't like guitar at all."

"Dude!" Jesse nudged him with his hip. "Watch your mouth." But the warning fell flat. Jesse was laughing too hard to do much admonishing.

"Go fuck yourself," Shaun muttered darkly. This game was stupid, and Jesse's little siblings were laughing at him. He didn't know why they had to play a stupid game. Why couldn't they get high?

When the song finished Shaun wanted to quit, but Jesse convinced him to try again. He turned the game on easy and spent a few minutes teaching Shaun how to play, much to everyone's amusement.

After three songs, Shaun could at least play on easy, but he'd had enough.

He took the guitar controller off, resisting the urge to throw it on the ground. The little girl snatched it from him.

"You suck," she said, setting off her twin again.

"He stinks too," Tyler loudly agreed.

Shaun glared hatefully at the little brats. He was no match for the look Jesse gave them.

"Don't you guys have any manners?" Jesse cried. "Why don't you two go to your room until you can be nice."

"No!" Allison stomped her little foot.

"Go upstairs or I'll tell Mom you wouldn't listen," Jesse threatened, and somehow—even though Shaun would have kicked anyone who threatened him like that in the balls—it seemed to do the trick.

"I hate you!" the twins yelled in unison. But it worked. They went upstairs, bickering back and forth the whole way.

"You too," Jesse said, turning to Sam.

"What'd I do?!" Sam yelled.

"Nothing. But you've had the living room all week. I want to watch TV with my friend."

"You're an asshole," Sam said. He scowled at his brother, but he was already getting up. He passed Shaun, assessing him with a loaded gaze. He followed the twin upstairs.

"Sorry about that," Jesse said. He sighed and took off his controller.

"It's okay," Shaun grumbled. "I don't like kids. I fucking hate 'em."

"Yeah." Jesse sat on the couch. "You do watch TV, right?" He fiddled with the remote.

"I guess." Shaun sat beside him. He kept a respectable distance between them. "You'd better not try to watch stupid reality shit."

"I wouldn't dream of it." Jesse grinned. He wiggled over so he could elbow Shaun in the ribs, and then he left his arm there, resting against Shaun's side!

Jesse settled on a channel. "*Ninja Warrior*'s on."

Shaun barely watched the stupid show. All he could concentrate on was Jesse's arm resting against his and wondering if maybe Kyle had had a point. Was Jesse hitting on him? He remembered Jesse pulling a similar stunt earlier on the bus. When he'd leaned his head on Shaun's shoulder and looked up at him with those striking blue eyes.

But it couldn't be possible.

Nobody like Jesse, someone so normal and attractive, would ever be into Shaun. Even if he was a homosexual, Jesse would have chased after someone else.

And Shaun already knew Jesse was straight. At least he thought so...

"She's cute." Jesse smiled slowly as a muscled girl worked her way through the obstacle course. The crowd cheered.

Shaun quirked an eyebrow. "That girl?" The girl on TV was super ripped.

"She looks like one of my exes," Jesse said, staring at the TV. "I mean, in the face! That chick looks like she's on steroids."

Shaun grunted.

"My ex was super cute, but also, a total prude. She wouldn't let me do more than feel her up, and we dated for like three months!" Jesse said.

"Wow," Shaun said blandly. "Sucks to be you."

Jesse laughed and elbowed him playfully. "Shut up. She gave me the worst case of blue balls. You have no idea," he said. He rested his arm against Shaun's again, totally unbothered by the lack of space between them.

Shaun debated whether he should move away or not. He was still thinking about it when the show ended, and Jesse started clicking through channels again. He passed a show with a hipster-type smoking a vape pen. It reminded him of the weed in his back pocket.

"Hey."

"Hmm?" Jesse glanced up from the TV. "What's that smile for?" He grinned automatically, responding to Shaun's devious look.

"I bought pot. Wanna smoke?"

Jesse's face lit up. He bounced on the couch, the TV forgotten. "Fuck yes! This is awesome!"

Shaun pulled the baggie out of his pocket. He opened it so they could smell the bud.

Jesse inhaled. "Nice," he said.

The sound of keys in the front door ruined the moment.

"Shit." Jesse grabbed the bag out of Shaun's hand and stuffed it between the couch cushions. The door opened, and a red-haired woman in scrubs entered the living room. She had a squirming baby in her arms.

"Hello, hello," she called in greeting. Her face was weary. She adjusted the baby on her shoulder in a practiced maneuver. She spotted Jesse and Shaun on the couch and turned in their direction. "Jesse, come take the baby."

Sighing, Jesse stood and took the crying infant from the woman. The lady in scrubs must have been his mother. And that must mean the baby girl, judging from the pink color of her onesie, was yet another sibling!

And then, another kid, a toddler this time, darted into the room through the woman's legs. He ran for the TV.

The toddler was different from the other kids, so much so that Shaun wondered if he was maybe someone else's kid. He saw Shaun on the couch and blinked shyly at him with big blue eyes.

"Hi," the toddler said cautiously.

"This is Shaun," Jesse said for his silent friend. "And this is my other sister, Lissa, and my other brother, Brian."

Shaun's mouth fell agape. *Five* siblings.

Jesse bounced his little sister sheepishly. "I know. Right?" he muttered.

"Nice to meet you, Shaun." Jesse's mom unloaded the baby bags and breezed into the other room. Shaun heard her rummaging around in what he assumed was the kitchen.

"Jesus," Shaun hissed when Jesse sat beside him again. "Is your mom a professional whore?"

Jesse snorted. "Don't be mean." He gave the baby in his lap a big, goofy smile.

"I'll be back in a few hours, okay? They don't need me for long." Jesse's mom reappeared from the kitchen. She munched on a granola bar. "I'll be back tonight." She waved at the kids and hurried out the front door.

"She's got work," Jesse explained.

"Yeah, okay." Shaun took his weed out of the couch, confident that an infant and a toddler wouldn't know what it was. He caught Jesse eyeing it longingly, but he put it back in his pocket. He wasn't doing drugs in front of little kids. Jesse didn't disagree. At least not verbally.

"I'm Brian," the little boy said, reintroducing himself. Shaun hadn't caught his name the first time, and he certainly didn't get it this time either.

"Yeah." Shaun attempted a smile but wasn't surprised when a grimace came out instead. Luckily, the kid didn't seem to notice.

"Today was art day in my class, and we got to draw anything we wanted. Wanna see what I made?"

"Ah..."

"Lemme go get it!" The toddler scampered off to get his book bag.

Jesse snorted. "Looks like you made a new friend."

"Fuck off," Shaun scowled.

Jesse laughed. He was clearly enjoying Shaun's palpable discomfort. He stood up, holding the baby on his hip. "I'm going to check on the kiddos upstairs. Can you watch Brian for a minute?"

"Are you serious?"

"Yeah, it'll just be for a minute," Jesse promised. "I'll be right back."

Well, if he was going to be *right* back.

"Fine," he huffed. Jesse grinned at him, then when up the stairs, the gurgling baby in tow.

"Look!" The toddler was back, holding a brightly colored picture. He heaved himself up beside Shaun, then handed him the drawing.

"Uh, nice job, kid," Shaun said diplomatically. Kids always drew the shittiest stuff, but Shaun wasn't an artist either. He was almost at the same art level as Brian.

"This is my mommy," he said, pointing out the tallest circular thing with stick arms and legs. You could tell it was a girl from the squiggly lines coming out of the circle's head region. He'd colored them a flaming red. "And these are the twins," Brian said, and he instantly gained a few points in Shaun's book for easily making them the stupidest-looking people on the page. They had matching buck teeth and swirlies for eyes instead of the black dots everyone else got. "I don't like them very much," Brian leaned in to whisper, his blue eyes huge.

"Me neither," Shaun agreed.

Brian perked up. "And Sammy is here." He poked a bloated-looking circle and laughed.

"Why'd you draw him so fat?" Shaun asked, a little surprised to find he was actually curious.

"'Cause he's a fat butt and he ate the last of my Halloween candy this morning!"

Shaun laughed.

"Oh, and I drew Jesse too. He's the best big brother ever. Don't you think?"

Shaun shrugged. "Sure." He didn't know what kind of brother he was, though he thought Jesse must be a fucking saint to put up with these kids all the damn time. "Where's your dad?" he asked, hoping to divert attention away from Jesse and discussing how great he was.

"I don't have a dad," Brian said sadly. He stroked the picture of his brother.

Shaun felt for the kid. "Sorry," he said. "I don't have one either."

Brian smiled, and even though Shaun didn't like to even think about his dad, he was glad he had if only to cheer the little blond up.

"Okay. Sorry." Jesse swept down the stairs, the baby on his shoulder. "Somebody messed her diaper. Yes, she did!" Jesse baby talked to the little girl. He kissed her wetly on the forehead, and the baby smiled and kicked her feet. "Hey, Brian? Do you mind if we have mac and cheese for dinner? The twins are hungry."

Brian seemed pleased with the announcement and bounced around in a very familiar fashion. "Yeah!" he said.

Jesse pulled a red-and-blue bouncy seat—which Shaun hadn't noticed until just then—out of an alcove and strapped Lissa in. He flipped the TV to a brainless kids show. "Watch Lissa for me, okay, Brian?"

"Okay."

"Can I get a hand?" Jesse asked, turning to Shaun. Cooking was the last thing Shaun wanted to do, but he nodded, his jaw clenched tight, and followed Jesse into the kitchen.

"I have to make three boxes," Jesse said, grabbing a pan from one of the cabinets and filling it with water. "Everyone's hungry," he said.

"How can your mom expect you to take care of five kids every day?" Shaun blurted as he watched Jesse bustle around the kitchen. He'd never so much as boiled water.

"Now that Sam's older, he can help out a lot more." Jesse shrugged, seemingly unbothered by his burden. "It's not fair of her, but what are you going to do? I love my annoying family. It's not like I want anyone else to take care of them."

Shaun sneered. "If my grandparents made me look after kids, I'd end up murdering them or some shit."

"You did okay with Brian," Jesse pointed out.

"I was sitting with him for like five minutes tops."

"Brian's sweet. He's special," Jesse said with a smile. He took a pack of hot dogs out of the fridge.

"Like retarded special?" Shaun joked.

"No, you asshole. Not retarded." Jesse playfully punched Shaun as he passed. He got out another pan and filled it with water. "He's just my favorite little brother, I guess. Even though he's always annoying me. I love him the most."

Shaun wasn't comfortable talking about love and was glad when he spotted Jesse adding the hot dogs to the water.

"What the fuck are you doing?"

"Hot dogs and mac and cheese," Jesse said as if Shaun were the stupid one. "Haven't you ever had it?"

Shaun wrinkled his nose dramatically. "No," he said. "Sounds disgusting." And this was from the boy who ate squirrel.

"It's not bad. You'll like it." Jesse laughed. "Now, do you still want to get high?"

"Seriously?" Shaun perked up.

"Sure. I mean, I can't get completely messed up, but I can get a buzz going, ya know. Mom'll be home eventually, and we can hang out on our own. Go to your house or something."

"No," Shaun snapped. "We'll stay here."

Jesse shrugged. He poked the waterlogged hot dogs with a fork. "Whatever. But hurry up. I don't want to do it in front of the kids."

"Yeah, all right." Shaun pulled out the weed and broke up one of the buds. He picked out the seeds and sprinkled the green on his rolling paper. Quickly, though very deliberately, he rolled the joint on the kitchen counter.

Jesse looked over his shoulder as he finished. "You got that from Kyle?"

"Yeah. His brother gets the stuff; Kyle just sells it." Shaun licked the edge and sealed the joint. "He's a freak."

Jesse's eyebrows shot into his hairline. "Why do you say that?"

"Because…" Shaun glanced at Jesse, wondering again if he was a fag like Kyle had suggested. He wanted to rant about Kyle, the dirty nasty whore, but now he was thinking it'd be in bad taste.

It wasn't that he had anything against fags. Not really. It just wasn't okay for people to think *he* was gay. They already hated him!

"Yeah? Because why?" Jesse prompted.

Shaun shook his head. "Never mind. Let's smoke." He took out his lighter and started to toke up.

"Woah." Jesse snatched the lighter from his fingers. "Outside," he said.

They slipped out the sliding glass doors and stood next to the house. Since Jesse still had the flame, Shaun handed him the joint.

Jesse blazed up. He inhaled deeply.

Shaun waited impatiently. He shifted from foot to foot as he watched Jesse enjoy his bud.

"Nice," Jesse sighed as he released a billow of smoke. He didn't cough. He seemed to know what he was doing.

"Give me some," Shaun said. He reached for it.

Jesse ignored his hand. He leaned in close, flipped the joint, and carefully pressed it to Shaun's lips.

Shaun cheeks heated up as Jesse's fingers brushed his chin. He held the joint between his lips and took a hit.

Jesse took it back when Shaun had a nice lungful. He blazed a second time.

"I thought you weren't getting wasted," Shaun said.

"Can't help it." Jesse coughed this time. He pounded his chest for good measure. "Fuck, I'd better get back to cooking."

Shaun snorted. He took the weed from Jesse and let him go back inside. He took a couple puffs on his own, preparing to go back to the chaos with Jesse and the children.

He could feel the weed taking over his mind; it had a calming effect, like water pouring over a raging fire. He snuffed the burning roach with a wet finger and put it carefully in his Ziploc. He hoped it wouldn't stink too bad.

Back in the kitchen, Jesse added the boxes of macaroni to the boiling water.

"I feel soooo much better," Jesse said. He giggled as he stirred the pasta.

"You're high," Shaun said. "Try to be responsible." He was joking, but Jesse snapped to attention and gave him a salute.

"Yes, sir!" he cried. "I am 100 percent capable, sir!"

Shaun snorted. He came a bit closer and peered into the saucepan. The noodles were boiling merrily.

Jesse sighed contentedly. "I'm glad you came over."

"You're glad I brought weed."

"Yeah, but it wouldn't have been as much fun without you," Jesse said. He smiled and leaned his head back against Shaun's shoulder.

Shaun hadn't realized he was standing so close. He tensed up and held perfectly still. He didn't know what to do. But for once, he felt very relaxed. Jesse had a shock of red hair over his eyes, and Shaun wanted to brush it away. His eyes were so pretty.

Jesse straightened up and went back to cooking. He didn't mention the intimate moment they'd just shared. He swept it under the rug like it was nothing.

Shaun kept an eye on Jesse as he finished preparing dinner. They were lucky; Jesse's siblings didn't notice anything was different. He laughed at everything though, and he kept touching Shaun a whole lot.

Shaun was concerned about the "gay" touching, but he was in a good mood. He didn't let it bother him.

After the kids ate and Jesse fed the baby, they moved into the living room to watch some TV. The twins played with their Nintendos on the floor while Brian watched over their shoulders. The baby was on a blanket doing something Jesse called "tummy-time." Jesse, Shaun, and Sam watched another stupid competition show, *America's Got Talent.*

Shaun was uncomfortable in the small enclosed space, but he'd calmed down considerably since the joint. He watched the idiotic talent show with a calm sense of resignation. Jesse was beside him; their thighs pressed warmly together.

It was eight when Jesse's mom came home.

Jesse jumped up eagerly as the younger kids swarmed to greet her. He grabbed Shaun's hand and urged him to his feet. "Mom, we're going to my room," he called over his shoulder and then tugged Shaun toward the stairs.

Shaun's hand was clammy in Jesse's. Red flags went up in his mind as Jesse led him to his room. What were they going to do in there? Alone. He let Jesse take the lead anyway. He was glad to be away from the teeming household. If Jesse tried anything, he'd kick him in the balls, he decided.

"I've got top," Jesse said when they entered his room, gesturing to the bunk beds. "Come on up." He hauled himself up the ladder and got situated in the nest-like bed.

"Uh…" It was weird being invited into another guy's bed, but it wasn't like there was anywhere else to sit. Shaun assumed the lower bunk belonged to one of the kids downstairs. So reluctantly, he climbed to the top bunk and sat cross-legged next to Jesse.

Jesse smiled at him.

"Sorry this is so weird."

"I figured it would be," Shaun said.

Jesse lay back on his pillow. "I have a pretty crazy family, don't I?"

"I guess."

"What's yours like? I know I can't ask about your parents, but…" Jesse trailed off, staring at the ceiling.

"Why do you even care?" Shaun asked cynically.

"I told you, didn't I? I think you're interesting." Jesse looked down the line of his body and straight into Shaun's dark eyes. "I think it's because you're so mysterious all the time."

"I'm mysterious?" Shaun choked. That was fucking hilarious.

"Yeah. I mean, everyone hates you, but nobody will say why. Kenny and Emily were laying into me at lunch, because I keep talking to you."

"Fuck them," Shaun said through his teeth. *Those fucking little bastards.*

"I don't give a shit what they say. I mean, for the most part, they're nice and I want to screw Emily at some point, but you're my best friend."

Shaun scowled. "I'm not your best friend. You don't know anything about me." Shaun didn't like the way his stomach flipped at Jesse's admission. He'd never been someone's best friend before. But more than that, he was surprised Jesse didn't know his secrets yet. He didn't understand why the others were being so hush-hush about everything. Ratting Shaun out was something petty Kenny would have enjoyed doing, but then again, maybe he was too afraid to even mention it. Maybe Shaun's fists held more sway than he'd ever imagined.

"Well...tell me, then!" Jesse cried in frustration. "How else am I supposed to know you if you never talk?!"

"I talk," Shaun grumbled.

Jesse laughed. "Tell me about your grandparents. Or your band. You pick."

Fuck this. Shaun sneered. This was fucking stupid. It wasn't like Jesse sat around explaining every part of his life. He hadn't even bothered to mention his five younger siblings when he'd invited Shaun over. But if Jesse were going to complain about it, then he might as well get it over with.

"Fine. I live with my grandparents. It sucks because my grandma is a complete bitch," Shaun said.

"Why?"

Shaun huffed. He forced himself to elaborate. "She doesn't like the way I am. She thinks I should be normal. You know, someone who goes to church and doesn't drink or smoke dope."

Jesse snorted. "Normal?"

"Yeah, well..." Shaun trailed off. "She didn't want me coming over tonight; she tried to ground me. Grandma knows what I get up to with the band. She thinks I'm with them now. She'll be pissed when I get home."

"Why? What do you do with your band? Fuck groupies and get high?" Jesse smiled dreamily.

Shaun snorted. "We don't have groupies."

"What about your grandpa?" Jesse continued, still looking curious despite Shaun's generic answers. Shaun imagined disapproving parent figures weren't all that rare.

He shrugged. "I don't know. He's okay."

"Oh fuck," Jesse whispered. His eyes widened comically.

"What?" Shaun said uneasily.

"Did you just say someone was 'okay'?"

Shaun punched Jesse in the arm. He didn't hold back, but Jesse took it admirably. He rolled on his pillow and laughed heartily. His eyes were closed, and there was a rosy color in his cheeks. Shaun was horrified to feel a warm rush of affection.

"Grandpa doesn't bother me," he explained. He felt obligated. "He lets me do whatever I want."

"Hey, it's okay to love your family, you know," Jesse said with a smile.

"Whatever," Shaun huffed. He didn't like answering questions about his personal life. "What about you?" he snapped. "Where's your dad?"

Jesse raised a brow at the change in topic, but answered nonetheless.

"He left after Sam was born. I guess he'd had enough of us," he said lightly. "Mom told us he was cheating on her with a girl in her twenties for like...years, and she didn't find out until he decided to divorce her."

"That's shit." Shaun scowled, a little upset that Jesse's dad would abandon him for some bitch. "So, what about the twins, and the other two? Whose are they?"

"You mean Allison and Tyler and Lissa and Brian?" Jesse laughed.

"Yeah, whatever." Shaun folded his arms. He couldn't be expected to know all their names!

"They're from different guys. Mom's been going through shitty boyfriends ever since Dad left. I think the only reason we moved out here was because she had a bad breakup with the last one, Joey. He'd proposed to her, and I was starting to think they might actually get married and that we'd be stuck in Detroit forever. Then Mom found out he was engaged to two other girls at the same time and that he was playing them all. Just because he fucking could." Jesse furrowed his brow. It was the first time Shaun had seen him upset. "He's an asshole. We're better off without him."

Shaun chewed his lip. He was embarrassed he'd asked such a sensitive question. There were a lot of things he'd rather not talk about.

"Sorry I asked," Shaun said awkwardly.

Jesse shook his head. "It's not a big deal. We're friends. We should tell each other shit."

"Yeah. I guess," Shaun said slowly, though he wasn't convinced. He still wasn't sure this was a good idea. Getting close to people never worked out in Shaun's book. But maybe Jesse could be different.

They talked for a while longer, about school, about girls, about different places they wanted to go. Jesse did most of the talking, but Shaun didn't mind. It was actually a relief.

It was after ten when they heard the kids getting ready for bed. It involved a lot of whining and complaining. The sound of it was like nails on a chalkboard.

"I'd better go," Shaun said.

"Aww, do you have to?" Jesse pulled a face. He looked a sad puppy.

"I can't stay forever," Shaun said. He was already climbing down from the bunk.

"You could stay the night if you wanted to avoid your grandma."

Shaun was surprisingly tempted, but when he imagined himself and Jesse sleeping side by side, he shivered.

"No. I'll see you later." Shaun made sure he had his stuff. He opened the door a crack. The coast was clear.

"I'll walk you out," Jesse said. He jumped down and followed Shaun into the hall.

Things had calmed down a bit downstairs. The younger kids were gone; only Sam was left in the living room, playing some shooting game.

"You guys are dicks," Sam said, his eyes never leaving the TV screen. "Mom said she smelled pot. You should have let me have some."

"It's been in Shaun's back pocket the whole time, doofus," Jesse taunted. "If you don't know what it smells like, then you don't need to smoke it."

"Fuck you," Sam growled, a tower of preteen rage.

"I'm not your supplier," Jesse said. "You don't know anything about it anyway. I know you've never even tried it."

Sam threw his controller down and stomped up the stairs. He hadn't even bothered to pause his game.

Shaun watched him go with amusement.

"He's not normally like that," Jesse said in apology. "He likes to show off in front of my friends."

Shaun grunted. He didn't care. He wouldn't have shared his stuff with that kid even if Jesse had begged him to.

Shaun headed to the front door.

"See you tomorrow?" Jesse asked.

"I guess," Shaun said awkwardly. He wished Jesse wouldn't have walked him out.

"Do you want a ride? I can borrow my mom's van."

"No. I'm good."

Jesse smiled wistfully. "Sit by me on the bus in the morning, okay?"

Shaun shrugged. "Sure. Whatever."

Jesse's lighthearted laughter followed Shaun all the way back home.

When he snuck back into the house, it was ten thirty. Ruth was fast asleep in her chair in front of the TV. She must have been waiting up, but luckily, she hadn't made it.

Shaun drifted by her and down the hall. He felt like he was floating on air. He hadn't even had that great of a time, but he felt so cheerful.

He had a strange urge to wash himself, and for once, he didn't avoid it. He floated into the bathroom and got the water running.

While he was cleaning up, he checked his cuts.

The ones on his arm looked okay. They were covered in scabs at any rate. It was the body's natural defense against germs and bacteria.

The one on his thigh was a different story, however. It was painful to the touch, and it was puffy and red. Infected.

Wincing in pain, Shaun scrubbed the cut with soap and water. He made a mental note to keep his knife a little cleaner.

Chapter Five

Jesse couldn't help himself. He was glad to see Shaun on the bus the next morning.

"Hey," he said pleasantly when Shaun stopped and stood over him in the aisle.

Shaun pressed his lips together until they were white and bloodless. He screwed up his face with intense contemplation. He seemed to be having an intense mental debate.

Jesse watched him, confused. What the hell was happening?

The bus lurched forward and the spell was broken. Shaun tossed his bag into his customary seat at the very back, and then he sat beside Jesse. *Right* beside him.

"Whatever," Shaun grunted, but he was fighting a smile.

Shaun smelled nice today. Like soap. His hair wasn't as tangled as usual. He was wearing a clean outfit too. A hunter-green thermal and dark jeans. Jesse bit his tongue seconds before he mentioned it. He didn't want to embarrass Shaun by implying he normally smelled or that his clothes were a mess. So, Jesse beamed at him.

Shaun looked away and avoided his eyes. He was clearly embarrassed, despite Jesse's attempt to spare him from that very thing.

Jesse felt his heart melt. There was something almost charming about Shaun that he couldn't quite put his finger on. The whole fuck-off-and-die vibe Shaun gave off wasn't as effective as he thought it was. At least, not to Jesse.

"Want to come over again today?" Jesse asked. It had been nice to have someone babysit with him, and Shaun, even when he was being a grouch, was better company than a bunch of children.

"You only want me to come over because I've got weed," Shaun said with a sour look.

"I wanted you to come over yesterday and I didn't know you had any," Jesse pointed out. Shaun made a face, but he dropped the issue. "So, can I expect you?"

"I fucking guess," Shaun said grudgingly.

Jesse smiled. "Good."

Jesse was an attractive, likeable guy who loved to socialize. He'd made lots of different friends over the years. There had never been a time he'd been attracted to someone like Shaun, though. He'd never had to beg someone to hang out with him.

Something felt right about snuggling up, physically as well as metaphorically to Shaun, though, and fuck what everyone else said or thought. Kenny and Emily both had tried to explain many times why he shouldn't talk to him, but Jesse wouldn't listen.

He didn't care if Shaun was "weird," or "mean," or if he'd been in random fights with the other kids in the past. He didn't give a damn. When Shaun was around, Jesse felt a whole lot better about...well, everything. And that's all that mattered to him.

Jesse saw something in Shaun that no one else in this town did. He knew there was something amazing waiting under the many layers of Shaun's icy exterior. He had a gut feeling he'd be rewarded in the end.

He brought up a random, school-related topic, talking just to talk, and Shaun listened, nodding in places, giving short "yes" or "no" answers when required.

The simple conversation about nothing warmed Jesse from the inside. No matter how uninterested Shaun appeared, Jesse knew he felt the connection between them. He was trying...just as hard as Jesse was to foster their budding relationship.

Jesse didn't want to put a name to it yet, but it was *obvious* they were destined to be best friends.

Once they got to school Jesse trailed Shaun to his locker and then surprisingly, Shaun urged Jesse to his own.

"C'mon. We don't have all day."

We? Jesse smiled; he liked that, Shaun putting them together, even if it was only in word form.

"So sorry." Jesse flashed a brilliant smile and led the way to his locker.

Astonishment was written all over Shaun's face. It took him a moment to catch up, but he did. He fell in step beside Jesse and then waited next to him while Jesse got his books for class.

Jesse could barely hide his amusement. It was almost cute how Shaun pretended he didn't care when Jesse could so clearly see that he did.

When the first bell rang, they split up to go to their classes, but Jesse wasn't bothered. They'd see each other soon enough.

The rest of the day went well. Kenny and Emily dropped the Shaun issue, and though Kenny seemed distant, Emily was normal. She spent the entirety of history, English, and lunch flirting with Jesse, which he saw as a win. He got the feeling Emily was hard to please, but she'd warmed up rather quickly. She'd been impressed with Jesse for coming to church Sunday and seemed even more so that he was going on Wednesday, as well.

If only all girls were so easy to please.

So, later, once Jesse got home and Shaun showed up, his clothes rumpled and his expression harried, Jesse was a little distressed when the first words out of his mouth were: "I can come over tomorrow, right?"

"I promised Emily I'd go to church with her," Jesse said sheepishly.

"What?" Shaun spat. He grimaced and wrinkled his nose with disgust. Jesse wondered if he'd been rejected by Emily or something. That's the only reason he could see for such a strong reaction.

"I have to," Jesse hissed, mindful of the kids within earshot. "If I want to get in her pants, anyway."

Shaun looked horrified but didn't say anything else. Jesse felt terrible. He'd been trying to get Shaun to participate in their little "friendship," and now he was turning him down the first time he asked to hang out. Feeling like he needed to make it up to him somehow, Jesse touched Shaun's shoulder and drew him upstairs.

"Don't bother us," he warned his little brother.

"Fuck you," Sam mouthed after them.

"I thought you had to babysit," Shaun bitched as he followed Jesse to his room.

"I trust Sam with the twins."

They climbed into Jesse's bed and sat side by side on the blankets. Shaun pouted. He looked miserable.

"Did you bring something to smoke?" Jesse asked.

"I thought we had to do it outside," Shaun said in a whiny voice. Jesse figured he was being mocked.

"As long as we only do it in here, Mom won't care," Jesse lied. There was no such rule, but he'd deal with the consequences later. And maybe spray some air freshener or something.

Shaun immediately took out his weed. He set up a rolling station in his lap. His shoulders slumped inward as he worked, and his expression remained unhappy.

"Everything all right?" Jesse asked cautiously. "You were upset before I even mentioned Emily."

"Grandma wants me to come to church tomorrow. She says I need to pray for forgiveness or some fucked-up shit," Shaun sneered.

"Oh, you should come!" Jesse cried. "It won't be so bad if we go together, I promise."

"I'm *not* going to church," Shaun growled. He'd finished rolling. He started to crush the joint between his fingers.

Gently, Jesse plucked it from Shaun's fingers and stole his lighter too.

"We need something to ash in," Shaun said.

Jesse reached down to the windowsill and grabbed one of Sam's empty soda cans. The kid was such a slob. Feeling mightily resourceful, he started blazing while Shaun watched him in silence.

"I fucking hate God," Shaun spat, and then weirdly, he lay down in Jesse's bed and snatched the joint back. He took in a huge lungful of smoke, struggled for a couple seconds to hold it in, and then coughed it out. It was a sloppy move, but Jesse heard you got higher if you coughed the shit up. Maybe Shaun was onto something.

"I hate God too," Jesse said, voicing one of the few thoughts he'd never shared with anyone before. He stretched out beside Shaun and got comfortable.

Shaun scowled at him. "Why? Your life is perfect," he said. "What do you got to complain about?"

Jesse snorted. "Seriously? My dad abandoned us for another woman. Then I got dragged across the country for years, watching Mom make mistakes over and over. I'm paying for those mistakes. I'm the one who cleans up her messes. I can't wait to move out, but at the same time, I'm afraid to leave the only family I've ever known. My life sucks."

Shaun turned his head. His wild, frizzy hair tickled Jesse's cheek. He looked deep into Jesse's eyes with so much understanding Jesse flung his arm around Shaun's chest and hugged him tight.

Shaun's whole body went stiff and Jesse let go. They lay side by side, their arms touching, their hips and thighs pressed together. They didn't look at each other for some time. They stared at the ceiling and lazily passed the joint back and forth.

Jesse smiled to himself. He felt oddly emotional. He was so glad he'd met Shaun. He decided there was no one else in the world like him.

A good hour passed before Jesse remembered the kids.

"We'd better get dinner ready," he said.

Shaun grunted, but he was already getting up.

Jesse was at the point where everything was hilarious. The twins took turns trying to make him laugh, an easy prospect to be sure. Sam continued to glare at Jesse for not letting him get high with the big boys, his scowl perfectly matching Shaun's. It seemed like Shaun had a hard time having fun no matter what he was on. Or maybe it was just the fact that he hated Jesse's siblings that had put the glum look on his face.

Monica came home in the middle of Jesse's dinner preparations. She handed Lissa to Sam, left Brian in the kitchen doorway, and hurried back to work.

"Hi, honey." Jesse was still laughing from Allison's latest knock-knock joke, but still managed to pick Brian up with some finesse. "Hey, Shaun?"

"What?" Shaun sat between the twins at the kitchen table. He looked highly uncomfortable.

"Help me out?"

Shaun pulled a face. "With?"

"Either take Brian or finish the veggies," Jesse said. He knew he was asking a lot from Shaun, but Sam had his hands full with the baby and Jesse couldn't hold Brian *and* get the green beans out of the pan at the same time. He hoped it wouldn't explode in his face.

Jesse heard Shaun get up, but concentrated on stirring the vegetables with his spoon.

"I don't want beans," Brian complained.

"We're having chicken nuggets and green beans, kiddo," Jesse said. "You've got to eat a couple bites at least."

"I hate green beans," Brian whined.

Suddenly, Shaun moved in behind them, his body mere inches from Jesse's. Jesse shivered as he felt Shaun close in. He had a distant memory, maybe it was a dream, of them standing like this only closer... Jesse turned his head and looked questioningly into Shaun's dark eyes.

Shaun leaned closer and lifted the toddler out of Jesse's arms.

Jesse let out a breath he hadn't even known he was holding. His heart did a somersault in his chest.

"I can't cook," Shaun said in explanation.

Jesse nodded and tried to calm his overexcited nerves. He drained the vegetables over the sink, then took the nuggets out of the oven. He got out some plates.

Shaun took Brian to the table and got him situated.

"You're Shaun, right?" Brian asked. "Jesse's friend."

"Yep."

"I remember you." Brian smiled and instantly began a conversation about his day in preschool.

Brian didn't fit in with the family. Sam was mean to him, and the twins followed suit without even trying. Monica had little time for the second-youngest member of the family, and as much love as Jesse gave the little boy, he still couldn't be around all the time.

Somehow Shaun must have sensed all of this. He had a pinched look on his face as he listened to Brian talk, but he gave Brian his attention. He had his arm on the back of Brian's chair and kept him close. The twins switched from telling jokes to picking on of Brian and his stories, and Shaun's hands balled into fists.

"Let him talk," Shaun said darkly.

Tyler stuck out his tongue, but he didn't interrupt again.

Jesse brought the food to the table. It took a few trips, but everyone was served and began to eat.

Sam put Lissa into the high chair, and Jesse took over. He fed her little bites of mushy baby food as he ate nuggets and speared some green beans. The twins fought over who had the most nuggets, and Sam ended up giving Allison an extra one so she'd stop complaining.

Shaun ate mechanically, and Brian mirrored his example, stuffing veggies into his mouth despite his so-called hatred for them.

Brian was in the middle of a story about their trip to the fair back in Detroit. It wasn't a very interesting story, but Shaun was all ears. He even managed to laugh when Brian mentioned the clown that had scared the shit out of Tyler.

"That's not funny!" Tyler yelled across the table at Brian.

"Shaun thinks so," Brian said back, surprisingly catty.

"Shaun's a weirdo! Sam told me about him!" Tyler cried. He threw a precious chicken nugget across the table at the toddler.

Jesse glanced at Sam, but he seemed unfazed. Shaun, on the other hand, glared daggers at Tyler.

"What did Sam tell you?" he spat. He switched his gaze to Sam, his dark eyes narrowing dangerously.

Tyler saw the look on Shaun's face. His eyes widened with fear. His lower lip trembled as he searched for words.

Sam smacked a hand over Tyler's mouth. "I didn't tell him anything," he said. "He's making stuff up."

"*Liar*," Shaun hissed.

The color drained from Sam's face. His eyes widened to match Tyler's.

Jesse jumped in. "Guys, enough. Quit fighting." Lissa sniffled at the raised voices and the sudden elevation of tension. She began to cry, her baby mush forgotten.

"I didn't say anything," Sam whined, but his hand still covered Tyler's mouth.

Jesse shook his head. "Take Tyler upstairs," he said.

"But—"

"Do it!"

"Screw you, Jesse." Sam grabbed Tyler's arm and yanked him from his chair. Tyler ripped his arm out of Sam's grip, but he followed to the stairs. Once they left the room, they started whispering loudly to one another. Their hushed argument faded as they went upstairs.

Shaun sat tensely, staring after Jesse's little brothers. Everyone at the table was quiet. Allison stared at her half-empty plate, and Brian watched Shaun fume in amazement. Lissa whimpered, and Jesse pulled her out of her high chair and rubbed her back soothingly.

"Allie, do you know what they're talking about?" he asked.

Allison looked up in surprise. "No," she said quickly.

It was obvious she did, and from the red staining Shaun's cheeks, he knew it too. Jesse refused to pull teeth to get an answer though. He didn't see the point. It would piss Shaun off more, he thought. So, he sent her upstairs after the boys.

Allison pushed her plate away and leapt to her feet. She escaped the kitchen in a hurry.

Shaun bared his teeth. "Your brothers are assholes," he said, and it wasn't clear who he was talking to. Jesse wanted to refute that claim, but Brian was already stifling a laugh.

"You like that?" Shaun smiled at Brian. "Sam's a dick," he said.

"...dick..." Brian repeated, setting himself off again. His hands barely covered his ridiculous giggles.

"That's right, kid." Shaun patted Brian's head. "And the twins are little fuck faces."

Brian laughed again, but Jesse had had enough.

"Shaun!" he cried. "Watch your mouth," he chastised, though there wasn't much heart behind it.

"Why? He likes it." Shaun ruffled Brian's blond hair. Brian squirmed and playfully batted after his hand.

"What am I going to tell Mom when she comes home, and Brian tells her all the new words he's learned?"

"Fuck if I know." Shaun shrugged. For the first time since he'd arrived, he was smiling. He turned to Brian and gave him another noogie. "You know you're not allowed to say bad words, right, kid?"

"I can say whatever I want," Brian said, looking at Shaun with a bit of the hero worship he normally reserved for Jesse. "Mom's got a fuck face."

Jesse glared at Shaun. "See. Look what you did."

"I told you I'm no good with kids," Shaun grunted. He sighed and attempted to make things right. "Kid, I get to say shit like that 'cause I'm older. Little kids like you gotta earn it."

"Why?" Ugh...the incessant question of "why." They could be here all day.

Shaun didn't have the patience for a long and meandering conversation. He said directly, "Because I fucking say so."

"But how come—"

"You be good or I won't be allowed to come over anymore."

Hmm, that seemed to work. Brian nodded, and Shaun rewarded him with a pat on the back.

"Good," he said, turning to Jesse with a grin. "See, that was easy."

The remainder of the evening was spent in the living room while the two high schoolers waited for Jesse's Mom to resurface.

Jesse was wrapped up in the baby but kept a close eye on Shaun and Brian as they watched a movie on TV. It was much too violent for a toddler, but Jesse didn't have the heart to make them change the channel. Shaun looked content sitting next to the three-year-old, explaining the violent nonstop action to the fascinated little boy.

The four of them looked like a happy little family, only unlike any of their real families they actually worked together.

Deciding to push his luck, Jesse lay back on the couch, cushioning Lissa on his chest. He stretched out and put his feet in Shaun's lap.

Shaun gave him an odd look, his dark eyes meeting Jesse's blue. But then somebody died a horrible death on-screen, and without a single protest Shaun went back to narrating the movie for Brian. Jesse's feet stayed where they were.

Warm and comfortably buzzed, Jesse fell asleep within minutes.

Jesse woke up when he felt Lissa being taken from his arms. The little girl fussed, and Jesse groggily opened his eyes.

"Mom?"

Monica stared down at him. "The house smells like pot."

"Oh. Right." Jesse was on the couch by himself. Where was Brian or Shaun?

There were footsteps on the stairs. Jesse sat up as Shaun reappeared at the bottom. Monica greeted him solemnly, and Shaun nodded cordially. He sidestepped so she could get by him and upstairs.

Jesse rubbed his eyes. "Where's Brian?"

Shaun folded his arms. He looked away as his cheeks got pink.

"You fell asleep," he said.

"Yeah, I was comfortable," Jesse said. Why was Shaun so embarrassed? He looked silly when he blushed. Jesse bit his tongue and tried not to laugh at his friend's predicament.

"Ah...the kid fell asleep on me too," Shaun said awkwardly. "I er...didn't know where he slept. I put him in your bed."

"Oh. That's fine," Jesse said with a laugh. "He's always crawling in my bed."

"Yeah." Shaun continued to avoid Jesse's eyes. He was steadily looking more and more uncomfortable. "I'm going to go."

"Okay."

Shaun passed Jesse on his way out the door. Jesse didn't necessarily want him to go, but his bed was calling to him. It didn't bother him Brian was already up there. He'd warm the blankets like a little furnace.

Then, Shaun touched his hair. He smoothed the unruly locks at the back of Jesse's head with a gentle hand.

Jesse swallowed and held perfectly still.

"See you tomorrow," Shaun said. He drew his hand back and hurried to the door. He slammed it behind him with an air of finality.

Jesse was still thinking about that weird touch when he got to his room. He exchanged his jeans for some PJs and climbed to the top bunk.

As Shaun had mentioned, Brian was fast asleep in the bed. He still had his clothes on, but he looked comfortable. Jesse decided to leave him be.

Jesse moved the toddler and stretched out beside him. He covered them in blankets and snuggled in. He closed his eyes.

It was one of the first times Shaun had touched him, completely on his own.

All the other times Jesse could write off as accidents or attempts at being playful. But this felt completely different.

Jesse was still trying to figure out what it had meant when he felt himself drifting off.

Of course, in the morning it had all been forgotten.

However, another question replaced it.

"What was Tyler talking about last night?" Jesse asked Sam that morning at breakfast.

Sam glared at him. Jesse couldn't tell if he was still upset about the whole "not sharing" the weed thing or if it was something else. He couldn't see what else Sam had to be mad about, but then again, he was dumb sometimes.

"I don't know."

"Yes, you do. Tyler said you told him something about Shaun."

There was a pause while Sam took a bite of his cereal. "You wouldn't believe me anyway," he said.

"What's that supposed to mean?" Usually, he and Sam were pretty close. Well, as close as a big brother and his little tagalong sibling could be. But Sam was never this closemouthed!

"You've been so bossy lately..." Sam trailed off, glaring at the last few Cheerios floating in his cereal milk. "And now you're hanging out with that weirdo..." he said sullenly. He picked up his bowl and took it to the sink. He dumped the remains down the disposal. "Never mind."

Jesse gaped at his brother. What the hell did he know? Sam left the room before Jesse could think up another question.

"You okay?" Shaun asked when he got on the bus later that morning. He seemed nervous again, and he didn't sit down until Jesse gestured for him to do so.

"I don't know. Sam's mad at me or something."

"Oh," Shaun sighed. "He's still being a little bastard, then?"

Jesse snorted. "Yeah, I guess he is."

"I wouldn't worry about it," Shaun said easily. He pushed his frizzy hair out of his eyes. "He's a cunt."

"Jesus!" Jesse laughed. "You don't have to be so harsh. He is my little brother, you know."

Shaun shrugged.

He wouldn't admit to it, but Jesse didn't mind the name calling. He felt Shaun was being rude because Sam, Tyler, and Allison knew the secret about him Jesse had been trying to find out since day one.

Jesse fought the urge to question Shaun. He knew it wouldn't turn out in his favor.

"Are you still going to church tonight?" Shaun asked. His eyes were fixed toward the front of the bus. Jesse followed his gaze and noticed Emily, Kenny, and the others getting on. He smiled and waved at them but stayed put. He missed Shaun's deep scowl.

"Yeah," Jesse said. "I told you, I want Emily to like me."

"What about the kids?" Shaun asked. "Are you going to leave them by themselves?"

"Why? Are you volunteering to babysit?" Jesse laughed, but got nothing back from Shaun. The other boy was as silent as a stone wall. "One of the women at the daycare runs a late-night service, I guess. Mom said it's kind of expensive, but she doesn't mind paying extra if I'm going to church."

"Hmm." Shaun seemed disappointed. "Did you tell her you're doing it to get in some girl's pants?"

"Yeah. Of course, I did." Jesse said. "And after that me and Mom discussed the best sex positions. She likes missionary, but I'm more of a reverse cowgirl fan myself."

For a second Shaun looked utterly confused.

"You dumbass. I'm joking!" Jesse elbowed Shaun as he began to laugh. Shaun frowned as he realized he'd been tricked. He elbowed Jesse back.

"Fuck you."

"Whatever, man. You can still come with me." But as soon as he'd said it, Jesse realized there was no way it would be possible. Kenny wouldn't even let Shaun in his truck for all Jesse knew.

But Shaun flat-out refused. He shook his head disgustedly.

"But what about your Grandma?"

"I'll go fuck around in the woods. Maybe I'll shoot something."

Jesse pouted. "I want to come."

"Then come," Shaun said.

"You know I can't. I already promised."

Shaun looked away. He glared darkly out the opposite window.

Jesse sighed. As much as he'd been looking forward to today, hoping to lay some of his better moves on Emily and impress her, he now couldn't wait until it was over. He'd never been so depressed to have a day off babysitting in his life.

Shaun was in a weird mood after they got off the bus. He was quiet in science and didn't say a word on the way to history. Jesse felt like he should stick with Shaun, and for once, he regretted making friends with Emily and Kenny and their crew. He felt somewhat obligated to spend time with them.

He debated what he should do. He tried to weigh the pros and cons of leaving Shaun on his own, but when history ended, he broke. He dutifully followed Emily to English and tried his best to seem interested in what she had to say. And to be honest, he had no idea what she was even talking about.

However, he did manage to tune into Emily's rambling conversation when he heard Shaun's name.

"What?" he asked, interrupting Emily's drawl.

She smiled. "Maybe we should talk about this later."

Jesse wanted her to repeat what she'd just said, but realized she was right. Now wasn't the time. English was about to start, and their teacher, Miss Stevens, was already writing on the board.

With a sigh, Jesse acquiesced.

When class was over, Emily gabbed about something different, though. As much as Jesse wanted to know what she'd been talking about, he couldn't find an opening to ask. Luckily, Kenny unknowingly picked up his sister's line of conversation a few minutes later at lunch.

"Are you still hanging out with Shaun?" he asked as soon as Jesse sat beside him.

"Ah...yeah," Jesse said. He poked the "mystery" casserole on his lunch tray and hoped Kenny wouldn't start grilling him.

"He hasn't tried to kill you yet?" Jordan leaned around Kenny to ask.

Jesse snorted with amusement. "No. Does he try to kill people a lot?"

It was just a joke, but the lunch table suddenly became deadly quiet. Jesse got the shivers.

"Does he?" he asked again.

"My brother knows this kid who used to live around here. He told my brother Shaun threatened to skin him alive. Just because he accidentally hit Shaun with his book bag," Jordan said. "That kid no longer goes to this school for that very reason."

"A couple years ago, there was a rumor that Shaun was killing people because like every few days he'd come to school with blood on his clothes," Sunny said dramatically. Lee and Rick nodded to verify her story.

"Once, Alicia told Shaun he smelled bad, and the next day she had a note in her locker. It was a list of all these weapons he had and how he was going to use them on her," Sara said, flipping her blonde hair over her shoulder. Alicia didn't say anything, but the disturbed look on her face said more than words could.

"And he fucking broke Eric's nose the other day," Kenny added, pointing to Eric who was sitting at the other end of the table. He was still rocking a splint on the bridge of his nose. "You saw his face, same as I did. That wasn't an accident."

"There's a million other stories we could tell," Emily said. She squeezed Jesse's shoulder. "We'd be here all day if we went through all the creepy stuff he's done."

That was quite a laundry list, but Jesse was hardly convinced. If this was the kind of stuff Sam had been telling the twins, then Jesse didn't care. Most of that was just Shaun's rotten personality showing through. Shaun couldn't help himself. Jesse had seen his mind work in real-time, without the judgment everyone laid at his feet. When Shaun felt cornered, it was a lot easier for him to be hateful and mean than it was for him to be a civilized human being. That was all. He wasn't a serial killer like everyone else seemed to think.

So, if everyone feared rumors and a few heated words, then Jesse could continue to ignore their advice.

Kenny wasn't finished. He went on, spouting more anti-Shaun gossip. Jesse tuned him out. He surreptitiously met his best friend's eyes across the lunchroom.

As usual, whenever he was with the in-crowd, Shaun glared at Jesse extra hard. But this time, Jesse met his eyes head-on. He smiled at Shaun and rolled his eyes in Kenny's direction. He wanted to get up and leave the popular table completely, but he didn't go that far. There'd be an uproar if he did something like that.

Shaun didn't look happy, but he did stop the whole death glare thing. If anybody else noticed them making eyes at each other across the room, Jesse didn't know. He didn't care either. Everyone was so busy discussing how much they hated Shaun, they were ignoring everything else.

"You're still coming with us to church tonight?" Emily asked when the bell rang at the end of lunch.

"Yep." Emily and her brother might be boring him to death with their rumors and gossip, but he still wanted Emily.

"That's so great. I wish more people our age were more passionate about religion."

Jesse's smile was strained. In the back of his mind he could hear Shaun mocking him.

"Did you tell her you hate God?"

Jesse shook his head to remove the disembodied voice. He promised Emily he'd see her later on the bus.

When they got to gym, it was raining outside. The coach decided they'd play basketball on the inside court.

Jesse, Kenny, and Eric trooped to the locker room to change. The other two were eager to get on the court, but Jesse took his time getting into his sweats. Shaun was absent and Jesse kept wondering when he'd show up.

It wasn't until they came out of the locker room that Jesse spotted Shaun talking with the coach. He watched them interact for a few moments, both parties growing progressively angrier. Then, Shaun turned and stormed out of the room.

"Wonder what that's about?" Kenny said, following Jesse's gaze.

Jesse shrugged. He was dying to know, but he fell in line next to his buddies and prepared to get picked for a team.

Shaun wasn't on the bus after school. Jesse wasn't totally surprised, but it was raining cats and dogs. Wind howled through the trees with ferocity, and lightning streaked across the sky followed by a bone-deep rumbling of thunder.

Jesse stared out the window as the bus trundled along the roadway. He wondered if Shaun had gone through with his plan to shoot things in the woods. He didn't know very much about guns—all right he knew nothing about them—but he didn't think using a weapon in this kind of weather was a good idea.

He wished Shaun had agreed to come with him.

"Are you sure you'll be all right by yourself?" Jesse asked Sam once they were home. Monica had had a similar conversation with him that morning. Sam had watched the twins on his own before. Nobody thought it was unreasonable for him to do it again.

"Yes," Sam said. He didn't look at Jesse, though. He was on the floor playing *Call of Duty*. The twins watched him from the couch, but they were already looking antsy.

"You don't have to be on top of them the whole night," Jesse said. "But you need to keep an eye on them."

"Yeah." Sam did some button mashing and cursed at his opponent on-screen.

Sam wasn't pay attention at all. Jesse stepped in front of the TV, and Sam threw himself to the side to see around Jesse's body.

"Dude! Move!" he yelled.

"Can I get you to listen for thirty seconds?"

"I'm listening!"

Jesse rolled his eyes. "Mom will be home early. By eight at the latest."

"I know!"

"She doesn't want you to cook anything. There're leftovers in the fridge. Nuke 'em in the microwave and clean up your mess."

"I know what to do, Jesse. Get out of the way!"

"And no more scary bedtime stories," Jesse said. He crossed his arms sternly. "Last time Tyler couldn't sleep for a week because you riled him up so bad."

"Are you ready to leave yet?"

Jesse glared at his snarling little brother. Shaun had a point. Sam *was* kind of a cunt.

Outside, a couple toots from a horn sounded.

"That's my ride," Jesse said. "I've got to go."

"Bye!" Allison called. Tyler wasn't one for goodbyes. He waved half-heartedly over his shoulder. He looked bored to death.

"Good riddance," Sam hissed under his breath, just loud enough for Jesse, still standing over him, to hear it.

"You're a brat." Jesse knocked the Xbox controller out of his brother's hands as he went by, enjoying his yell of annoyance. He might have cursed him as well, but Jesse was already out the door.

"Hi," Emily said as Jesse jumped in the truck. It was still pouring, and he shook himself off, doing a good imitation of a dog. It was warm in the cab and the music was loud again. "Turn that down," Emily said to her brother.

"Hey, guys." Jesse grinned at the siblings.

"I hope you're ready for this," Kenny said. "I think you'll have to meet everyone today. No more hiding in the back."

"What?"

"I told my parents you were coming, and they told the pastor. He loves new guests," Emily gushed. "Mom and Dad want us all to sit together up front."

"Oh?"

"You'll see!" Kenny said with an evil smile.

The church was a tiny, one room kind of deal. The dirt parking lot was packed. After they found a spot, the three of them rushed through the rain and the puddles and pushed past the heavy wooden doors.

The church looked larger inside than out. It was well lit. Globes of light hung from the vaulted ceiling. Beautiful stained-glass windows lined the wall behind the pulpit. The room was divided by two rows of pews, most of them full of parishioners. An older gentleman in black, the pastor, roamed the aisle. He greeted people in the pews with a sunny smile.

"Are you taking him?" Kenny asked his sister.

"Yep. Find Mom and Dad." Emily took Jesse's hand. She dragged him down the aisle.

"Pastor Noel!" Emily said as they approached the old man. The gray-haired pastor beamed. "This is my friend, Jesse. He just moved to town."

"I think I saw you in the back on Sunday too, how lovely," Noel said. "You moved into the old Welch place?"

"Bertie Welch was my grandfather," Jesse said.

The pastor squeezed his shoulder. "I didn't know Bertie all that well, but we had a small service after he died."

Jesse nodded. Monica had driven down to attend. To claim his house too.

"Would you mind if I introduced you to everyone?" Noel asked. "I think that would go over nicely."

"Uh, sure." Jesse rubbed the back of his neck. He was already feeling hot and itchy. It looked like half the town was here!

"Good, good." Noel put his arm around Jesse, and Emily seemed to melt into the crowd. Before Jesse knew it, he was standing in front of the entire church, being introduced to a room of strangers. Jesse, his face burning with embarrassment, smiled and nodded as choruses of hellos and welcomes came from the crowd.

"I think we embarrassed the poor boy enough for one night," Noel said, and the audience chuckled with agreement. "Emily? Could you help Mr. Welch back to his seat?"

Emily appeared at Jesse's elbow and took his hand. She led him down the aisle and into a pew near the front. She sat him next to Kenny, taking his other side. An older couple was on Kenny's other side, and they leaned forward to introduce themselves as Emily and Kenny's parents, Mr. and Mrs. Taylor. Jesse gave them a stupid smile. *Fuck*, his head was spinning!

Service started, songs were sung, Jesse stared at the pastor and tried to follow along. Beside him, Emily praised and worshiped aloud, totally involved. She kept a tight hold on Jesse's hand and tried to get him involved as well, but Jesse continued to feel overwhelmed, out of place, and a tad embarrassed. He couldn't wait for this to be over.

It only lasted an hour, though the service felt much longer than sixty minutes. When Pastor Noel wrapped it up, the room erupted into casual banter. Mrs. Taylor, a beautiful blonde woman, invited Jesse to dinner.

"Let us meet your new friend," she said.

"I appreciate the offer, ma'am, but I've got five brothers and sisters waiting for me. I ducked out of babysitting to be here."

He couldn't have picked a better excuse. Mrs. Taylor smiled brilliantly and invited him over to dinner another time. Rain check!

"Do you have to go home?" Emily asked once she, her brother, and Jesse were back in the truck.

"I'm sure my brother's terrorizing the twins by now."

"Those poor things," Emily said.

"Talk about lame," Kenny snorted.

"Shut up, Ken!" Emily said, giving her brother the evil eye. "Jesse? Did you hear Pastor Noel announce the youth dance? It sounds like so much fun."

"I must have missed it," Jesse said sheepishly.

The ride back was short, and Jesse all but leapt from the truck when they got back to his place.

"Can you come next week?" Emily simpered.

"Let me make sure, before I promise," Jesse said.

"See you tomorrow?"

"Of course."

Emily smiled as Jesse shut the door. He waved and off they went.

Fuck, that was uncomfortable, Jesse thought as he headed inside. The entire time, he'd felt tense and awkward and he'd wanted to escape. He didn't want to go back to church. Emily had annoyed him the entire time.

"Back already?" Sam muttered. He was still playing *Call of Duty.* The twins were gone, and Sam had moved to the couch.

"What the fuck was I thinking? Church?" Jesse sat beside his brother. "I had to get out of there."

"Yeah, that sounds pretty boring."

"Can we double-team this?" Jesse asked, gesturing to the screen.

"Thought you'd never ask." Sam grinned. "Glad Mr. Meanie isn't here. You're making the strangest friends, lately."

"He's not mean," Jesse said. He grabbed the second controller before his brother could elaborate. "C'mon! I want to play."

"I'm going to murder you," Sam said, and the two boys got to it.

*

"I did it!" Jesse said the minute Shaun was within earshot.

"Did what?" Shaun asked. He hesitantly took a seat beside him, but Jesse barely noticed his reluctance. He was eager to share his harrowing journey into the dreaded religion.

"I did church," Jesse elaborated with a smile. "It was brutal, but Emily loved it. I even got to meet the parents."

"Great," Shaun said sourly.

His rotten mood drew Jesse's attention. Shaun was scowling, and he looked deeply unhappy. He was wearing the same clothes he'd had on yesterday, and everything had a fine splattering of mud on it now. His hair was tangled again and even messier than usual.

But what got Jesse's attention the most was the weird bulge under his sleeve.

"What's that?" he asked. He poked the bulge.

Shaun hissed. "Don't do that!"

"Sorry." Jesse held up his hands, indicating he wouldn't be poking any further. "But what is it?"

Shaun hesitated, but finally pulled back his sleeve. Jesse gasped. A bloody mass of gauze covered Shaun's arm from wrist to elbow.

"What happened?!" Jesse's voice went up an octave. It looked like Shaun had suffered a serious injury in the hours they'd been apart. "Oh my God!"

"I ah..." Shaun held his mangled arm out, surveying it calmly. "I went hunting...like I said I was going to—"

"And did that?" Jesse touched Shaun's elbow gently, drawing his arm into his lap. He couldn't see what sort of damage had been done through the gauze, but there was so much blood!

"I fell," Shaun said.

"On what? A knife?!"

Shaun stiffened and pulled his arm back. He yanked his sleeve down over the bandages. "It's fine," he all but growled.

"Can you even move your hand?" Jesse asked in a panic.

"Fuck you." Shaun lifted his arm, held his hand in Jesse's face, and then proceeded to wiggle his fingers.

"You're wincing!" Jesse cried. "Stop! You'll make it worse." He cradled Shaun's hand between his own, but Shaun wouldn't allow it. He yanked his hand from Jesse's.

"I'm *perfectly* fine," he declared.

Unconvinced, Jesse continued to prod. "Let's go to the nurse when we get to school. I'll come with you," he pleaded, deeply disturbed by the whole thing.

"Don't need her. I already had my grandpa look at it."

"Did you really?"

Shaun folded his arms and didn't answer.

"You're impossible! Do you know that?"

Shaun was a hard person to like. He was gruff and mean, rough around the edges if you will. Stubborn to a fault, unable to take any sort of criticism without biting your head off. He was also stupid and too proud to take well-meaning help from anybody.

"Shut up," Shaun grumbled.

Frowning, Jesse did just that. Shaun certainly made it hard for anyone to get close to him, but Jesse was more than up for the challenge, even if Shaun annoyed the crap out of him half the time.

Jesse could be stubborn too.

"So, are you done talking to me now?" Shaun snapped at the end of chemistry. Normally Jesse was talkative and energetic during the one class they could sit by each other, but today he'd been stone silent.

"I didn't know I was allowed to. I thought you wanted me to shut up," Jesse said. He was angry still, but mostly he wanted Shaun to stop being such an asshole. There was no reason for Shaun to brush him off like he had. Jesse was only trying to help.

"You're a fucking dick, you know that?" Shaun said, though he sounded more defensive than anything else. All this over some hunting accident?

"How am *I* being a dick?" Jesse asked in exasperation. "I'm trying to help you."

"I—" Shaun rudely pushed past him, hitting Jesse with his backpack. "C'mon," he growled.

Rolling his eyes, Jesse followed Shaun into the hall.

"Just drop it, all right? I'm fine," Shaun said when they were halfway to history.

"Shaun..." Jesse whined, grabbing his good arm.

"Don't touch me, fag," Shaun hissed, pulling away and marching off toward the classroom. Hurt, Jesse trailed behind him.

"Are you all right?" Emily asked the second Jesse sat beside her.

"Yep. Fine," he lied, figuring if Shaun could get away with it, then he should be allowed to as well.

Class was boring. They were studying World War II. Jesse pretended to take notes as he stared at the back of Shaun's head. It was so unfair he had to sit all the way up front.

Once, Shaun turned and caught Jesse looking at him. As much as Jesse had wanted his attention, he found himself avoiding the piercing eye contact that seemed to see straight through his soul.

"We were all wondering if you can hang out with us on Friday again," Emily said when they were on their way to English. "You had fun last week, didn't you?"

"Oh, yeah." Jesse hadn't thought about it. He'd assumed he and Shaun would spend time together like they had all week. They might be able to do something after Monica came home too. Maybe they could go to Shaun's place to get away from all the kids. He was sure Shaun would be over his little funk by then.

"Is that a yes?" Emily fluttered her eyelashes.

"I'm not sure—"

"We could pick you up at eight. Like last week. You don't have to babysit all night, right?" Emily asked.

"I don't know—"

"Think about it, okay?" Emily pushed. "It was fun having you at the party last weekend and doing church on Wednesday." She touched Jesse's arm. She squeezed it in an overtly friendly gesture that made him feel as though he'd been caught.

"It was fun," he said. He felt obligated to say so. Emily was smiling at him and batting her lashes so hard it was a wonder her eyes hadn't popped out of her head.

"I wanted to ask you something..." she said. Her hand tightened on Jesse's arm, and they slowed almost to a stop. Someone pushed past them to get down the hall, and Jesse coaxed her along.

"What?" he asked. They were almost to English. The weight of the conversation was strangely foreboding. It was uncomfortable.

"Well, I was just wondering..."

The hesitations and pauses were too much. Jesse took a deep breath. "What were you wondering?"

"Remember the youth ministry dance the pastor mentioned?"

Jesse shrugged. "Sure."

"Do you want to go with me? It's on Saturday."

"As like a date?" Jesse blurted. They were in front of their classroom. Right in the doorway.

Emily, her hand still firmly attached to Jesse's arm, pulled him inside. She led him to his desk and waited for him to sit.

"If you wanted to call it a date, well..." She fidgeted with the purple scrunchie around her wrist. "I wouldn't mind."

"Oh." Jesse cleared his throat. This was what he'd wanted, right? Time alone with Emily? An actual, honest-to-God date? "Sure. We could go to that."

"Great." Emily grinned. "It's a date, then."

"Yeah. Great," Jesse said. He watched Emily stroll to her desk. She looked coyly over her shoulder and winked.

They sat next to each other during lunch. Emily talked excitedly about...something. Jesse found it hard to focus on her sometimes. She arbitrarily jumped from one topic to another. She talked about a movie the gang wanted to see on Friday and then began discussing the merits of high heels and flat shoes.

"I don't know, my legs look good in heels. I like the extra height too," she said. "But flats are so cute. My older sister got me a beautiful silver pair in New York. They're so trendy," she gushed.

"Hmm." He didn't have an opinion. He didn't care what a girl had on her feet.

"Maybe I'll wear them Saturday. I mean, they're way better to dance in, right?"

"Uh-huh."

Emily smiled. She went on with the one-sided conversation with little heed for Jesse's boredom. The dance, the dance, the dance... The more she talked about it, the less Jesse wanted to go. It wasn't supposed to be a big deal, but Emily was making quite a fuss.

Kenny cornered Jesse before gym. "So, you're taking my sister to the dance?" he asked. They entered the gym and cut across the basketball court to get to the locker room.

"Oooh!" Eric taunted. "Ken's going to have your balls, dude!"

"Why? Emily invited me," Jesse said. "Was I supposed to turn her down?"

"Did you want to?" Kenny said as they walked into the changing area. "You ignored her all through lunch. You looked bored."

Jesse ruffled a hand through his hair. "I didn't know what to say. She was talking about shoes."

"She mentioned a lot more than that," Kenny said. He pulled his gym stuff out of his locker. "I guess I was the only one who was listening."

Jesse kept quiet. He pulled his change of clothes out of his locker too, and tugged his T-shirt over his head. He was completely embarrassed. Kenny was a pretty cool guy, but he got the vibe that if he fucked up in any way with Emily, Kenny would kill him.

"Anyway, I'm glad you're taking her to the dance," Kenny said. Behind him, Shaun stomped into the room and went straight to his locker without sparing anyone a glance. Jesse watched him from the corner of his eye. "Emily told our parents last night she was going to ask you. They thought it was a good idea."

"Um, that's good," Jesse said.

"Did she mention you're invited to dinner before the dance?"

"Oh, no. She didn't say," Jesse said.

"Oh fuck!" Eric laughed. "First date and you're already meeting the parents!"

Shaun had his back to the room. He was stuck in a half crouch over his gym bag. His body was completely still. Jesse bit the inside of his cheek. Shaun was *listening*.

"Uh, I already met them," Jesse said. "Yesterday. At church."

Eric chuckled and smacked him on the back. Jesse winced. "Don't worry then, no pressure."

"Shut up, you know what they're like," Kenny said. "They might have stopped the whole thing if they hadn't seen you Wednesday. They think going to church means you can be trusted."

Eric snorted and Kenny glared at him.

Jesse rubbed his stinging shoulder. He glanced nervously in Shaun's direction.

Shaun jerked his yellow-stained hoodie over his head and yanked the hood up. His back was tense and angry. His shoulder blades stuck out like knives.

Kenny put his arm around Jesse's bare shoulders. Jesse jerked in surprise.

"C'mere," Kenny said in a low, dangerous tone. He drew him in close. "I like you, Jess, but you'd better be nice to my sister," he said, his eyes serious and unwavering. Jesse blinked. "Just because my parents are easy to win over doesn't mean I am."

Jesse swallowed. He'd made a huge mistake. He should have gone after Sunny or maybe Alicia. Neither of them had brothers who would beat him up. Or at least he didn't think they did.

"You're good, dude. Calm down," Kenny laughed. He cuffed Jesse on the arm. "I'm just warning you."

Jesse grabbed his gym shirt and pulled his arms through the holes. He was tired of the roughhousing. "Yeah, okay," he said awkwardly.

Behind them, Shaun hurled his bag into his locker. He didn't turn around, but Jesse got the feeling he was pissed. He slammed his locker shut with a resounding bang.

"What's wrong with him?" Eric said under his breath. Everyone stared at Shaun. They all watched as he balled his hands into fists and stormed from the room.

Jesse sighed. "Nothing's wrong," he said, but he suspected he knew what was up.

"He's a loser," Kenny said with a dismissive shake of his head.

"No, he's not," Jesse said. "He's just—"

"A freak?" Eric supplied.

"No," Jesse snapped, trying not to get angry. "He's moody today."

That made Eric and Kenny laugh. Jesse scowled as he finished changing. He hadn't meant to make everyone laugh. He ignored the two jocks as best he could. Sometimes, they were dicks.

Today, it was nice out. The sun was drying up the rain from yesterday. The coach led them out to the field to play touch football. He was in charge of teams today, and he divvied everyone up, putting an equal number of good players on both teams to keep it fair. Jesse kept sneaking glances at Shaun, wondering—hoping more like—that they'd get put on the same team.

The coach didn't put Shaun on a team. Jesse was on the verge of getting pissed off. The dumbass teacher had forgotten Shaun completely. But he needn't have worried. Once the teams had been decided, the coach pointed a finger at Shaun and glared at him expectantly. Jesse had no idea what that was supposed to mean, but Shaun did. He turned and walked off toward the edge of the field. He gradually picked up his pace until he was running. Jesse watched Shaun run a lap around the field. He was red-faced and angry. He started a second lap and wasn't slowing down.

"Okay, guys, let's play," the coach said, ignoring Shaun and his laps. Everyone else ignored him too. It seemed this was a semiregular occurrence.

Jesse was decent at football. He wasn't paying much attention, but he managed not to completely embarrass himself. He found it impossible to keep his eyes off Shaun, though. He wasn't very good at running. He didn't know how to pace himself. He ran hard for as long as he could before he slowed considerably. When he passed close by, Jesse could see how exhausted he was. Shaun sweat buckets, and he looked like he was about to collapse, but he never went slower than a jog. The one time he tried, the coach yelled across the field for him to stop slacking. It was the only time he'd acknowledged Shaun's struggles, and Jesse felt another spike of anger on his friend's behalf.

Thankfully class ended soon, and the coach called everybody back inside. Shaun stopped right where he was and collapsed back in the grass.

Jesse went straight for him. Eric and Kenny tried to call him back, but Jesse waved them off. He needed to check on Shaun. Maybe it was dumb, but he didn't care. He had a bounce in his step as he rushed to Shaun's side.

"Why did he make you do that?" Jesse asked as he approached. He sunk into the grass at Shaun's side.

Shaun was covered in sweat; his face was dripping wet, and his hair was matted and fucking reeking. His hoodie was completely soaked with perspiration.

"I—I had to—do it—instead—instead of—detention," Shaun wheezed.

"What?" Jesse peered into Shaun's weary face.

Shaun held up a hand and sat for a few moments, breathing hard. Jesse sighed and waited for a better answer. He looked around.

They were completely alone in the field. There wasn't a soul in sight. The manicured lawn of the school stretched before them. The football field and the stadium seats broke up the monotony of green. There were yellow corn fields in the distance and wide swaths of trees. The same thick and unruly jungle behind his and Shaun's houses bordered the school property. Jesse felt vulnerable staring out at all the wide-open space. He scooted closer to Shaun and put a hand on his knee.

"Coach Vance made me run laps for skipping class. He does it to everyone, but I'm the only one that has to run the whole period like that," Shaun said after a brief rest.

"You could get sick running like that," Jesse said with concern. "You should at least get to stop for water or something."

"I'm fine, Jesse," Shaun said. He'd denied Jesse's help, again, though he wasn't as rude about it as he had been that morning.

"We are friends...aren't we?" Jesse asked after another minute of silence.

"Yeah?" Shaun said slowly, almost reluctantly. He wiped his face with his sleeve and quick as lightning, his expression turned into one of determination. "I fucking told you we are."

Jesse fought a smile. "Then is it okay if I care about you?" he asked. Shaun paused at that. He looked shyly into Jesse's eyes. "Friends can be worried about and want the best for each other. Right?"

"I don't know," Shaun admitted after a significant pause. He looked away uncomfortably.

"How about you take my word for it? It's okay if you let me worry about you. Nothing bad will happen if you let me."

Shaun cradled his arm to his chest. "I don't want you to see it," he blurted.

"What's that?" Jesse asked. He rubbed Shaun's knee in encouragement.

Shaun looked at Jesse's hand on his leg. He was surprisingly calm about the unwarranted touching.

"I don't want you to see," he said softly.

It took a moment for Jesse to parse the meaning of Shaun's softly spoken words. But then, he realized what Shaun was referring to.

"Your arm?"

"Yeah," Shaun said. He pulled his knees to his chest and wrapped his arms around them. He let out a deep, shaky breath and buried his face in his arms. He looked fragile and helpless.

Jesse's heart filled with sympathy. He scooted closer until he could rest his head on Shaun's shoulder. He put his arm around his damp back and rubbed it reassuringly.

"All right," he said gently. He didn't like it, he wanted to help, but he knew fighting over it wouldn't make anything better. "You don't have to show me."

Shaun's fingers touched the edges of Jesse's hair. "I don't want you to be worried," he said gruffly. His back rumbled against Jesse's side. It tickled a little. Jesse hugged Shaun tighter and closed his eyes.

"That's what good friends do, so just get used to it," he said pleasantly. He'd fully expected Shaun to push him off, especially after the "fag" comment earlier. But Shaun's fingers hesitantly rubbed the back of his neck and slid into the springy red hair at the nape of Jesse's neck. He wasn't pushing Jesse away. This felt...intimate.

"Hmm," Shaun hummed. Jesse could feel his breath on his ear, and he shivered. It felt good. Weird but good.

"I'm so late to my last class," Jesse said to distract them both from their weird embrace. Shaun's fingers were still rubbing the back of his neck, ghosting through his hair. He didn't want him to stop.

"Want to skip?"

"Yeah."

Without a second thought for his clothes in the locker room or the fact Emily would be expecting him to sit with her on the bus home, Jesse stood and gave Shaun a hand up.

They held hands for a few seconds. It was an accident. Jesse had been trying to help Shaun stand up, and Shaun, a little off-balance, needed Jesse's hand for extra support.

But it had happened, and for some reason Jesse didn't let it go like he normally would. He kept thinking about it as they walked home.

Since it was early and Jesse didn't have to be home anytime soon, when they got to Shaun's house, Jesse asked if he could come in.

Shaun tensed immediately.

"My grandma's home."

"So? You've met my whole family," Jesse pointed out.

"I don't want her to meet you," Shaun said sourly.

"Well..." Jesse struggled to come up with something that would get him into Shaun's house. He didn't want to leave. "I'll be rude, and I won't even look at her," he said. "Or you could sneak me in?" he suggested, on the verge of begging.

"My room's a mess," Shaun said. He tugged his long sleeves over his hands.

"And mine's clean?" Jesse laughed. "C'mon," he pleaded. "I'm so tired of being cooped up in my house. Let me come over."

Shaun sighed loudly. He was losing his patience. "I don't want you to come in," he said, his teeth gritted. "I'd rather be at your house."

Jesse pouted. He should have seen this coming. Shaun was such a private person. It would kill him if anyone found out he had a normal bedroom, filled with dirty clothes, useless junk, porn, and posters with lame bands and chicks on the walls.

"All right. Fine." He didn't want to argue. "But you'll be over later, right?"

"Yeah." Shaun sounded defensive again.

Jesse almost huffed but he managed to catch himself. "See you then," he said. He headed home. At least he'd get a shower and a chance to change out of his smelly gym clothes. That was a definite plus.

Jesse got home in short order. He stripped in the bathroom and jumped in the shower. Sometime between washing his hair and masturbating, he remembered his date with Emily. He'd completely forgotten about it. He hadn't even mentioned it during the walk home when Shaun had mentioned her—or the "snobby bitch" as he called her.

He dried off and walked naked to his room. There, he had to hunt for something to wear. Nothing he owned was clean. He'd have to do a load a of laundry over the weekend, he thought. He found a pair of his brother's jeans, which were a little tight in the crotch but otherwise fit, and put on a T-shirt and a hoodie.

As if on cue, the minute Jesse finished dressing, the doorbell rang. He ran a hand through his damp hair and then ran downstairs to answer the door.

Shaun stood on the front step. In comparison, it didn't look like he'd done more than change out of his gym stuff. His hair was just as tangled and frizzy as ever. Jesse wondered where he'd gotten that wild mop of hair.

"Hey," Jesse said. He opened the door and invited Shaun inside.

"I got a little left," Shaun said as he stepped inside. He held up his baggy of weed. He'd brought his pipe this time. "I don't usually smoke every day. I need to get more."

"I'll buy this time," Jesse said quickly. He didn't want to become a leech. He was using more than his fair share anyway.

"No," Shaun said firmly.

Jesse blinked in confusion. "What do you mean, no?"

"Don't talk to him. Kyle's a faggot," Shaun said as he moved into the living room.

"What?" Jesse asked, now thoroughly bewildered. "He's not gay."

"How the fuck would you know? You only met him once."

Okay, now that was weird.

"How do you know that?"

Shaun stood with his back to Jesse. He drew his shoulders into himself. "He told me. He met you at that party," he said.

Jesse circled around Shaun. He avoided Jesse's eyes, but allowed Jesse to take his arm. He coaxed Shaun to the couch and urged him to sit. "I wanted to repay the favor and buy us something to smoke," Jesse said. "What does it matter if Kyle's gay? I'm not going to suck him off or anything."

"You'd be surprised," Shaun grumbled. He sat stiffly on the couch. He held the baggie and the pipe in his lap. "He might talk you into it. If he gives you a good price."

"Oh, fuck you." Jesse shoved Shaun into the arm of the couch with all his might. Shaun grunted but otherwise, he didn't react. "What do you think I am? A prostitute?"

"If you turn gay, we can't be friends anymore," Shaun said flatly.

"Where is this coming from?!" Jesse couldn't believe they were having this conversation.

"You heard me."

Jesse sucked his teeth. "So, now you're homophobic?"

"I'm not afraid of gays!" Shaun said in a huff. He turned and looked Jesse in the eye. "I don't want people thinking I'm gay for being around them!"

Jesse snorted. He couldn't help it; he started to laugh. "Is that all?"

"Fuck you," Shaun growled. He opened his baggie and packed the bowl with the remains of his weed.

"Nobody thinks you're gay," Jesse said. So that explained all the "fag" stuff. Why he always got nervous whenever Jesse touched him.

"Yeah right. I'm sure they told you I'm weird and that I'm a fag," he said. He yanked a plain black lighter from his pocket and sparked up. He didn't hand the smoke to Jesse like he usually did, but Jesse was too interested in the present conversation to care.

"They do not! Do you want to know what everyone says about you?"

"Fuck you! I know what they say about me! I've lived with it—!"

Jesse laid his hand over Shaun's, stopping him midrant. "Nobody thinks you're gay."

Shaun glared down at their hands. "Are you fucking sure?"

"Yes," Jesse said with confidence. "They think you're dangerous. I've been warned multiple times to stay away from you. Everyone thinks you'll murder me or something."

Instead of relieving him, that only seemed to make Shaun angrier.

"Fuck them *all.*"

"Yeah, fuck them," Jesse said. "I know you wouldn't hurt anybody."

"You don't know shit."

"Gee, thanks." Jesse snatched the pipe from Shaun. He leaned back and took a puff. Monica was going to *kill* him for smoking in the living room. "I try to cheer you up and you insult my intelligence."

"You don't get it," Shaun snapped. "If people think I'm a fag, my life will be even worse than it is now. Around here, being gay gives people the license to do just about anything they want. That's why Kyle's in the closet. He knows, just as well as I do, what'll happen to him if he's ever outed."

"What'll happen to him?" Jesse asked.

Shaun shook his head. "Don't worry about it."

Jesse rolled his eyes, but Shaun continued.

"They hate me because I'm not like them. They hate me because they're afraid," he said bitterly. "But if they think I'm a cocksucker? It'll be too fucking much for them."

"You act like they're going to behead you," Jesse said with a little laugh. "This isn't the old west. Gay people have rights now."

Shaun was silent for so long Jesse was sure he was being ignored. He drew himself up, ready to defend the whole LGBTQ community, when Shaun spoke.

"I promised my grandparents I'd make it to senior year," he said solemnly. "They were expecting me to graduate, but fuck that. I've only got a couple more months; then I can drop out and leave this place for good. I'll never have to think about this hell hole, or anyone in it, ever again."

Jesse didn't know what to say. He thought Shaun sounded crazy.

They passed the pipe between them a few more times until they ran out of weed. It was just in time, too, as seconds later Sam came in the front door.

"Hey, stoners," he greeted sarcastically. His eyes darted to Shaun. He surveyed him with an unfriendly expression on his face. "Skipping school to smoke? Are you gonna drop out next?"

"What's it to you?" Jesse still remembered the weird way Sam had been acting that morning. He was being bossy? Well, maybe Sam could go fuck off.

"I don't know. I always thought it'd be cool to have a delinquent for an older brother."

"Oh, yeah. Good one." Jesse gave him the finger. "Fuck off."

Sam started up the stairs. He grinned the whole way, like he'd accomplished something insurmountable.

"Jerk," Jesse muttered.

"What's his problem now?" Shaun asked nonchalantly, like he didn't care, and really, it was very possible he didn't.

"I don't know. You, probably."

"Oh." That drew Shaun up short.

"Don't worry about it," Jesse said.

The rest of the night flowed into the same routine they'd had since Monday. The twins came home, hassled Shaun until he'd had enough and Jesse sent them upstairs. Monica dropped the babies off, and amusingly enough she placed Brian in Shaun's lap.

"I think you've got a new fan. All Brian ever talks about is his cool new friend."

Shaun flushed. He ruffled Brian's hair and then moved the toddler off his lap and onto the couch between him and Jesse. Brian smiled worshipfully up at the big boys.

Monica had even brought pizza for everybody, so Jesse didn't have to cook again.

"Oh, and, Jesse," Monica said as she carried the pizza boxes into the kitchen. "I can smell that weed a mile away. Keep it away from the kids, will you?"

Jesse nodded dumbly. He was embarrassed they'd been caught; not that they'd tried to hide the evidence. Still, the lecturing note in his mother's voice was unpleasant.

For some reason, cutting up a piece of pizza for Lissa reminded Jesse of the dinner and date plans with Emily.

"I'm going on a date with Emily on Saturday."

"Oooh! Jesse's got a girlfriend!" Allison and Tyler sang at the same time. Sam shoveled a piece of pizza into his mouth. He didn't look interested.

Shaun went deathly silent. He set his pizza down. His face twisted into a grimace.

Jesse had been expecting this. He could have lied about the whole thing, but he didn't want to keep secrets. "I know you hate her and all but—"

Shaun slammed his fist on the table. The plates rattled. Brian's empty cup toppled and rolled to the floor.

"Seriously?" Jesse said.

Shaun glared at him darkly. A glare that carried a hatred and anger so deep-seated Jesse was literally floored. He shut his mouth.

Brian looked between them with complete surprise. The twins seemed to be holding their breath, waiting for an explosion. Sam suddenly looked interested. He watched the scene unfold as he continued to munch on his slice of pepperoni.

Jesse stood up. He wasn't doing this in front of everyone. "Sam, watch the kids," he said. He gestured for Shaun to follow him out of the room, and Shaun leapt up immediately. His chair skidded over the linoleum and he kicked it out of the way.

They reached the privacy of Jesse's room. He shut the door behind them, took a deep breath, and turned to face Shaun.

"What's your problem with Emily?"

At least Shaun didn't play coy; he immediately spat, "I *hate* that bitch."

"Right. So, one minute you're afraid everyone's going to think you're gay, then you flip out when I get a girlfriend? Do you have any idea how contradictory you are?"

Shaun glared at him. "Emily's a cunt," he hissed.

"Why do you hate her so much?" Jesse asked. He was trying to remain calm. "Did she turn you down or something?"

Shaun bared his teeth and snarled. "I would *never* ask that dirty whore on a date."

Jesse stepped up and shoved Shaun in the chest. Shaun stumbled over a pile of clothes but caught himself with a growl of frustration.

"If you touch me again, I'll *smash* you," Shaun growled.

Jesse dropped his arms to his sides. The anger he'd felt moments before had drained from him and left him cold. He couldn't believe he'd pushed Shaun like that.

Shaun balled his hands into fists. His body vibrated with restrained fury. He was ready for a fight.

"Why are you doing this? Why can't you be happy for me?" Jesse said in a little voice. He felt queasy. All this over a stupid date? "I thought we were friends."

"I never wanted a friend," Shaun said. He advanced on Jesse, forcing him back without even laying a hand on him. "And I don't need you in my fucking face."

"But—"

"Leave me the fuck alone!" Shaun cried. "You will anyway. Once you start cozying up with that *slut*." With a pained look, Shaun shouldered past him and left the bedroom. There were a few seconds of silence before Jesse heard the front door open and slam.

Shaun was gone.

Shaken, Jesse sat on the edge of Sam's bed.

Shaun was jealous, Jesse thought. He was jealous of Emily.

He was afraid Emily would take Jesse away. The idea Jesse would end up hating him like everyone else did made him physically ill.

So, in other words, Shaun cared. He didn't want Jesse to disappear. He didn't want to be alone, even though he constantly acted like he did.

Once again, Jesse came head to head with Shaun's pride and his distrust in the world. It cut between them like a knife through butter.

Jesse was determined to make a difference. He wanted to be the most important person in Shaun's life. Jesse didn't fully understand why. It was clear Shaun had never had a friend before, and though Jesse saw a deep injustice in that fact, it wasn't the only reason. There was something else there. It was in Shaun's reluctant smiles, his possessiveness toward Jesse, the shy way Shaun touched him...

Jesse tried not to think about that though. Remembering Shaun's hesitant touch made him feel dizzy and hot.

Jesse had never felt this strongly about anyone—

"Did you guys break up?" Sam poked his head into the room. He gave Jesse a big, shit-eating grin.

Jesse flushed. "No! Fuck you!"

Sam laughed and ducked back out into the hallway.

Jesse listened as his brother's footfalls faded. He sighed. He wanted to go after Shaun. He wanted to talk to him. He wanted to make him understand that he meant more to Jesse than Emily did, but Jesse knew he had to let Shaun cool off. He knew if he tried to make Shaun see reason, he'd react with more anger.

"Is Shaun mad?"

Jesse glanced up as Brian shuffled into the room. He looked disappointed.

"Yeah," Jesse said. He patted the edge of Sam's bed. Brian climbed up next to him and leaned into his side. "He'll get over it though."

"He said we were gonna watch *Rambo* today," Brian whined.

"You can watch it later," Jesse said. He brushed the toddler's hair back in a soothing manner. "Shaun will be back soon."

"Like real soon? Like maybe today?"

"Not today," Jesse said. "Maybe tomorrow."

They'd see Shaun tomorrow, Jesse said to himself. Jesse would see him first thing in the morning after all. But for now, Jesse had to stay here. He was reminded of his responsibilities downstairs when he heard Lissa start to cry followed by Sam's muffled yelling. With a groan, he got up to investigate.

The next day Jesse waited eagerly for Shaun to get on the bus. He'd spent the night before, after putting Sam and the twins in time-out for antagonizing Lissa, coming up with a speech. He was rather proud of it. He considered writing it down, maybe getting it published into a self-help book called *How to Take Care of Your Impossible Best Friend.*

When the bus stopped in front of Shaun's house, Jesse waited impatiently for him to get on. The driver paused, waited a moment, then shut the door and drove to the next stop. No one got on.

That was weird. Was Shaun sick or something? Jesse had only known him for...about a month. Maybe he skipped class sometimes; but that didn't make sense either. If anything, Shaun's mean grandma would have made him go.

Maybe he was avoiding Jesse and the bus ride. Maybe his grandparents were driving him.

That was it, Jesse decided. Shaun would be in second-period chemistry, his usual dour self. Jesse wouldn't be able to deliver his speech in class, but he could wait.

When the bus stopped next, Emily, Kenny, and the others got on. Emily's face lit up when she saw Jesse sitting by himself. She led her brother to the back of the bus, and their friends followed.

No one commented on Shaun's absence.

Everyone started talking at once. They wanted to go out tonight, and Jesse was invited. Emily and Sunny mentioned a new movie everyone wanted to see in theaters. There was going to be another get-together afterward.

Jesse didn't want to outright say he wasn't interested. He wasn't though. He wanted to make up with Shaun. He made an excuse about babysitting and said he wasn't sure whether he'd be able to get out of it or not. Kenny gave him a weird look, but Emily told him to "wait and see." Maybe Monica would give him the night off again. Jesse didn't want to be too obvious. He didn't want everyone thinking he'd rather be with Shaun babysitting than with the popular kids at a party. He did though. Whether he'd admit to it or not.

So, he put up with Emily's excited chatter. He didn't turn her down. When they got to the high school, he followed her and Kenny into the building. He kept his eye out for Shaun, but they didn't run into each other.

During first period Jesse wrote and discarded several notes for Shaun. Jordan was curious. He looked over his shoulder more than once as Jesse wrote and wrote. He asked sarcastically if he was writing love notes to Emily.

It seemed everyone knew about their date. Jesse was embarrassed too. He'd never felt so much pressure for a first date. He wasn't even sure he was interested in going anymore.

The note was a love letter, all right. It was full of a lot of emotions and heartfelt promises. Shaun would turn bright red when he read it. The thought made Jesse smile.

When math class ended, he stuck the note in his pocket and got ready for a confrontation. He ditched Jordan as soon as he could and hurried to the chemistry room.

Shaun wasn't there when Jesse arrived. He tried not to be discouraged. He took his seat and sat straight up with his back rigid. He waited expectantly for Shaun to amble in, scowling at everything in creation.

The late bell rang, but still Jesse waited.

And he waited through history.

And through lunch.

And gym.

But Shaun wasn't in class. He wasn't in the school at all.

Jesse was hurt. Shaun didn't seem like the kind of person who would run from his problems, but he'd skipped school entirely to avoid another confrontation.

On the bus ride home Jesse sat beside Emily. He wasn't happy about it, but he tried his best not to look bored as he listened to her talk about the hilarious movie they were seeing tonight. She wanted Jesse to come. She was adamant about it.

Jesse was unwilling to commit to a night out, but he promised he'd call if he was able to escape his babysitting duties. He told her not to count on it.

That shut her up.

When Jesse and Sam got off the bus, Jesse didn't even bother going into the house. He turned and started for Shaun's.

"Where are you going?" Sam called after him.

Jesse didn't respond. It seemed obvious to him where he was going, so he kept walking. The grass grew in unruly patches between the properties, and the weeds tangled in his shoelaces and brushed against his bare arms.

Jesse slowed as he neared Shaun's lawn. He didn't know what he should say.

He was divided. He wanted to reprimand him for skipping school. He also wanted to beg for his forgiveness. He didn't want Shaun to avoid him anymore.

He was still deciding what to say when he crossed the gravel driveway. There were a couple jolly gnomes and a fat frog among the shrubbery. Jesse shoved his hands in his pockets and studied the ugly decorations. He chewed his lip and steeled himself. He didn't want to be caught standing on Shaun's doorstep. He climbed up the porch, lifted his fist, and knocked.

The door was jerked open. Jesse stepped back to make room.

An old woman—Shaun's grandma Jesse realized—held the door open. She was the spitting image of Shaun. They had the same frizzy hair, the same dark penetrating eyes, and the same wide mouth. The only real difference was that her hair was gray, and she was heavyset. Oh, and she was a woman, of course.

"Who are you?" Shaun's grandma asked in a shrill voice. She furrowed her thick brows and looked him over with apathy.

"I'm ah..." Jesse fidgeted under her stare. He should have been used to getting stared at considering all the time Shaun spent staring at him, but her gaze didn't feel as...familiar as Shaun's did. "I'm here to see Shaun. I'm a friend of his...from school."

The old woman snorted like a pig. She crossed her pudgy arms. "Who are you?" she said again. "Shaun doesn't have any friends." Jesse fought not to cringe. He was already starting to see why Shaun disliked her. He'd known her for five seconds and already thought she was crude.

"I'm new in town. I live down the road." Jesse pointed the way he'd come and the old woman looked over his shoulder skeptically. "Shaun's been helping me babysit."

Shaun's grandma laughed. "Shaun? Babysitting?"

Jesse shrugged. "Yeah?"

When Jesse didn't immediately back down and change his story, the old woman's amusement drained away. She scratched her rounded chin. "He did say he was at a friend's house this week," she admitted.

"He was talking about me. I'm Jesse." He considered being a gentleman and offering his hand for a shake, but the old woman had her hands on her hips now. He decided against it. "Is Shaun home?" he asked instead.

She sneered. "Oh, don't you know?"

Since when had this conversation become a guessing game? "No...?"

"Shaun left this morning. Said he was going to band practice." She rolled her eyes and looked skywards. "The good Lord has his work cut out with that boy."

"He's...with his band?" Jesse said.

Shaun's grandma glared at him. "Isn't that what I just said?"

"Well, yes, but I mean..." *Why didn't he tell me?* The question sounded pathetic. He bit his tongue before he could finish the thought.

"Didn't he tell you?" Shaun's grandma asked, unintentionally rubbing it in.

Jesse shook his head.

"Well, he'll be gone all weekend. He and those cretin friends of his are practicing today and playing a show tomorrow night."

"Tomorrow?!" Jesse leapt at the old woman. "Saturday night?!"

Now Shaun's grandma was really looking at him funny. "Are you all right?"

"Do you know where they're playing?" Jesse pleaded.

Shaun's grandma pursed her lips. "I have no idea where my grandson is. Do you think he'd forget to tell you where he was going and then tell me?"

"I—"

"That brat has no consideration for anyone but himself. He's just like his father," she said sourly. "I'll tell you one thing, boy, don't expect too much from my Shaun. All he cares about is his music, his weed, and pissing me off."

The old lady stepped back and shut the door, but Jesse wedged his foot in the doorjamb.

"Wait," he said.

The old lady gave him a vicious glare, but there was no way Jesse was missing the chance to see Shaun play. He *had* to find him.

"Do you know where they practice?"

The old lady crossed her arms again. She stuffed her hands under her armpits. "Not in the slightest."

"Do you know where they're going to play?"

"Some bar."

Jesse sighed. "Well, do you at least know what the band's called?"

That that struck a chord. "Oh, it's something silly..." Shaun's grandma shifted from one slippered foot to the other as she thought. "Execute...something."

"Execute Something?" That was weird.

The old lady wrinkled her nose. "Execute Invasion," she said. The words were poison in her mouth. "He carved it into the wall one night. I had Eli plaster over the whole thing."

"Oh."

"Hmm. Now, if you're done asking questions, I've got better things to do."

"Sure," Jesse said. He pulled his foot out of the jamb. "Thanks."

The old woman grunted and then slammed the door in Jesse's face. Jesse shrugged off the lady's rudeness. He spun, hopped off the porch, and raced home with a new purpose.

Sam was on the couch when he got back, playing Xbox.

"Where's your friend?" he asked nosily, but Jesse was already running upstairs to be alone. He didn't answer.

He looked up every bar, club, and restaurant within fifty miles on Google. He went down the list, making calls.

It took close to two hours, but finally, *finally*, Jesse found the place. Execute Invasion was headlining tomorrow night at a biker bar thirty miles away.

Jesse was so excited! He wondered if Shaun had any fan girls or if there'd be a mosh pit. Maybe there'd be an awesome after party with booze! Whatever the case, Jesse couldn't wait to see his best friend.

Emily's ears must have been ringing. Just then, Jesse got a text from the girl and their Saturday night plans came rushing back. Fuck...he was supposed to go on a date tomorrow night!

I know you said you couldn't come tonight, but I was just checking, Emily texted.

Jesse stared at the message. He was drenched in guilt. He felt like Emily watched him through the screen.

I'll find out when my mom comes home, Jesse texted back. *She'll be here soon.*

Jesse had been planning on skipping out on tonight completely, but he was reconsidering that decision. Maybe he owed it to Emily, and it wasn't like he had anything better to do tonight. He had no way of finding Shaun's practice space with the scraps of information he'd received. He'd have to wait until tomorrow to make his move.

Cool, Emily said. *We can pick you up, if she says you can come out with us.*

Jesse sighed and put his phone down. Why was he doing this? He wanted Shaun's friendship more than he wanted Emily. Hell, he wasn't sure he needed a girlfriend at all. Hadn't that been the main goal?

Jesse stayed in his room, contemplating his life choices. He could hear the twins downstairs, but it didn't sound like Sam needed any help. The sound of cartoons floated from the living room.

About an hour after Emily's text, Jesse heard the front door open followed by Monica's voice. Feeling obligated, Jesse dragged himself down to greet her.

"Mom?"

"Hey, Jess." Monica crouched in front of the twins, giving them hugs. She looked around Jesse curiously. "Where's your friend?"

"Band practice," Jesse said.

Brian totted out from the kitchen with a juice pouch. "Shaun's not here?" he cried. His cheerful face instantly crumbled.

"He's busy tonight," Jesse told him.

"*Noooo*," Brian whined. He tried to get around Jesse and upstairs, possibly investigating the veracity of the claim for himself. Jesse scooped him up and held him tight.

"Really?" Monica said. "I was going to give you the night off. I made up an excuse and skipped out early tonight."

Jesse sighed. Well, looked like he was going to the movies.

"Don't sound too disappointed," Monica chuckled.

"I'm not. I got invited to a movie," he said.

"Sounds fun," Monica said. She moved into the kitchen. "I'm going to start dinner. Sam, can you keep an eye on the baby?"

"*Can you keep an eye on the baby?*" Sam repeated in a whiny voice. "When do *I* get a night off?"

Jesse escaped to the bedroom with Brian in his arms. He flipped the little TV on for the toddler and sat down to send a text to Emily.

Emily was ecstatic. She said they'd be over to pick him up in less than an hour. The movie started at seven.

Jesse wanted to cancel the plans for the dance tomorrow, but he couldn't muster the courage. He'd have to sit through an entire movie with Kenny glaring daggers at him. *Fuck,* why had he thought dating Emily would ever be a good idea?

"Is that Shaun?" Brian asked. He sat on the floor, watching Jesse text from the edge of Sam's bed. "Is he coming over?"

"No, honey. I told you he's busy tonight. I'm going to see him tomorrow," Jesse said. He put his phone away and gestured for Brian to sit in his lap.

The toddler had a long face, but he got up and climbed into Jesse's arms. "Are you going to his house?"

"I'm going to see Shaun play with his band. At a bar."

Brian's face lit up. "I want to come!"

Jesse shook his head. "You can't. Little kids aren't allowed. It's a place for grownups."

Brian pouted. He pushed Jesse away and stomped out of the room in a toddler rage. Jesse heard him making a mess with Legos in the nursery.

Jesse sighed. He shouldn't have promised him he'd get to see Shaun today. It wasn't fair.

He picked something clean to wear and got ready to go. He changed the TV to something semi-interesting, a paranormal show, and waited for his ride.

Forty minutes later, he heard Kenny's truck pull up in the driveway. He always had his music up way too loud.

Jesse went out to greet his friends before they came to the door. He just wanted to get this over with.

"I'm so glad you can come with us!" Emily said as Jesse got in the truck. She threw her arms around him and squeezed him tight.

"Yeah, me too," he said. He patted her back awkwardly.

Emily kissed him on the cheek and took his hand. She didn't look at her brother, but Jesse did.

Kenny watched them like a hawk. It was unnerving. Jesse felt his palm start to sweat, but he didn't let go of Emily. He was afraid to.

They met up with the crew at the movie theater in town. It was a small place. They were showing four movies on two screens.

Eric and Sara were ahead of them in the ticket line. Eric paid for his girlfriend, and Emily whispered in Jesse's ear.

"They're such a cute couple."

Jesse had cash in his pocket. He felt obligated to pay for Emily. She squeezed his hand and rested her head on Jesse's shoulder as he got tickets for two.

Next, they followed Rick and Lee to the concession stand. Lee wanted popcorn.

"He takes such good care of her," Emily cooed.

That was his cue. Grudgingly, Jesse forked over another ten bucks for a bucket of popcorn and a drink for Emily. They were surrounded by couples!

When the lot of them shuffled into the theater, Jesse got squeezed between his date and Kenny. He held the bucket of popcorn on his lap, in extreme distress. Emily insisted on holding Jesse's hand the entire time. It was a territorial thing. She was staking her claim. Jesse felt like his skin was crawling with ants. He didn't have a free hand to scratch though. He was miserable.

The movie started and so did Emily's relentless chatter. She was a big talker during movies, it seemed. Everything that happened, Emily had some sort of opinion or comment. It was beyond distracting.

Beside him, Kenny laughed at the corny jokes on-screen. On the other side of him, Eric and Jordan tossed popcorn back and forth. Emily sipped loudly on her straw. She never *stopped talking.*

By the time the credits rolled, Jesse had a major headache. He hadn't watched the movie. There had been so many conversations going on, food flying, Sunny kept kicking the back of his seat, and Lee ran to the bathroom a hundred different times...

He was done with these people. He wanted to go home.

"Come to the party with us," Emily mewled when they got back in the truck.

"I've got a terrible headache," Jesse said. He squeezed the bridge of his nose for effect. "I wouldn't be any fun."

"You weren't any fun at the movie," Kenny said.

"Ken! Don't be such an asshole," Emily cried.

"He didn't laugh a single time," Kenny pointed out. "You sat there like a rock."

Jesse shrugged. "I don't feel good. Must have been something I ate at home."

"Must have been." Kenny gave him a side-long look, and Jesse resolutely looked away.

"I hope you feel better by tomorrow," Emily said. She drew Jesse's clammy hand to her lips. She kissed it tenderly. "The dance is going to be so much fun. You can't miss it."

This seemed like the perfect opportunity to escape the unwanted event, but Jesse felt Kenny's eyes on him. His glare was tangible. It was a lot like the death glares Shaun subjected him to. Only, Jesse was scared of what might happen if he dared to challenge it.

Jesse cleared his throat. "I'll be all right," he said. "I need a good night's rest. That's all."

On the ride back to Jesse's, Emily detailed the dinner Saturday night she had previously failed to mention. It was another meet and greet with the parents. How wonderful.

"Can you be at my house? Around six?" she asked.

"Sure." Jesse was already feeling the panic set in. "I can borrow my mom's van."

"Great! I'll send you the address later tonight."

They dropped Jesse off in front of his house. Emily had to climb out to give Jesse enough room to escape.

"Don't be late tomorrow," Kenny said as Jesse slid out the passenger door.

Jesse paused. "I won't."

"You'd better get lots of rest tonight," he said, giving Jesse a pointed look. "Don't disappoint my sister."

Jesse swallowed. The *fucking* pressure! "I—I won't."

"Kenny. Don't be a creep," Emily chastised. She put her hand on Jesse's lower back and drew him away from the truck.

"Don't worry about him," Emily said. "He's not coming to the dance. He won't bother us."

"He's not bothering me," Jesse said. His lips stretched into a thin smile.

"Well, I think he's being a pain," Emily said. She shut her eyes, took a deep breath, and then forced a smile on her face. "I'm looking forward to tomorrow."

"Me too," Jesse said. His throat was closing up. How was he supposed to get to the dance *and* the biker bar? He couldn't miss either.

Emily leaned in and kissed Jesse softly on the lips. It was chaste. It wasn't anything to write home about, but they had kissed. Right in front of Kenny. It seemed like a power move.

Emily smiled brilliantly when she pulled back. It wasn't forced. Her eyes twinkled in the moonlight, and Jesse felt his heart thudding in his chest, not from excitement, but from absolute terror. He *had* to make tomorrow night work. He *had* to try. Kenny would skin him alive if he messed this up.

The nervous anticipation built overnight. Jesse tossed and turned in his bed. He wished Shaun had mentioned he was playing a show Saturday night... He suspected if he had, Jesse wouldn't be in this stupid predicament right now.

But he hadn't and now Jesse had to figure everything out himself.

Jesse got up around noon. He wished he could have slept in longer. The sad part was he could have; Monica had taken the kids for a shopping trip. The house was empty and silent. Jesse was too anxious to enjoy it.

By five, Jesse was a nervous wreck. He was close to calling Emily and canceling.

Shaun's band started playing around nine. The bar was almost an hour away. There was no way he could do the dance and still make it to the bar in time. He had to decide. He'd have to ditch Emily...or take her along.

He decided taking Emily was the route least likely to get him killed. So, Jesse got cleaned up, combed his hair, dressed in his nicest button-up and jeans ensemble and showed up at Emily's house at six on the dot.

"Jesse!" Emily threw open the door. She wrapped her arms around him. "I'm so glad you came."

Emily was dressed in a pink frilly dress and her silver flats. Her hair was in a fancy up-do and she wore little earrings in the shape of crosses. In other words, her outfit was completely inappropriate for a biker bar.

"I said I'd be here," Jesse said, hugging her back weakly. He was so damned nervous!

Emily's house was big. The layout was similar to Jesse's, though it was much nicer both inside and out. The living room screamed class and refinement with its polished hardwood floors, pristine white furniture, artfully arranged flowers on the tables, and the beautiful black-and-white photographs of the countryside on the walls.

Then Emily's parents stepped into the room. He instantly started to sweat.

"Hello, Jesse, nice to see you again." Emily's mom stepped forward. She was tall and dark-haired. Her delicate features resembled Emily's. She hugged Jesse in greeting. He stiffened and bore it silently.

"You too, Mrs. Taylor."

"Call me Sue, sweetheart," Emily's mom said kindly. She could probably *smell* his unease.

"I'm Paul." Emily's dad introduced himself next. He clapped Jesse on the shoulder. "Our daughter's quite taken with you."

"I like her too," Jesse said in a daze. Paul smiled toothily in reply.

The four of them stared at each other for a moment. Jesse felt sweat beading along his hairline.

Sue clapped her hands together. "Kenny won't be joining us tonight. He went out for a drive. We know you two lovebirds have a fabulous night planned, so let's get dinner started." She smiled. Everyone was fucking *grinning*.

Mr. and Mrs. Taylor swept into the other room.

"C'mon, Jesse," Emily called.

Jesse took the brief reprieve to wipe the sweat from his forehead. He expected his plans for the night wouldn't sit well with either parent. The thought twisted his stomach into knots. How the *fuck* was he supposed to eat anything?

Luckily, dinner wasn't finished. Sue served sparkling water and cheese and crackers in the dining room while she tended to the roast in the kitchen.

Jesse was seated across the table from Emily. Paul sat at the head of the table and his wife was seated at the opposite end, at the only free space available.

Jesse had never been in a house nice enough to have a separate room for dining. The formality of it, from the fancy place settings with linen napkins, multiple forks, and the crystal wine glasses, to the strict seating arrangements made Jesse more nervous than ever. The three of them—mostly Emily and her father—chatted about the dance while Sue clattered around in the other room. Jesse was uncomfortable. His mouth was dry, and he savored his bubbly, nonalcoholic drink. He was so glad no one was making him talk about himself. That relief was short-lived, however.

Dinner was served. Salad, a roast with potatoes and carrots, and a basket with dinner rolls. Once everyone was seated and dishing food onto their plates, Emily's parents began to grill Jesse.

They asked a million questions about his family and their move from Detroit. They wanted to know about Jesse's progress in school and asked him in-depth questions about his future college and career plans. Jesse made most of it up. He had no plans; he wasn't interested in college and had no idea what kind of career he would fall into. He was embarrassed by his single mother, her failed relationships, and being one of her many offspring. He pulled it off though. Everyone listened with extreme interest as he lied about his grades and talked about wanting to be a doctor. The hard work his mother did at the hospital had sparked his interest, and his siblings were his inspiration.

When Jesse was close to finishing his roast the most important question of all came up. Sue asked about Jesse's beliefs.

Did he have faith? Was his mother a Christian? Was he baptized? Had he shared the love of Jesus Christ with his siblings?

Jesse, for the most part, believed in God. But they certainly didn't have a good relationship. He'd never spent so much time talking about him either. The stupid, circular conversation went on for what felt like forever when it had only been twenty minutes. He didn't want to say the wrong thing, but then again, what did it matter? The worst thing that could happen was Emily being barred from the date tonight, and that would solve all of Jesse's problems anyway!

"Mom, Dad, I hate to interrupt, but it's getting late," Emily said after another of Jesse's stilted answers. "We'd better get going. The dance is starting. We don't want to miss out on the fun."

"Goodness, I'm sorry," Sue laughed, sounding anything but. "We've been interrogating you for over an hour, haven't we?"

"That's all right," Paul answered for Jesse before he could even open his mouth. "It's not often Emily brings a boy home. We're just curious."

"Er...yeah," Jesse said.

"Well, can we go now?" Emily gave her father a pleading look with her hands clasped together.

Paul smiled at his daughter. He studied her in silence. After a moment his eyes moved to Jesse.

Jesse didn't feel comfortable under his scrutinizing stare. He'd rather face Shaun's death glare any day.

Paul cleared his throat. "You know the rules, Emily. Home by eleven."

"Thanks, Dad!" Emily went around the table to kiss her father on the cheek. She wasted no time. She rounded the table, took Jesse's hand, and yanked him out of the room. She stopped to grab a dainty purse on the coffee table, and then they were rushing out the door.

"Sorry about them," Emily said once they were in the van. "They'll soften up once they get to know you."

"Oh, good." Jesse started the engine.

"You looked so nervous! Maybe I can make it up to you tonight," Emily said with a laugh.

Jesse didn't know what she meant by that, but when he checked the dashboard and saw it was five minutes past eight, he firmed his resolve.

"Would you mind if we skipped the dance?"

Emily's smile dropped.

"What kind of girl do you think I am?"

"What?"

"Do you seriously think I'll fuck you just because you picked me up and spent two hours sucking up to my parents?!"

Jesse blinked. "Uh, no. But there is somewhere else I wanted to go."

"Like back to your room?" Emily snapped. "I can't believe you!" She tossed her head like an angry horse. She looked strangely fierce all in pink with her hair flying around her.

"No..." Jesse didn't want to admit where he was planning on going. He knew Emily wouldn't approve. But she certainly wasn't happy now.

"I don't understand. Where would you rather take me than to the dance you promised?"

"A show," Jesse blurted, hoping to shut her up. "I wanted to see a band."

"A band?" Emily narrowed her eyes. "Where is this band?"

"Well..." Jesse accidentally bit the inside of his cheek. He tasted blood. "It's far. It's like a forty-minute drive. We have to go now, or we'll miss the beginning." He glanced at the time again. Another three minutes had passed. "It starts at nine."

Emily stared him down. "You'd better not try to get me drunk."

"No. Of course not."

"And you'd better not take advantage of me."

Jesse had no plans to "take advantage" of anyone. For the first time tonight, he was being totally honest.

"I won't," he said.

"All right then," Emily said. Her expression softened.

Jesse let out a breath he hadn't known he'd been holding. He shifted his free hand through his hair, ruining its neatly combed appearance.

"It's just that..." Emily started. "The guys around here expect you to put out after a couple dates. I went out with you because I thought you'd be different, only..." She laughed. "I thought you were trying to get in my pants before the night had even started."

Jesse shook his head. "No." He'd totally given up on getting laid. There was a good chance she wouldn't come out with him again, either, once she found out whose band they were going to see.

"Guess we'd better hurry then. We've only got an hour," Emily said.

"Right." Jesse backed out of the driveway and headed toward the freeway. It was the fastest way to the bar according to the directions off Google.

It was 8:10. Jesse stepped on the gas.

Emily was quiet for most of the ride. She turned her attention to her phone. Jesse knew this had been a bad idea, but there was no turning back now.

Jesse tightened his grip on the steering wheel. He was so close to seeing Shaun... The only thing that separated them was distance, and Jesse was rapidly closing the space between them. He was almost embarrassed how intensely he longed to be in Shaun's presence. He missed him terribly. Maybe it had only been two days, but Jesse was anxious to make sure everything was right between them.

He hoped there wasn't a bouncer at this place. The bar's reviews said it was a total shithole frequented by a local biker gang. It was understaffed, the lighting was bad, but the drinks were cheap. Jesse figured if Shaun was allowed inside, he and Emily would be able to sneak in too.

Close to the exit, Jesse made a wrong turn that costed them fifteen minutes. He cursed his bad luck and did an illegal U-turn to get back on track.

Jesse scoured the landscape until he found the place. It was right off the highway. There was no visible signage indicating the name of the place, but Jesse knew this grungy bar was it. The parking lot was filled with bikes. It looked like the whole gang had showed up. A few semi-trucks were parked in the back, as well.

"Are you sure this is it?" Emily asked. She'd looked nervously out the window. They were they only van in lot. She pulled at the edge of her dress.

"Yeah." Jesse felt her pain. He hadn't dressed up all that much, but he imagined they would stick out like sore thumbs. "Ah...do you want to wear my hoodie?" He fished around in the back seat for the sweatshirt he'd spotted earlier.

And then he actually found it.

"Oh." It was Sam's hoodie. It had stupid anime characters all over it.

Emily glanced at it, looked back at bar, and then snatched it up. "It's better than nothing," she said.

Nobody tried to stop them as they walked through the door a quarter after nine. There was no staff guarding the door, no bouncers with wrist bands, nothing. They were late, but just in time as far as Jesse was concerned.

The most amazing guitar riff reverberated across the room as they stepped into the gloomy bar. There were people everywhere, bikers in their leathers, a couple of cowboys at the bar, old fat men in suspenders. Jesse scanned the room, but none of that caught his eye.

Shaun looked incredible.

The normally sullen and pinched-looking boy stood on a stage against the back wall. His legs were spread in a power stance, his back curved as he bent over his guitar. His head was down, and his mop of frizzy hair obscured his face. His fingers flew over the fret board as the most amazing sound came from him! Jesse couldn't look away.

"Shaun?" Emily said. "That's who we're here to see?" She sucked her teeth, but with a sigh she possessively grabbed Jesse's arm and drew him toward the stage.

Just then, Shaun threw his head back and...well, not to sound gay or anything—because Jesse was definitely straight—but Shaun looked fucking hot. His eyes were shut as he swung his guitar around and nodded his head to the music. He was completely lost in the sound. Sweat beaded on his pale skin and ran down his throat. His whole body moved in rhythm.

Emily found a table and pushed Jesse toward a chair. He stumbled and looked down so he could find his chair.

Once he was seated and Emily was squeezing in beside him, he looked up and met Shaun's wide and surprised eyes.

Caught, Jesse grinned.

The corners of Shaun's mouth twitched upward ever so slightly. He fumbled, and for a few beats, he and Jesse stared at one another, caught in a beautiful musical haze. Then Shaun tore into his guitar again. He went back to doing his thing. He dropped Jesse's gaze and just like that, the spell was broken, and Jesse was able to take in his surroundings.

The other band members weren't all that great.

Well, that was a little harsh. From what Jesse could tell, the music was solid. The drummer was pretty good, though he looked bored sitting behind his drum kit. The bassist was all right. He smirked at some cute leather-clad girls near the stage. The guitar, of course, was perfect in every fucking way. No complaints there. But the singer? He sucked. He was clearly drunk. He seemed more interested in yelling and screeching into the microphone than singing in melody.

It was bringing the whole thing down.

"The singer sucks," Jesse said into Emily's ear.

"Uh...they're all pretty bad," Emily said, and Jesse felt himself bristle.

"Shaun's great," he said, turning away. He didn't care what Emily thought, but he'd rather she kept her mouth shut if she was going to say stupid shit like that.

"I'm going to get a drink. I'll be back," Emily said and promptly disappeared.

Jesse barely noticed.

The song ended, catching Jesse by surprise. There was a round of half-hearted applause from the bar. Jesse made sure he clapped as loud as he possibly could, and when Shaun spared him another incredulous look, he put his fingers in his mouth and whistled.

For a second, Jesse was sure Shaun was going to laugh, but then he looked away.

"Okay, guys…" the singer slurred. He gripped the mic stand like it was the only thing keeping him up. "Here's another original for ya. It's called 'Swallow the World.'"

Shaun cut through the last of the singer's intro with another insane guitar riff. Jesse squirmed in his seat, fighting the urge to scream out loud like a stupid fan girl.

He'd totally known Shaun was cool…ever since he'd met him. But now that they were friends… That awesome figure on the shitty stage, oozing musical genius, became this unattainable god or something! It was hard to believe he'd had that boy in his house, had him lying in his bed every day the past week, smoking weed with him like it was no big deal. Jesse was star struck.

"Hey, I got you one," Emily said. She plopped a beer down in front of him and then returned to her seat. She sighed heavily and continued to be an enormous buzz kill.

Shaun's band played two more original songs and then did a few covers.

Jesse continued to be amazed by his best friend. He never wanted this moment to end, but at the same time, he couldn't wait for them to finish the setlist so he could go and talk to Shaun. The desire to be at his side was overwhelming.

Emily looked bored. Her mood slowly shifted to angry as Jesse continued to ignore her.

After what seemed like hours and mere minutes all at once, the singer said good night to the audience and was applauded off the stage. He went straight to the bar.

The other band members started breaking their shit down. Shaun purposefully didn't look Jesse's way, but he was moving unnaturally slow like he was waiting for something.

"I've gotta go say hi." Jesse excused himself. "I'll be back," he promised before he ran to the stage.

He twisted his way through the tables. They were close together and packed with bikers, but nothing was keeping Jesse from Shaun.

"Oh my God! You were so good!" Jesse cried once he was within earshot. Shaun straightened up and pushed his wild hair back with an absent hand. He stared down at Jesse, the slight smile from earlier teasing the edges of his lips. Jesse had tried to convince himself the entire walk over not to, but he pulled himself up the side of the stage and threw his arms around Shaun. He hugged him tightly.

"Jesse!" Shaun hissed. His hands rested heavily on Jesse's shoulder blades. He was tense, but he didn't push him away.

Jesse let go. He straightened up with a laugh, hoping to brush off the awkward moment. "You should have warned me you were so awesome." He smiled hugely. "I had an idea, but...wow. You're amazing, Shaun."

Shaun blushed. He looked around shifty-eyed. No one but Emily, the bassist, and the drummer were looking at them though. The drummer looked like he was trying not to laugh.

"C'mon." Shaun pulled him off the stage and to the side, giving them a little privacy. At least it was dark over here.

"You were," Jesse said once they were more or less alone. "I've never seen anyone play that good."

"You're a jackass," Shaun said. He grinned, showing his teeth.

Jesse opened his mouth. He wanted to say all the things he'd saved up since Thursday night, but nothing would come out.

Shaun was sweaty and flushed. His dark eyes were charged with an incredible energy. He radiated confidence and power. Jesse stood in front of a total stranger. A sexy, impassioned stranger.

They stared into each other's eyes. Jesse looked deep into the dark and swirling depths, searching for traces of the boy he knew from school. He looked so deep he felt himself falling into those eyes. His head spun.

"Whoa," he muttered. He looked away. He had to. He reached out and grabbed the wall to steady himself.

"You okay?" Shaun was at his side in an instant. He raised a hand to help, but he never touched Jesse. His hand hung there in the air, suspended. Jesse stared at it instead of meeting Shaun's questioning gaze.

"Fuck you, I'm fine," Jesse mumbled. He shook his head and tried to reorient himself.

"Fuck you too," Shaun shot back, good-naturedly. "How'd you find me anyway?"

"I went to your house after school," Jesse said. He chanced another look at Shaun. "Your grandma told me you'd skipped class to practice for tonight's show."

If Shaun minded him going behind his back to talk to his grandmother, he didn't show it. Instead, he looked confused.

"She doesn't know where we play."

"Yeah, I had to call every bar in a hundred-mile radius, looking for one headlining Execute Invasion." Jesse poked Shaun in the chest. Shaun's mouth curled up at the edges. He looked smug. "Don't laugh at me. I came all the way out here, just to see you," Jesse said, his voice softening unconsciously.

Shaun was smiling at him, as much as he ever smiled anyway, and everything felt like it was back to normal. Shaun wasn't mad, Jesse was joking around, they were talking like they'd never argued in the first place, but something felt off.

"Are you all right?" Shaun cocked his head to the side as if he could assess Jesse's health by looking at him from a different angle. "Do you want me to take you home?" he asked softly.

"I...ah..." Jesse hesitated. Not because he didn't want that. He did. He wanted Shaun to take him home. He wanted Shaun all to himself, but... "Emily's with me."

"Yeah." Shaun's face darkened at the reminder. "I saw her."

"I wouldn't have brought her but..." Jesse felt like an asshole admitting that aloud, but it was the truth.

"Don't tell me you dragged her from that fucked-up church thing and brought her here?"

Jesse shrugged. "We didn't even make it to the dance."

Shaun smirked. He glanced toward the crowded part of the bar where Emily sat, and continued to look smug. Jesse didn't follow Shaun's eyes. He hoped Emily wasn't looking their way.

"She thought I was bringing her here so I could take advantage of her," he admitted. "I thought she was going to beat me up."

"I think she still might," Shaun said cryptically. He was still looking over Jesse's shoulder.

"Oh fuck...is she watching us?" Jesse bit his lip. He *knew* Emily was staring at them... It was like he was chatting up a cute girl while his girlfriend furiously watched. This wasn't the situation at all, but he still felt horrible.

"Oh yeah. She looks pissed."

"Fuck," Jesse cursed under his breath.

"C'mon. I'll take you home. You don't have to go with her," Shaun urged. He looked intently at Jesse. "We can get the fuck out of here...together." He breathed. He sounded desperate.

Jesse bit the inside of his cheek again.

"Ow," he muttered. He rubbed his bottom lip as he considered what to do. Shaun watched him with narrowed eyes. "I drove," he said slowly. "I can't leave the van...I can't ditch her."

Shaun looked angry. He straightened up and squared his shoulders. An invisible barrier shot up between them.

"I'm—" Jesse fought the urge to apologize. "Can I come over tomorrow?"

Shaun sneered. "Don't you have to go to church with your little girlfriend?"

Jesse had, in fact, promised to sit with Emily and her parents Sunday morning. Why did he keep promising people shit?!

"After church," he clarified.

Shaun looked displeased and Jesse was sure he'd refuse, but he nodded shortly. "Tomorrow. When you're done with Emily."

"Okay." Jesse smiled brilliantly. He leaned forward. He wanted to hug his friend again, or at least touch him, but he abandoned the idea when Shaun bristled and his whole body tensed. Jesse sighed. He gave his friend one last long look and then turned to go back to Emily.

Emily sat right where Jesse had left her. There were two dirty-looking guys in leather vests sitting on either side of her now. They were trying to get her attention. Emily ignored them completely. She only had eyes for Jesse, and she glared at him angrily as he approached.

"C'mon, sweetie, tell us your name," one of the guys said as Jesse neared the table. He looked like a real badass with a bandana on his head and tattoos covering his prominently displayed arms. His friend chuckled under his breath.

"Yeah, we helped you get those beers. We can tell you're looking for a good time." This biker was completely bald. He had a huge beard and both ears pierced.

"A girl doesn't come to a bar all dressed up to ignore everybody," the first biker said.

Jesse stopped next to the table. He didn't know what to do.

Emily glared at Jesse. She didn't make eye contact with either biker, even as they leaned into her face to get her attention. "We need to talk," she said, poking her finger at Jesse.

"Um..." Jesse hovered next to the table, staring into Emily's angry face. "Want to go outside?"

The two bikers laughed.

"Yes," Emily said. "Now."

"Honey, why would you go anywhere with that little boy?" the bandanaed biker asked sarcastically. "Why don't you come sit with us?"

Emily turned and emptied the remainder of Jesse's beer on the biker's head.

"Screw you," she said. "I'm not going anywhere with you!" She dropped the bottle on the floor and jumped up. She ran at Jesse and spun them toward the nearest exit. They ran.

"Shit! Why did you do that?!" Jesse yelled over the sound of the two bikers screaming after them.

"Get back here, bitch!"

"We're going to teach you a lesson!"

Jesse and Emily burst through the front door, and together, they sprinted for the van.

Jesse unlocked the doors. They jumped in the vehicle, and he slammed the keys into the ignition.

"Hurry up!" Emily yelled. The bikers had brought their friends along. Five of them spilled into the parking lot.

Jesse started the engine and reversed from their spot. The bikers spotted them instantly. The group swarmed the van.

"This is so fucked up," Jesse hissed under his breath. He shifted into drive and punched the gas. They flew past the bikers and whipped onto the road. In seconds, the bikers and their bar were lost in the rearview mirror.

"Did you have to do that?!" he yelled. Emily was catching her breath. She glared at him.

"They were trying to pick me up!" Emily cried. "You didn't even notice. You were too busy obsessing over *Shaun*." She made a face, like the name passing her lips made her sick.

"Fuck..." Jesse had screwed up tonight. He should have made an excuse and canceled. He could have said he had to babysit or that he was sick or...something! Emily and Kenny would have gotten over it eventually.

"I need to tell you something important...if you'll listen," Emily said after a moment of silence. She'd calmed down. She even attempted to look earnest when she met Jesse's eyes.

Jesse looked away, back at the road. It was getting late. Before, when they'd been driving up here, there had been other people on the road but now it was all but deserted. Emily had an eleven o'clock curfew, and it was just past ten thirty now.

Jesse sped up until he was going almost twenty over the limit.

"It's about Shaun," Emily said.

Jesse looked at her. "What?"

Emily rolled her eyes. "You're obsessed with him."

"I'm not," Jesse said forcefully. "We're friends. That's all."

Emily shook her head. "We've all told you he's not friend material. We've all told you to stay away from him too, but you've totally ignored us."

Jesse furrowed his brow. How was this important?

"To you, Shaun must seem...like a...normal person," she said slowly.

"Normal?" That wasn't exactly how Jesse would describe Shaun. Who was normal anyway?

"Shaun's not normal, Jesse," Emily said firmly. "And now that we're dating, I can't stand by and let you be friends with someone like him."

Jesse pulled a face. Shaun was right; Emily was a cunt sometimes. She and her friends wanted to make Shaun this terrible boogeyman so he wouldn't spend time with him anymore. What did it matter to them who he hung out with?!

"What are you going to say, Emily? Are you going to tell me about that time Shaun shoved someone and insulted them? I don't care about that dumb shit."

"No," Emily said. "I'm going to tell you a story."

Jesse snorted. "A story?"

"It's like an urban legend around here," Emily said tautly. "But it really happened. I saw it happen."

Jesse ground his teeth together. "It?"

Emily tucked her hair behind her ears and turned so her back was to the window. She looked at Jesse straight-on. "When we were kids, like seven or eight, Shaun and I were in the same classroom. I think it was first grade.

"One day, Shaun came to school, and he was... covered in bruises and cuts." Emily touched her face. "He had a black eye and a split lip... I mean, it was obvious he'd been beaten."

"Was he being bullied?" Jesse asked. He felt bad, but this was hardly a story worth telling. It wasn't particularly damning. Jesse got in fights sometimes too. He hadn't been seven or eight at the time, but Shaun was different.

"Yeah. They thought some older kids might have messed with him. Even back then Shaun had a mouth on him." Jesse smiled at that. He bet Shaun had been a real hell-raiser as a kid. "But Shaun denied it," Emily said. "He said he was fine, and honestly, besides the bruises, he seemed okay. They hadn't even taken him out of the classroom at this point, because he was so calm."

"They couldn't get Shaun to name any names. So, they took him to the nurse to get patched up, and they called his parents to pick him up."

"You mean his grandparents," Jesse said.

"No, his parents," Emily said. "He didn't live with his grandparents back then. He had a mom and dad like everyone else. Once."

Jesse's eyebrows climbed into his hairline.

"Well, his parents never picked up the phone," Emily said. She paused dramatically before dropping the bomb. "They were both dead."

"Oh." Jesse had guessed something bad had happened to Shaun's parents. He hadn't known if it was abandonment or death or just a bad fight that kept Shaun from his natural mother and father, but since Shaun had had such a bad reaction to even the word "parents," Jesse had never tried to figure it out. But they were dead? Both of them?

"They didn't just die, Jesse," Emily said. "His mother was murdered by his father. Then he killed himself." The girl in the pink dress looked utterly horrified. She had her hand pressed to her chest. "I won't go into the details, because I don't know them all, but I guess Shaun's father came home from work, beat Shaun until he couldn't move, and then turned on his wife. He stabbed her; I think. He killed himself next. He slit his throat and bled to death. And you know what?"

"What?" Jesse whispered.

"Shaun watched the whole thing. And he came to school the next day because he didn't want anyone to find out his parents were dead. He'd wanted to keep it a secret."

For some reason, that gave Jesse the chills.

"I saw him, Jesse. He was completely normal, talking and acting like he always did. He wasn't bothered by it at all. He went away for a while. He wasn't in school for a couple of months, but when he showed up again, he was living with his grandparents. They brought him to church sometimes, and in Sunday school, our teacher tried to get him to talk about his parents and you know what he said? He started talking about how he'd kept his father's bowie knife. The one his dad had used to slit his throat. Said he liked to keep it close because it reminded him of his dad."

"You're lying."

"I'm not!" Emily cried. "Something is deeply wrong with that kid! He hasn't killed anyone, Jesse, but he's threatened people...he's hurt them...who knows when he's going to snap." Emily snapped her fingers for effect. "He'll go crazy one day. Who knows what he'll do!"

"Not...everyone with crazy parents grows up to be a mass murderer, you know," Jesse said weakly.

"I know, but you've got to admit he's pretty weird. I mean, what kind of kid watches their parents die right in front of them, and concludes they'd better not tell anyone?"

"I—I don't know," Jesse said. He thought about the menacing look Shaun got in his eyes, sometimes. It wasn't...normal. It was like a vicious animal looking at helpless prey. Jesse had never seen a look like that before, and maybe it was because Shaun had seen things other people had not. Things Jesse had never even imagined. With a sick feeling in the pit of his stomach, he remembered Shaun showing Brian that violent movie, explaining all those gory deaths in graphic detail. He shuddered. Was Shaun a psychopath?

"I didn't want to say anything. None of us did because, frankly, it's a sick story," Emily said. "He'll kill me if he finds out I told you. He gets really upset when anyone brings it up."

Jesse's eyes widened. "Thanks for telling me."

"You're welcome." Emily was completely relaxed now. She leaned back against the window. "I hope you'll at least think about keeping your distance."

Jesse shrugged. Even now he wasn't ready to write Shaun off that easily.

Emily looked at the dash. "We're going to be late," she said.

"Oh." Jesse had forgotten. He sped up a little more. There weren't any cops way out here anyway.

"It's okay. I'll just make up something," Emily said.

"They'll never let me take you out again," Jesse said with a laugh. It was funny because he wasn't really that upset.

"You can convince them you're a good Christian boy tomorrow. Just go along with whatever I say."

Jesse sighed. He'd already resigned himself to church early the next morning.

"I'll be there," he said with an unenthusiastic smile. If she noticed the lack of feeling behind it, she didn't mention it.

Chapter Six

Shaun watched as the bikers chased after Jesse and his idiot girlfriend. He'd noticed the two, leather-clad mongrels messing with Emily long before Jesse had. He'd hoped she'd join up with them and go have a gang bang, but apparently, she wanted Jesse more. Shaun wasn't surprised. He understood the sentiment.

He was worried. He jumped off the stage and peered out the nearest window. He'd beat some biker ass if they were bothering Jesse.

An intervention wasn't needed. Jesse and Emily drove out of the lot in what he recognized as Jesse's mom's van. The group of bikers waved their fists and spat profanity, but they didn't continue the chase.

"Who the fuck was that?" Danny asked when he returned to the stage.

Shaun shrugged. His guitar was in its case and the cords to his amp were reeled in. There wasn't much left to do by this point, but he put his head down and made himself look busy to avoid questioning.

He wasn't getting away with it that easily.

"Yeah, who was that?" Ben cut in. "Was that one of your friends from school?"

"Yep," Shaun said.

"Why was he hugging you?" Danny asked, and Shaun bristled and squared his shoulders.

This was exactly why he'd been avoiding questions! Why had Jesse had to hug him like that?! Why couldn't he have waited until they were alone to do stupid gay shit like that?!

"I don't know," he grumbled.

"No, seriously, he was all over you!" Danny laughed.

"He liked the set, I guess," Shaun said in a lame defense.

Danny snorted with amusement. "Too bad the ladies don't react the same way, huh? You might actually get laid sometime." There was a significant pause, and Shaun held his breath as he shifted his guitar and amp around. Danny watched him for a moment and then burst into laughter. "Maybe you're fucking that guy."

Shaun kicked his amp out of the way and lunged at Danny. His hands went around the asshole's throat. Danny's laughter was cut short. His eyes popped out of his head.

"Shaun!" Ben hissed. He stepped between the guitarist and the drummer and shoved Shaun back a few paces. Shaun, wild-eyed and burning with anger, clenched his fists open and shut. He wanted to *kill* Danny for saying that!

"We're not fighting on stage," Ben said. He pushed Shaun again, back to his guitar and his amp. "Go load that up and I'll get you a beer."

"Fuck you, Ben," Shaun said darkly, but he followed his directions. Danny rubbed his throat, but he still looked terribly amused. He'd stopped laughing at least.

"You're not...fucking that guy, right?" Ben asked after the equipment had been loaded into their individual cars. Danny and Will were at the bar, getting even drunker, but he and Ben sat at a table in a dark corner. The girls Ben had been flirting with all night were a few tables over, still trying to catch his eye, but unfortunately for them, Ben only flirted for fun.

"What are you talking about?" Shaun was on his way to drunk and was feeling quite nice. He kept thinking about Jesse and how cool it was he'd ruined his first date with Emily to come and see him play. The thought made Shaun smile.

"That guy you were talking to," Ben said. "He isn't your—"

"He's my best friend," Shaun said with a smile. He completely missed Ben's insinuation.

Ben smiled back, gently. "I didn't know you had any friends."

"Just him," Shaun corrected, in case Ben started to think he was popular or something.

He was ugly, people hated and were afraid of him... It didn't matter if he was a great guitarist, or that he was in one of the most brutal death metal bands in two hundred miles; none of that mattered to anyone at school.

And then came Jesse, out of the blue. Jesse liked him for no reason at all, really. He'd seen past all of Shaun's bullshit and actually gave a shit about the person he was underneath.

Jesse was special.

Shaun smiled again.

"Man, I don't think I've ever seen you smile so much," Ben pointed out. "It's kind of creepy."

"Screw you," Shaun said, not letting the bassist's words affect him. He wished Jesse could have stayed and gotten drunk with them, but Ben wasn't so bad. In fact, Ben was the closest thing to a friend Shaun had ever had before Jesse. Shaun wished he'd introduced his two friends to each other, but the moment had passed.

"Hey! You guys!" Will stumbled over with a giggling blonde on his arm. "This is my new friend..." He paused as he waited for the girl to introduce herself.

"Lily," she said. Her shirt was so lowcut, her tits almost spilled out as she leaned over the table.

"Lily's invited us back to her friend's house for a party." Will squeezed the blonde closer to him. She giggled and Will dropped his arm to grab her ass. "Wanna come with?"

Ben shook his head. "I've got to get back to Angela."

"What about you?" Will glanced in Shaun's direction.

"No... I should get back," Shaun said. He didn't want to go to some stranger's house... He had to be home early tomorrow for Jesse.

"Back to your grandma and grandpa?" Will asked in a stupid baby voice. "Whatever." He turned away, pulling the blonde along. Shaun disinterestedly watched them go.

"Are you okay to drive?" Ben asked. He'd only had one beer, which was pretty ridiculous since the owner who'd booked them had given Will a bunch of free beer tickets.

"Yeah, I guess." Shaun finished his drink. He really didn't want to go home. He usually liked to stay out until Sunday, but he'd put up with Ruth's bitching and Eli's well-meaning advice if it meant he got to see Jesse a little sooner.

After he'd stormed out of Jesse's room the other day, he'd wanted to go back and apologize the second he got home. It wasn't that he was sorry for insulting Emily, because he wasn't. Realizing most of his anger was because he was jealous, though, hadn't been pleasant. The discovery had enraged him, embarrassed him, and made him extremely worried if Jesse found out the depth of his...feelings...for him that he'd be abandoned.

Nevertheless, Shaun had spent their time apart obsessing over Jesse. He was getting used to it too, but he was also sickened by how attached he was. It wasn't normal to need him all the time. The desire to have Jesse all to himself was overwhelming. It wasn't healthy...plus it seemed incredibly gay. But right now, Shaun wasn't worried about it.

The entire ride home Shaun replayed Jesse's rapt expressions in his head. Jesse had barely looked away from him the entire night, and even though Shaun had tried not to stare at him, he'd felt Jesse's gaze caressing him, stroking his ego with a tender hand.

The house was quiet when Shaun got home. He snuck into his room, scowling around the now clean space. Fuck Ruth. It was his room. Why couldn't he keep it dirty?

Whatever. He was tired. He wasn't in the mood to take a shower, or even change, so he flopped back on his bed and kicked off his boots.

He was half-asleep when his arm started itching. Groggy, he yanked his sleeve back.

The nasty cut he'd added to his collection a few days ago stared back at him. It was healing nicely since Jesse had bugged him into cleaning it out and bandaging it properly, but it must have been pulled open while he played. It was oozing dark blood.

"Fuck," he muttered. He winced as he scratched the edges of the wound. The blood smeared across his scarred forearm, and he wiped it on his stomach. He'd have to get a shower in the morning before Jesse came over.

He pulled his sleeve up and ignored the throbbing. He eventually fell asleep.

"You're home early." Shaun sat up. His eyes focused on a figure in the doorway. It was Ruth. He grumbled and rolled out of bed. He trudged to the closet and picked out something clean to wear.

"You're bleeding," Ruth tutted as she watched Shaun pick through his clothes. "You're not a child anymore. This little 'habit' of yours has to stop."

"I don't know what you're talking about," Shaun growled. He ripped a black thermal shirt off its hanger.

Ruth pursed her lips together. "Your friend was looking for you on Friday."

"I know. He came and found me," Shaun said, almost to himself. He smiled softly as he moved to the dresser to get a pair of pants and some underwear. He had an urge to be clean and presentable, or at least not his usual ogre-like self.

"What?"

"Nothing." Shaun gathered a pair of hunting pants. They were patterned with leaves and bark and shit like that. He found boxers and some clean socks and then pushed past Ruth on his way to the bathroom. She squawked with indignation.

"Excuse you," she sneered.

Shaun dumped his armload of clothes on the bathroom counter. "Jesse's coming over today. If he knocks, let him in," he said, then slammed the bathroom door.

Shaun undressed in front of the mirror. He didn't normally like to look at himself, but he was feeling particularly self-conscious today.

His body was covered in cuts. The one on his arm wasn't too bad. There was dried blood surrounding it from last night, but it had scabbed over. The old one on his thigh had closed in a red, angry line. For a while, it had been touch and go. The wound had festered with pus for days. Shaun had poured a whole bottle of alcohol on it and wound it up tight in gauze.

He scrubbed his skin harshly under the shower. His body was an ugly mess of cuts, bruises, and scars. Lots of scars. He was embarrassed, but he rarely regretted them. They always felt so good to make.

He dried off and dressed the wound on his arm. He didn't want Jesse to see any blood or to ask any questions. He put his clothes on and made sure everything was covered. He ran a comb through his hair, even though it was hopeless. It wouldn't lay flat. He looked better though, and he was eager to see Jesse, no matter how queer it sounded.

Shaun was in remarkably high spirits when he returned to his bedroom. He was slightly disappointed Jesse wasn't already here. At least he'd get to greet him personally.

The thought was a magical cue; there was a knock at the front door. It couldn't be anybody but Jesse. Shaun got up to answer it.

"Hey," Shaun said as he opened the door. He smiled.

"Hi." Jesse stood with his hands twisted in front of him. Distress rolled off his form in tsunami-sized waves. He snuck a cautious look at Shaun and then glanced away. Shaun felt his stomach drop. Jesse *knew*.

"I'm going to kill that bitch," he growled. "It was Emily that told you, right?"

"Yes, but... Please don't," Jesse pleaded. He reached out for one of Shaun's clenched fists, but Shaun jerked his hand out of reach. "She...thinks she's doing what's best," he said in a tiny voice.

"Fuck her," Shaun said and then after a pause, "And fuck *you*."

"Shaun..."

Eli poked his head into the kitchen. His face lit up. "We have company," he said.

Shaun bared his teeth. "Why don't you just *go*," he hissed, now thoroughly pissed off.

"No," Jesse said. "I wanna talk."

Eli edged into the room, eager to insert himself into the conversation, but that was completely unacceptable. Shaun growled with frustration, grabbed Jesse's arm, and yanked him outside.

"I don't know why I fucking invited you here. There're too many people home," Shaun muttered as he dragged Jesse to the garage.

"You've been to my house, right? Five brothers and sisters and a nosy mom," Jesse said with a nervous laugh. "Where are we going?"

"Somewhere we can be alone."

The garage was cluttered with just about everything but a car. There were gun racks mounted to the back wall. Eli's workbench of tools and a massive jigsaw were on the wall to the right. Across from that was Shaun's guitar and his amp. It was his practice space.

Shaun let Jesse go the moment they entered. He went straight to the swivel chair by the bench and sat down. Jesse stood in the middle of the dusty room. He kicked a loose screw on the floor.

"What do you want?" Shaun asked.

"I..." Jesse fidgeted. "I just—"

"Want to know if it's true?" Shaun finished for him.

Jesse met Shaun's eyes. His top teeth worried his lower lip. "Yeah."

"Why? So you can tell everyone at school that I'm a freak?" Shaun snapped.

"I'm not going to tell anyone!" Jesse said adamantly. "Nothing between us has changed. I don't think any less of you," he said, and Shaun sneered. "I promise if you don't want to talk about it...that's fine. I won't ever bring it up again."

Shaun clutched the arms of the swivel chair. His fingers went white from the pressure. He didn't want to talk about his parents. The chance Jesse would betray him was high, especially if he kept hanging out with that bitch Emily.

But Jesse was his friend. He'd been worried about Shaun when he hadn't shown up for school. He'd gone out of his way to see Shaun play. Jesse stood in front of him now, looking fearful but determined and Shaun was vaguely impressed. What the fuck had gone through his head after Emily had told him the urban legend of Shaun's parents? They all thought the same thing... Shaun was a psycho and one day he would snap and become a mass murderer. Why was Jesse even here?

Shaun decided to bite the bullet. "I always knew there was something wrong with my parents," he began. He stared Jesse straight in the eye, silently daring him to look away. Jesse didn't. "They got married young, just out of school because Mom was pregnant and that's what you do when you're raised Catholic.

"That baby was stillborn."

Jesse sucked in a breath of surprise.

"A year later they had me," Shaun scontinued. "I was a surprise. An unhappy one. They hated each other, and neither of them wanted a baby, but they were too...fucked up to just get a divorce and move on with their lives. So, my entire childhood was spent watching them argue," Shaun said bitterly. "When I was growing up, my mom started seeing other men. She brought them home sometimes when Dad was at work, but more often than not, she went out to see them and she'd leave me home by myself for hours because she couldn't be bothered. She wasn't a good mom.

"Dad was a drunk. I don't think I have a single memory of him being sober. He worked odd jobs but never held anything down for long. He was too addicted to the bottle to care about stuff like showing up for work," Shaun said. "He knew my mom was cheating on him. He'd call her a whore and smack her around. He seemed to enjoy it. It was fucked up, Jesse. Nobody but us knew what was going on in that house," he said and Jesse looked away. His bottom lip trembled.

"When I started school, Mom spent more and more time with her boyfriends, and the arguing between my parents got more violent. When I was five, Dad broke Mom's arm. When I was six, he broke her ribs. When I was seven, he knocked her teeth out."

"Oh God," Jesse winced. "Where you around when it happened?"

"Of course," Shaun said. "They never did anything in private."

"Why didn't she just leave?" Jesse asked.

"I swear she was a glutton for punishment," Shaun said. "But she listened to her parents. They pressured her to stay in the marriage. They were *assholes,* but they fixed her teeth and brought us food when Dad was out of work. They paid our bills when my dad couldn't. They must have known about the abuse, but they were more concerned about the *sanctity* of marriage. My mom wanted to please them. So, she worked around their rules as best she could."

"The people in there?" Jesse pointed back toward the house. He looked horrified.

"No," Shaun said. "My mom's parents wanted nothing to do with me after my dad...after everything happened. They moved away and washed their hands of us. Ruth and Eli are my dad's parents."

"Oh."

"Just shut up and let me finish," Shaun said impatiently. This story brought up so many bad memories and feelings, but there was no way he was going to stop now.

"A few weeks after I started first grade, I came home from school and Mom was up in her room throwing clothes in a bag. She said she was leaving. Her face was bruised up. Dad must have beat her after I left for school." Shaun's expression grew pinched as he remembered the last conversation he'd ever had with his mother. "She said she didn't care what happened to me and my dad and that we could all go to hell. She said she couldn't stand to be here anymore."

"She said that to you?" Jesse asked softly, sounding more hurt than Shaun had ever been.

"She didn't like me. It was obvious," Shaun said. He wished he felt sad over the injustice, but ultimately, he felt nothing. "By then I'd lost all allusions of what a good mom was supposed to be."

"I'm sorry, Shaun," Jesse said in a gentle voice.

Shaun shrugged. "Dad came home right in the middle of our conversation. He'd been out getting more beer, and he was already upset. I've never seen him so upset.

"Mom got this really scared look on her face, and she closed up her bag really fast, grabbed it, and ran downstairs like she was going to run out. But Dad caught her first.

"They were yelling and screaming at each other. I don't remember what they were saying. There was a thump and Mom's voice went quiet.

"I stood in their room, listening to my dad yell and yell and have nobody answer him. I heard his footsteps coming up the stairs and down the hall. He carried Mom over his shoulder, and she was unconscious. Her eyes were closed, and her face was blank. I stood there in a panic. I was stupid. I should have hidden in the closet, but it was too late. Dad saw me standing in his room, and he dropped Mom.

"I didn't like her very much, but I was scared," Shaun muttered. He dug his fingers into the armrests of the chair as the most traumatic event in his life played out in his mind. "I'd never seen my mom like that. There was blood coming out of her mouth and she wasn't moving. I thought she was dead."

"Was she?" Jesse whispered.

"No. Not yet. I tried to touch her, but Dad, he...he hit me across the face and knocked me to the ground. I was only a kid then. I would have hit the bastard back, but I wasn't strong enough. He overpowered me easily and kicked me over and over. He screamed at me. He told me I ruined his life and shit. I cried and begged him to stop, but he kept kicking me until I went silent."

Jesse moved like he was going to come forward, his hands held out in a vaguely comforting manner. Shaun shot him a glare. He needed to get through this without Jesse's useless pity. Jesse caught the message and stayed where he was.

"I crawled into the hallway. My body hurt all over. I could barely move," Shaun said. "Dad gave up on me once I was out of the way. He didn't come after me."

"Shaun—"

"Shut up," Shaun snapped. Jesse's blue eyes were teary, but the story was at its climax. "He shut the door, but it bounced open again. The frame was broken from all the times he and Mom had slammed it, but Dad didn't notice. He picked Mom up and tossed her on the bed. He pulled her dress up and climbed on top of her. He raped her.

"I had a perfect view from the hallway. I was horrified, but I barely even blinked. I watched the entire thing play out."

"Jesus," Jesse cursed under his breath.

"Mom woke up in the middle of it and struggled to get away. Dad, he...he screamed at her and held her down. He hit her in the face again and again until she was still. His fists were bloody, and I couldn't make out her features anymore. There was nothing but blood," Shaun said. "Then he fucked her again. This time, he finished."

"When he got off her, he looked around the room for something. He pushed stuff off tables, tore through their drawers, and then he pulled out his hunting knife. I don't know why he had it in their room. It belonged in the closet downstairs with the hunting supplies, but he had it under some clothes in the dresser. He took it out and laid down on top of Mom. He whispered something in her ear, and I don't know if she was alive to hear it, but he talked for so long that I started to relax. I thought it was over and that Mom would go to sleep and Dad would go back downstairs and get drunk. I thought everything would be normal again. But then he sunk his knife into her stomach. Then he stabbed her in the chest. He stabbed her until blood dripped off the edge of the bed and pooled on the floor.

"I cried," Shaun admitted. "I'd seen death before. Dad and Grandpa had taken me hunting. I'd watched them gut and skin all kinds of animals and I hadn't thought much of it, but seeing my own mother bleeding out was the worst thing I've ever seen."

"...Jesus..." Jesse said again. His hand was over his mouth. Shaun wondered if he was going to be sick.

"And then Dad fucked her again, going real slow like he was savoring it. I kept waiting for Mom to push him off and tell him it hurt, but she didn't move. She was dead. Very dead. When he was done using her body he laid back and stared at the ceiling for a few minutes. I was afraid to look away. I was afraid to move and get his attention, so I lay there, watching him, hoping he wasn't going to come for me next, but then he stuck his knife in his throat and he made the most horrible choking sounds. He jerked around on the bed and writhed in agony. His feet tangled in the sheets, and he pushed the blankets to the floor. The knife fell out of his hand and blood gushed out of his throat. He stopped moving."

"What did you do?"

"I fell asleep there, waiting for them to move," Shaun said slowly, refusing to look Jesse in the eye. "When I woke up the next morning and they were still lying in bed, I couldn't believe it. How could they be dead? They *lived* to make my life miserable. And suddenly, they were gone? Just like that?

"I was stupid, I convinced myself, if I went about my normal day, my parents would wake up and everything would go back to normal," Shaun said. "So, I picked myself up, got ready for school like I did every morning, and before I went to the bus stop, I took dad's knife."

"Why?"

"I kept thinking when they woke up, Dad might try to hurt Mom again or that she would hurt him in retaliation. I wanted to remove the temptation." Shaun looked at his pale, scarred hands. He remembered holding that bloody knife, all those years ago, his childish fingers trembling with the evil power inside it. "I washed it off and hid it under my mattress. I knew they'd never look in my room.

"Later, when the police questioned me, I didn't tell them about it," Shaun said. "My grandparents took me back to the house to get a bag of clothes and anything else I wanted. That's when I took the knife," he said. "It was all I had of my previous life. My parents were gone, the house was taken away, and for a while, I had to go live in a home, a place for crazies..." Shaun scowled. "I still have it. That fucking knife makes me sick when I touch it, but it's just as well. I feel sick most of the time."

Shaun stopped talking, realizing with some amusement this was the most he'd said in a long time. He hadn't said this much since he was eight and he'd had to tell the police what had transpired in that bloody bedroom. The irony hit Shaun hard.

His throat felt sore.

"I wish that hadn't happened," Jesse said. Shaun glanced up. Jesse stood before him, watching him tentatively. His eyes weren't full of the disgust and pity he'd expected but understanding, concern, and, yes, fear, but Jesse knelt in front of Shaun's chair and looked up at him sincerely. "But I'm glad you told me. I'm glad you..." Jesse trailed off. He stared into Shaun's eyes, and then, slowly, he slid his arms around his middle and rested his head in his lap. "I'm glad you're here...with me."

Shaun blushed about a hundred different shades of red in the span of a few moments. Jesse was hugging him again, which was embarrassing, but not so bad. Guys hugged each other sometimes. Not a lot, but sometimes. But Jesse had his face pressed to Shaun's crotch, and far from being grossed out by his best friend's proximity, Shaun found himself fighting the urge to pop an erection.

"Jesse?" Shaun moaned. Gently, he shifted his fingers through Jesse's soft, auburn hair.

"I'm sorry." Jesse sat up. His eyes were wet, but he hadn't let any tears fall. Shaun's arousal intensified as he studied Jesse's pained expression. He felt a stifling wave of guilt as his cock grew harder.

"C'mere," Shaun said gruffly. He opened his arms.

Jesse crawled into Shaun's lap. Shaun sighed and wrapped his arms around Jesse. The chair wasn't made for two. It was a tight fit. It took some wiggling to get comfortable, but Jesse settled with his arms around Shaun's neck, his knees digging into his hips. Their dicks were mashed together.

It was bad enough having Jesse so fucking close, but Shaun really started to regret his decision when Jesse started to cry. He pressed his tear-stained face against Shaun's chest and held on tight.

"This is incredibly gay, you know?" Shaun said, and indeed, he was half-erect. Jesse sniffled and moaned, and for some reason, Shaun thought it was sexy. He knew he'd have to add a cut to his collection for this sick behavior, but for now, it felt good to hold Jesse close. Horribly, disgustingly good.

Jesse laughed; his breath was hot against Shaun's neck. "What's gay about me sitting in your lap?"

"You're fucking retarded if I have to explain."

Jesse turned his head. His lips brushed against Shaun's throat. Shaun froze.

"You scare me a little."

Shaun frowned at the whispered confession.

"I could never have watched something like that and...function normally."

"I'm not normal," Shaun said bitterly. "Everyone says I'm a freak."

"I don't care. I don't think you're...that weird," Jesse said.

"Fuck you."

"If I was here when that happened, you wouldn't have had to go through it alone. I wish I'd been around," Jesse said sweetly.

Shaun didn't wish for that at all. "You would have run away from me, just like all your other friends did," he said. "You'd hate me like everyone else."

"Nope," Jesse said. He clutched Shaun tighter.

"Yes, you would," Shaun said firmly. "Trust me."

"Never." Jesse laughed at Shaun's growl of frustration, and with a heave, Shaun pushed him out of his lap and onto the floor.

"Ow!" Jesse cried as he sprawled out on the concrete floor. He glared at Shaun, tears still on his face, but after a moment of intense glaring between the two, Jesse snorted and stood up. "I guess spilling your heart out doesn't make you any nicer. I'll remember that next time." He punched Shaun on the shoulder. "That hurt, you bastard."

Shaun smirked, totally unrepentant. He was glad the awkward story time and the even weirder lap-sitting and hugging were over. He could go back to pretending he didn't feel anything besides friendship for Jesse like he had been for weeks now. Everything would be fine. As long as Shaun kept lying to himself.

"So…" Jesse looked around the room until his gaze fell on Shaun's guitar. "Can you show me how to play?"

"Tsk, you think I could teach you?"

"Sure. Why not?"

Shaun narrowed his eyes. "Guitar isn't easy like that stupid game at your house. There's more to it than pushing fucking buttons."

"I know that!" Jesse cried. "I could be good at guitar."

"Yeah, okay." Shaun plugged the guitar in. He motioned for Jesse to pick it up.

"If I could ever be as good as you, that'd be amazing." Jesse shredded his fingers across the fretboard. Shaun plugged the amp in, and the most horrible sound emerged as Jesse continued to strum. It was like a dying crow.

"Hold up!"

Jesse stopped playing. He stuck out his tongue. "No good?"

Shaun shook his head. "If you're going to do this, do it right, dumbass." He circled around Jesse until he stood behind him. "Hold it like this." He slipped his arms under Jesse's and reached around to pull his hands into the right position.

"Like that?" Jesse's smaller hands flexed under Shaun's.

"Yeah," Shaun breathed. He was really close to Jesse. His auburn hair smelled like apples. Shaun pressed a little closer, even though he knew he shouldn't.

"What do I do?"

"You do your fingering here," Shaun said, squeezing Jesse's left hand over the fret board. "And you strum here." He did the same to the right. His chest was pressed firmly to Jesse's back. There was nothing between them but a couple layers of clothes.

Jesse turned his head to look over his shoulder. "Play something," he said.

Their faces were dangerously close, but Jesse was so short their lips didn't line up. It was a small relief, because if they had, Shaun wasn't sure what would have happened.

But that was stupid. Nothing would have happened, Shaun thought grimly.

Jesse moved his hands under Shaun's. He was trying to escape, and Shaun dropped the guitar in his haste to release him. Jesse caught it before it fell. He held the Gibson in his hands as he waited for Shaun to take it back.

Shaun blushed. "I thought I was teaching you." He snatched the guitar from Jesse and slid the strap over his head. He took a deep breath and then let his fingers fly. He ran through a riff from his favorite song. It was a difficult verse, and Jesse watched him in awe. He clapped when Shaun finished.

"I knew you'd be good," Jesse said with a grin.

"Whatever." Shaun thrust the guitar back at Jesse and proceeded to teach him a few basics. He had to try...really, really hard to keep his patience. He made sure to keep his distance too.

A future career in teaching was definitely out of the question, but with only a few harsh words, Shaun showed Jesse a few chords before both of them grew too frustrated to continue.

"Told you," Jesse said after an hour of work. "Told you I could play."

"You know what? You don't get to say 'I told you so' until you're as good as I am," Shaun sneered.

Jesse laughed. "Sometimes I really hate you." Though of course that statement was thrown right out the window when Jesse slipped his arm around Shaun's waist and hugged him again, too quick for Shaun to push him away, but slow enough for his face to heat in embarrassment.

Fuck! Why couldn't he stop blushing?

"What can we do now?" Jesse asked as he stepped back. "Please don't make me go home. I got the whole day off from my horrible family."

Shaun shrugged. He hated the majority of Jesse's family. Especially the twins and the older one, Sam. They were all fucking shit heads, as far as Shaun was concerned. Though the baby wasn't all that bad. He didn't know enough about her to hate her, but she did do an awful lot of sniffling and crying when she wasn't being held by Jesse, which was annoying. Brian was the only one Shaun actually liked. Though he'd never admit it aloud. Jesse seemed to be on the same wavelength. "Brian misses you," he said.

Shaun didn't know what to say. He shrugged again.

"He threw a fit when I told him I was going to see you Saturday and he couldn't come."

"Good thing you didn't bring him along," Shaun said with a frown. "Bars aren't for little kids."

"Thanks, Captain Obvious." Jesse poked Shaun in the ribs. Shaun batted his hand away. "I wasn't going to. I'm not an idiot."

"Could've fooled me. You are dating that insufferable bitch."

"Emily is pretty insufferable," Jesse said. They slipped out of the garage and back around to the front of the house.

Shaun led him inside. "I warned you," he said.

"Yeah, whatever." Jesse rolled his eyes. "But you have to come over Monday after school or Brian's never going to talk to me again. He thinks I'm keeping you all to myself."

"Aren't you?" Shaun asked. The kitchen was empty, and he steered Jesse through to the living room, which was just as deserted. He sat Jesse on the couch. TV was a normal activity. They could watch TV.

"I guess I am." Jesse sat down stiffly. He waited for Shaun to sit beside him and then cuddled, actually fucking cuddled, into his side. He relaxed with a sigh.

"What are you doing?" There was no question if Shaun should bring up the strange behavior. It flew out of his mouth.

"Using you as a pillow? Is that all right?" Jesse asked casually. Shaun nodded dumbly in response. "What's on?"

"Ah..." Shaun stretched and grabbed the remote off the coffee table with the tips of his fingers. He didn't want to disturb Jesse. He was comfortable. He flipped the TV on. Clint Eastwood was on the screen in a cowboy hat. "Westerns," he said.

"This is pretty good. I saw it once." Jesse rested his head on Shaun's shoulder and settled in to watch.

A soft, tickling started in Shaun's belly. It felt like butterflies fluttered inside of him.

Jesse knew the truth about him. The truth that had turned the entire town against him. Shaun had been waiting for this day. He'd been waiting for Jesse to shrink away in fear and disgust, but it wasn't happening.

Jesse still smiled with him, laughed with him, watched him with eager eyes. He still touched him, much to Shaun's distress. Jesse still wanted him.

The tiny spark of interest Shaun had felt that first day when Jesse had introduced himself, all bouncy energy, smiles and laughter, flared into a feeling that, while unfamiliar, was recognizable.

Unnamable, because he didn't want to give it a name, embarrassing, because he didn't want to admit it, but recognizable.

It wasn't love. Not yet, but it was close.

Shaun had never felt like this before. He felt helpless. He let Jesse lean against him as they watched *The Good, the Bad and the Ugly*. He listened to Jesse's comments, but he didn't say much in return. He concentrated on the warmth of Jesse's body. He couldn't do much else.

Jesse was a drug and Shaun was totally intoxicated.

During the dramatic standoff, Eli walked into the room.

"What are you boys watching?"

Jesse straightened up and moved away from Shaun. His eyes went wide. "We're watching a movie," he said quickly. He sounded guilty.

"Clint Eastwood, eh?" Eli asked.

"It's almost over," Shaun snapped. The arm Jesse had been cuddling against was unbearably cold. Fuck, why had Eli chosen to come in *now*?

"I didn't mean to interrupt," Eli said, but the smirk on his lips proved anything but.

Shaun glanced at the TV. The credits were rolling. They'd missed the end of the movie. "What do you want?" he hissed.

Eli held up his hands. "I was just wondering who you've got in here with you," he said. He glanced meaningfully at Jesse. "That isn't a crime, is it?"

"Yes," Shaun growled.

Jesse gave him an exasperated look. "I'm Jesse," he said.

"Pleased to meet you." Eli held out a hand, and Jesse shook it politely. "I'm Eli. Shaun's grandpa."

"Um...hi," Jesse said, smiling sheepishly.

"Okay. You've met. Now what do you want?" Shaun didn't like this. He'd been having a nice time when it was just him and Jesse. He didn't need Eli butting in.

Eli looked slightly affronted. "Grandma isn't in the mood to cook tonight. I'm taking her to the diner. Do you two want to come?"

Shaun made a face. "No," he said viciously.

Jesse elbowed him. "Don't be so rude," he chided.

"Don't worry. He's always like this," Eli chuckled. He ruffled Shaun's messy hair.

Shaun violently tore out of Eli's reach. "Stop it!"

"Don't worry. Your hair couldn't get any worse," Jesse joked. He reached up to ruffle Shaun's hair, as well, but Shaun caught his hand and laced their fingers together. He pinned their entwined hands to the couch and gave Jesse a threatening look.

"Are you sure you two don't mind being alone for dinner?" Eli asked in such a way that Shaun immediately let go of Jesse's hand and glared death at the old man.

"We'll be all right," Jesse said, obviously missing the insinuation. "Won't we, Shaun?"

"Fuck you both," Shaun growled. He was close to getting up and storming to his room, abandoning Jesse, but he didn't think it would have the effect he was hoping for.

Besides, Eli was done interrogating them. He smirked at Shaun and then went into the back room to call for Ruth.

"C'mon. Let's go to my room...at least until they leave," Shaun said. He got up and all but ran down the hall.

Jesse was right behind him. They entered Shaun's room without running into anyone else.

"Wow," Jesse said. He looked around. "Are you a closet OCD or something? I don't think I've ever seen a guy's room that was so clean."

Shaun made a face. "Eh, my grandma cleans when I go away. I hate the smell of air freshener." He turned the stereo on.

There wasn't much to do in Shaun's room. He didn't spend a lot of time here, and when he did, he was usually getting high or sleeping.

Jesse found the stack of CDs beside Shaun's dresser. He sorted through the collection.

"Oh fuck! This is good," Jesse said. He picked out a few CDs. "Ha! I can't believe you have this!"

Shaun snatched the latest CD out of Jesse's hand. He put it in the stereo.

"Maybe you don't have shitty taste," Shaun said.

Jesse sang along and started to head bang. He looked ridiculous.

"Bye, kids!" Eli called through the door. "We're leaving."

"Go away!" Shaun yelled back. He sat on the bed and watched Jesse head bang his way through an entire song. Shaun laughed when it ended, and Jesse stumbled to the bed and collapsed beside him.

"My head hurts," he moaned.

"Yeah, well, you're doing it wrong," Shaun pointed out. "You're lucky you didn't break your neck."

Jesse groaned. "Ow. I think I did."

Shaun snorted.

"Do we have any smoke left?" Jesse sat up and asked excitedly.

Fuck. "No. I forgot to get more," Shaun muttered. Between their argument Thursday, practice Friday, the show Saturday, and Jesse and all his distractions, he'd forgotten about Kyle.

"Can we get some now?" Jesse asked.

"No." Shaun didn't want Jesse anywhere near Kyle. It was stupid and selfish to want to keep his best friend to himself, but Shaun had it in his head that Kyle would steal Jesse away if given the chance. Shaun had told Jesse Kyle's secret, but he'd never tell him the whole messy story between them. He just knew he had to keep Jesse away from the dealer. Kyle was a fucking snake.

"C'mon. Please! I'll stay in the car. I won't talk to him if that's what you're afraid of!" Jesse begged. He rolled onto his stomach and pressed his hands together in a classic beggar's pose. "Please."

"You're turning into a pothead," Shaun sneered. "I'll get some tomorrow."

"Shaun!"

"I said no!"

"C'mon, please!" Jesse begged.

Shaun felt his resolve crumbling. He wondered if Jesse knew how undone Shaun felt around him lately. Jesse batted his long pretty lashes, his shining blue eyes hopeful and bright.

Shaun flushed. "For fuck's sake," he muttered under his breath. "Will you shut up if I say yes?"

"Yes." Jesse grinned broadly. "So, can we go now?"

Shaun wasn't happy with it, but Jesse promised he wouldn't talk to Kyle. As long as Shaun kept the visit brief, it'd be fine.

Eli and Ruth had the Ford, so they'd have to take Ruth's old van. It was prone to breaking down, and Shaun didn't use it for that very reason. Kyle's house wasn't far though, and plus he was kind of hoping it *would* break down so they wouldn't have to go.

Shaun made Jesse wait outside his room while he rummaged around in the box under his bed for money. Jesse was having a hard time staying out.

"What's the big deal? Do you have porn under there?" Jesse laughed from the hallway.

"Jesus, you'd think you were afraid to be alone." Shaun hesitated and then grabbed sixty bucks. His stash was beginning to dwindle. Even with the semiregular payments from Execute Invasion.

"I'm not afraid," Jesse said bravely. When Shaun returned though, he grabbed onto his arm for an unusually long moment. They were practically holding hands.

"What are you doing? Let go." Shaun shook Jesse's hand off his arm. How was he supposed to forget about his stupid gay feelings if Jesse kept touching him?

"Sorry, I just...I feel weird." Jesse drew his arm back. He looked at Shaun under his lashes. "After your story, I mean."

"Mmm." Shaun pocketed the money and headed to the front door. He didn't address Jesse's comment until they were in the van and he'd found the keys—conveniently sitting on the dashboard. "Maybe you do need something to smoke. Something to calm you down."

"Ha, yeah. That was the idea," Jesse said. He touched Shaun's arm again as he slid the key into the ignition. This time, Shaun let him hold on. Jesse fisted a bit of Shaun's sleeve. It seemed to comfort him.

Kyle's house was ten miles down the road. It was another rambler, a lot like Shaun's. At least from the outside. Kyle's family didn't bother to keep the place clean, like Ruth did. And nobody insisted on putting up pictures of Jesus and little statuettes of the cross in every room.

"Wait here," Shaun said firmly as he parked in the drive.

"I will," Jesse said. With a sigh, he gave Shaun's arm back.

Shaun patted his retreating hand like you would a cute dog. He got out and marched determinedly to the front door. He faltered when it opened before he reached the porch.

Kyle was in the doorway. "Hey, sugar," he said. His normal put-together appearance was mussed. His eyes were red. He looked incredibly stoned.

"Hey." Shaun eyed him warily. "I want to buy."

"Mmm. You finished that whole bag in less than a week?" Kyle asked. He looked over Shaun's shoulder, toward Ruth's van. "You were sharing, weren't you?" He smiled slowly.

"None of your business," Shaun muttered. He felt his face get hot.

Kyle laughed. "Come in, honey." He stepped back and welcomed Shaun into the dirty kitchen. "Let's go in the back."

Now that Shaun had a good look at Kyle, he realized he was barely clothed. He was wearing cutoff shorts that clung to his ass indecently, and a short tank top that barely covered his stomach.

Shaun wrinkled his nose. "What are you wearing?"

"This?" Kyle did a little twirl. "Daddy dressed me up," he said.

Shaun tried not to gag.

"Don't judge. Most people call before they show up. I would have changed if I knew you were coming," he said.

The setup of Kyle's house was similar to Shaun's. The kitchen connected to a small living room, strewn with beer bottles and other miscellaneous trash. Down the hallway was a bathroom, the master bedroom and two other smaller rooms. Before they could get further than the living room, Kyle stopped to talk to a rough-looking man sitting in a chair in front of a blaring football game. He was heavyset, though not fat per se, with long black hair under a baseball hat, a scruffy beard, and a wife beater. Shaun recognized the man as Kyle's stepdad.

"I've got a customer, Daddy," Kyle said. He climbed into the man's lap and kissed him on the cheek.

"You gonna take care of 'im?" the redneck asked. His hand crept up Kyle's bare leg and toward his ass. Shaun watched, sickened.

"Yes, Daddy." Kyle kissed the man's other cheek before he slid off his lap. As he did so, it provided the perfect opportunity for Kyle's stepdad to grab his ass. Kyle squealed like a girl and pulled away with a laugh. "C'mon." Kyle tried to take Shaun's hand, but he stepped away and folded his arms. If Jesse couldn't hold his hand, who the fuck did Kyle think he was?

Kyle didn't seem terribly wounded. He shrugged and led the way to his room. Or at least Shaun thought it was Kyle's room, but from the posters of half-naked girls on the walls, Shaun realized that it was his brother's.

Kyle went to the dresser. "Oh fuck...where'd he—" He rifled through the top drawer. "Shit...here it is."

He pulled out his brother's stash of weed, packed neatly in a metal box. The scale and a box of heavy-duty baggies sat on a desk across the room. Kyle sat in the computer chair and leisurely apportioned some bud into a bag.

"So, is Jesse with you?"

"He's in the van," Shaun said shortly.

"Why's he out there?" Kyle asked sweetly. "He should have come in. We could have smoked first."

"I don't want him anywhere near *you*," Shaun said sharply. As soon as he said it, though, he wished he could take it back. He bit his tongue.

"Why's that?" Kyle dropped what he was doing and turned to get a good look at Shaun. For the first time since middle school, he looked genuinely pissed.

"I don't—" Shaun shut his mouth. He didn't want to look too protective. It was bad enough he had to deal with his own up and down emotions when it came to Jesse; he didn't need Kyle interfering.

"What is it, honey?" Kyle soothed. He left the half-filled bag of weed and got closer to Shaun. "You can tell me anything."

"The fuck I can," Shaun said through his teeth. He stood his ground, but he was extremely uncomfortable. Kyle wasn't touching him, but he was close enough for Shaun to feel the heat coming off his scantily clad body.

"I wish we could be friends again," Kyle whined. He tried to touch Shaun's arm, but Shaun shook him off immediately. "I still don't understand why we can't talk anymore." Kyle tried again, going for Shaun's other arm this time.

Shaun ripped away. His blood boiled. "Because I don't want to *fuck* you," he hissed. He wished he could have avoided this stupid conversation. Besides never becoming friends with Jesse, he didn't see a way. Kyle's presence in his miserable life had always been a given, and Kyle *loved* to tease Shaun.

"But why not?" Kyle asked. He cupped Shaun's cheek and stepped closer. Incredibly close.

He was taller than Jesse, and his lips lined up perfectly with Shaun's. Shaun was gratified to feel none of the conflicting emotions he'd felt earlier with Jesse. That meant all the gayness he felt for Jesse was an isolated incident and thus easier to get rid of. Here and now, with an actual gay guy, he felt next to nothing, unless disgust, horror, and maybe a bit of amusement counted.

"Because I'm *not* gay." Showing an amazing amount of restraint, Shaun smacked Kyle's hand away. "And if I was, I wouldn't fuck you anyway. You're a whore. Now get my goddamn weed so I can leave."

"Is that what you think of me?" Kyle had the gall to ask. He put his hand on his hip and pouted ineffectively.

Shaun gave him an exasperated look.

"All right, all right." Kyle dropped his stance and moved back to the desk. He finished weighing and bagging the weed in record time. He handed over the bag and then held out his hand for the cash.

"Be careful, sugar," Kyle warned him, slipping Shaun's money into the waistband of his cutoffs, like a stripper.

"What's that supposed to mean?"

"However you want to interpret it," Kyle said cryptically.

Deciding to ignore the thinly veiled threat, Shaun left Kyle's house without another word. He didn't respond when Kyle's stepdad called out a friendly goodbye.

"That took a long time," Jesse whined as Shaun got back into the van. Jesse looked like he'd been squirming with impatience for quite a while. He immediately latched onto Shaun's arm.

"Fucking Kyle..." Shaun shook his head. "He was giving me a hard time."

"He was?" Jesse's hand tightened around Shaun's arm. "What'd he do?"

"I don't want to talk about it." Shaun started the van and backed down the drive. At the last second, he decided to go somewhere else. He turned in the opposite direction of home and started to drive.

Jesse was oblivious. He clutched Shaun's arm and sang—badly—along to a country song on the radio. Shaun didn't like country music, but he enjoyed listening to Jesse mess up the lyrics.

Ten minutes later, Shaun spotted an old gravel drive. It was overgrown and almost invisible from the road. But Shaun knew it by heart.

The house Shaun had grown up in was no longer standing.

Nobody had lived there after what had happened. It wasn't haunted or anything, not that Shaun believed in that kind of thing. His parents had been so miserable he was sure their spirits were long gone.

The house had sat empty for years after the murder/suicide. Nobody had been interested in buying it, not even out-of-towners who had no idea of its terrible past.

Shaun had gone to see it sometimes when he was younger, riding his bike the twenty miles or so just to look at it.

Eventually it had burned down.

They'd said it was arson. Dumb kids playing around. No harm done.

Shaun hadn't felt all that upset about it. He'd always hated that place. Just looking at it had instilled a stomach-gnawing unease. He remembered all the times he'd wanted his parents to go away, to stop fighting, to shut up and die, and then they had. They'd been dead and Shaun had watched it happen.

He hadn't been back since the day it'd burned to the ground.

There was nothing left now. Just an empty lot filled with weeds and tall grass. He barely recognized it.

There was an old For Sale sign by the road, alongside a No Trespassing sign, but there wasn't anyone to deny him the right to park here. Just for a few hours.

Jesse was singing. He looked around curiously.

It was getting late, and the sun had already set. Shaun couldn't tell if Jesse had noticed the signs or not.

Shaun pulled the van up to the charred foundation of the old house and cut the engine. Darkness settled around them.

"Oh fuck. It's dark," Jesse said. His face glowed in the green light from the console.

"Yeah," Shaun said. "I didn't feel like going home."

"Me neither." Shaun didn't know if Jesse was talking about his home or Shaun's, but he didn't ask for clarification.

"C'mon." Shaun climbed out of the driver's seat and crawled into the back of the van. The back seats were pushed down from the time Eli had hauled their new armchair from the Goodwill. There was plenty of room to lie down. Jesse sprawled out beside him.

"Too bad you don't have a moon roof," he prattled. "We could see the sky."

Shaun unlatched the van's back hatch. As it swung upward the dark sky came into view. The stars of twilight winked into existence.

"There's more stars here than in Detroit. Or in...well, anywhere that I've ever lived before," Jesse said as he stared into the night sky. "It's beautiful."

"It's all right," Shaun said. He was distracted. He pulled out the pot and packed his bowl. He was glad he'd decided to bring his pipe. "Wanna go first?" he asked once everything was ready.

"Light it for me?" Jesse propped himself upright on his elbows.

Shaun brought the pipe to Jesse's lips. He struck the lighter and Jesse obediently puffed. When Jesse leaned back, Shaun took a hit and watched Jesse hold on to his smoke.

"You gonna breathe sometime soon?" Shaun asked. Jesse was getting red in the face.

Jesse pursed his lips. He attempted to release the smoke in a cool ring, but ended up coughing and sputtering like an idiot. Shaun couldn't help but laugh.

"I saw that going better in my head," Jesse said as tears of exertion ran down his cheeks.

"You're an idiot," Shaun told him fondly.

They shared the pipe for a while, talking about nothing in particular. Shaun got tired of doing everything while Jesse lay back and enjoyed his buzz, so he lay down beside him and got comfortable.

It was quiet after that, for a while anyway. Shaun packed the bowl again and handed it to Jesse. He flopped onto his side as he smoked. They both laughed at how clumsy he was. When Jesse got himself under control again, he broke the silence.

"Where are we?" he asked.

"This is where I used to live," Shaun said. "The house burned down, but this is where it was," he clarified before Jesse could ask.

Jesse must have suspected because he didn't look the slightest bit surprised. Of course, he was high. "Are you scared to be here?" he asked instead.

"No," Shaun said quickly, then, "I don't know. Maybe." He thought about it for a moment more, shyly meeting Jesse's inquisitive gaze. "It used to make me sad to be here."

"Not now?" Jesse took Shaun's hand. Their fingers laced together. Shaun blamed it on the weed when he clutched Jesse's hand like a lifeline.

"You're here," Shaun admitted. Those two words made him feel extremely vulnerable, but for once, he wasn't embarrassed. Jesse seemed pleased, and really that was all that mattered, Shaun realized with an uneasy pang.

"Let's be best friends forever, okay?" Jesse said with a dreamy smile. "When you leave town, I want to come with you."

"You do?" Shaun's eyebrows shot into his hairline. "But what about—"

"Just promise you'll take me with you," Jesse said. "Promise me."

Shaun didn't want to promise anything he couldn't 100 percent guarantee. It scared him Jesse would want him too.

But Jesse...he was special.

Maybe he wasn't special to his mom, who had five other bratty kids, or to Kenny, who had so many friends he didn't know what to do with them, or to Emily, who kept trying to twist Jesse into her view of the perfect boyfriend, but to Shaun, Jesse was one of a kind. Shaun didn't know if he *could* leave Jesse behind the way things stood now.

"I—yes," Shaun said. "We'll get out of here together." As the reluctant promise was drawn from him, a weight settled across his shoulders. He didn't feel burdened; he felt reassured.

Wordlessly, Jesse scooted closer and tossed his arm and his leg over Shaun. He gave him a full-body hug.

"Hmm," Shaun mumbled. He put his arm around Jesse. He felt good tucked against him like that, and as Shaun rubbed his back, he felt a sense of contentment so strong he found himself laughing again, for the second time in less than an hour!

Jesse pulled back. He was laughing too.

Shaun knew the moment was over as they separated, but he wasn't sad. On the contrary, he was happy. He knew he'd have Jesse tomorrow and the next day and next month as well. Maybe next year too, if he was lucky. He'd never been so optimistic in his life. It felt good to look forward to something for once.

Beside him, Jesse rolled onto his back again and tried to name the constellations. Shaun smiled as Jesse get several wrong in a row. He didn't correct him.

They were still holding hands.

*

Shaun wasn't surprised when Jesse was affectionate on the bus Monday morning. He was embarrassed, though, especially when Jesse tried to grab his hand. Shaun nudged him away.

"What's wrong?" Jesse asked.

"Not..." As much as Shaun felt obligated to keep the gayness to a minimum, he really didn't want to. At the very least, they had to be private about it. "Not in public," he whispered.

Jesse looked at him. His pretty blue eyes filled with hurt. "But—"

"Don't even try to say you hold other guys' hands, because I know for a fact that you don't," Shaun snapped.

Jesse pouted, but he didn't argue. He changed the subject to school.

When Emily got on the bus, Shaun was relieved. She sat in the front with her brother and her friends. He'd feared that now she and Jesse were dating—were they dating?—she'd try to sit with them. She did wave at Jesse though.

Amusingly, Jesse wasn't paying any attention to her, so her wave went unreturned.

Jesse was more like his usual self in chemistry. The class did a boring review session for a test later in the week. They were playing Jeopardy with the review topics. Shaun and Jesse were on the same team, and really, Shaun felt bad for the two other people in their group because neither of them knew a single answer.

"Melting ice is an example of what kind of change?" Mr. Barnes asked Jesse.

"C'mon, this is easy," the stupid blond bitch, Sara, whispered. If she knew the answer, it really must have been easy, but Jesse bit his lip and thought hard.

"Uh...what is a chemical change?"

Sara sighed as Mr. Barnes shook his head. He moved on to ask the next group. Jesse had lost them two hundred points.

"Shit! Sorry! I told you I'm bad at chemistry," Jesse said to the group. He smiled at Shaun. "Guess we'd better study, huh?"

"You can study if you want," Shaun said. He'd never put much effort into school. Why start now?

Jesse stuck his tongue out. "You'll help me," he said smugly.

Shaun tried not to smile like a loon. He felt stupidly pleased, though. He would help Jesse study, if that's what he wanted.

They walked to history together, like always. When they got to class, Jesse didn't immediately retreat to his seat in the back. He lingered by Shaun's.

"I wish I knew Mr. Barnes was giving suckers to the winning team." Jesse pouted. "I like suckers."

"You don't need any sugar," Shaun said. "You're hyper enough as it is."

Jesse poked him in the chest. "Just because you said that, you owe me a bag of suckers."

"I do?"

"Yes."

The bell rang. Shaun noted the distress on Jesse's face. He stored it away for later.

"Guess I'd better find my seat," Jesse said reluctantly. He stretched his arm out, like he was going to touch Shaun again, but he pulled away at the last second. He scampered to his seat next to Emily.

Shaun was glad he'd aborted the attempt.

Last night after he'd took Jesse home, Shaun had made a deep cut in his hip. It hadn't felt as good as it usually did, but it had certainly got him in the right mindset.

He didn't need to be thinking about Jesse that way. Didn't need to be holding his hand and getting erections around him. It was wrong.

Everything Shaun did was wrong, and in his mind, the punishment fit the crime perfectly.

He tried to ignore how old that argument was getting. He tried to forget how worn down he felt, telling himself he was dirty, that he didn't deserve to touch Jesse, and that he shouldn't pollute him with his sick mind.

The only person that had ever wanted him was a whore with conditions. Shaun told himself that over and over. He didn't want to let himself forget.

Class ended and Shaun didn't wait for Jesse. He went to his next class without looking back once.

When lunchtime rolled around, Shaun was still hating on himself. He went to his usual table, the only one consistently devoid of students, and pulled out his bagged lunch. Yuck. Another PB and J.

"Hi." Jesse set a lunch tray on the table.

Shaun jerked in surprise. He dropped his sandwich. "What are you doing here?" he asked.

"Emily was being a bitch. I'm sitting here until she cools down." Jesse sat right next to him, leaving very little space between them. Shaun scooted a few inches away.

"What'd she do now?"

Jesse watched him move away with sad eyes. "I don't know; she's mad I'm still hanging out with you. She thought telling me your story would make me hate you." Jesse gave him a significant look which Shaun artfully ignored.

"Dump her already. There's gotta be a better girl you can mess with." He tried to ignore the extreme hatred that welled inside him at the thought of Jesse hooking up with another girl. Any girl.

"Yeah," Jesse said. "I'm regretting this whole thing. I mean...she was different when I first met her. She was quiet...kinda nice. Now she's..." Jesse trailed off. He looked across the cafeteria at the girl in question. She was talking with Sunny and ignoring him completely. "I don't know; she's bossy and kind of boring."

Shaun snorted. "You just found that out? I told you not to go with her."

"I should have listened," Jesse said. He sighed and ran his fingers through his hair. "Now I'm afraid if I hurt her feelings, Kenny's coming after me. I don't think he wanted me to go out with her in the first place."

"Kenny's an asshole," Shaun spat. "He's no better than his fucking sister."

Jesse smiled sadly. He laid a hand over Shaun's. "What'd they do to you?"

Shaun stared at their hands. He considered saying a lot of different things, but he shook his head. He didn't want to complain. "They're just so high and mighty," he said. "They think they're better than me because they have money and their parents give a shit about them."

Jesse squeezed Shaun's hand. He removed it right after, but Shaun's hand tingled. He missed Jesse's touch already.

"They're scared of you. People are stupid when they're scared."

Shaun didn't want to let them off the hook, but he let it go. He drew his hand into his lap and shrugged noncommittally. He hated everyone, but there was no reason to turn Jesse into a cynical, hateful person because of his own personal biases.

They switched topics. They talked about music and guitars as they ate. Jesse was serious about learning how to play. Shaun was glad there was something he could share with him that Jesse couldn't get from anyone else. They made plans to practice.

Shaun didn't want to admit it, but he thoroughly enjoyed having someone to talk to during the most social part of the school day. He'd never longed for social contact before, but he was going to miss it now that he knew what it was like. He hoped Jesse never went back to the popular table.

After lunch, they walked to gym together. Shaun had gotten used to Jesse hanging with Kenny and Eric, but he didn't have any interest in them today. The coach put them on different touch football teams, but Jesse stuck close to Shaun the whole time.

"Jesse! C'mon!" Kenny yelled as he ran past them on the field.

Jesse waved at him, but he didn't speed up. He kept pace with Shaun's lackluster trot.

They were supposed to be doing...something. Shaun didn't know what. He knew nothing about football. It was a stupid game, and it required too much running. He chose to show his masculinity in different ways, anyway, like hunting. He realized walking after his team wasn't his purpose as a cornerback, but he didn't care.

Jesse was a motormouth. He talked about the horrible movie he'd been forced to see Friday.

"You would have hated it. It wasn't funny at all," he said before he launched into detailed descriptions of the weak humor.

Shaun didn't like comedies, but he was amused Jesse thought he knew enough about him to decide whether he'd like something or not. It was presumptuous, but sweet, nonetheless. And he really hated that fucking word...*sweet*.

The coach blew his whistle and called the game. Everyone headed back to the locker rooms. Shaun and Jesse fell behind.

"Do you have to skip next period?"

"Why?" Shaun asked.

"It sucks riding the bus by myself," Jesse said.

Shaun arched an eyebrow. "You're not alone. Your brother's there; your friends are there. So's your girlfriend," Shaun said. He couldn't help the face he made when he mentioned Emily.

Jesse shrugged. "Yeah."

They entered the locker room. Jesse had stashed his stuff in Shaun's locker, and he went straight there. Shaun slowed. Kenny and Eric glowered at him. They looked away when they realized they'd been noticed. Jesse followed Shaun's gaze, but he was too late to see the nasty looks on their faces.

"C'mon. Give me my clothes," Jesse said. He tugged on Shaun's combination lock.

Shaun put the code in. He could feel Jesse's friends glaring at him. It felt like needles pushing into his skin.

"So, can you ride the bus with me?"

"No." Shaun elbowed Jesse out of the way and opened the locker. "You're being gay again," he said.

"I am not," Jesse said. He bumped Shaun with his hip in retaliation.

Shaun stepped back and let Jesse get his change of clothes. He wondered what Kenny and Eric must be thinking. He and Jesse were awfully cozy. Talking nonstop, sharing lockers, touching each other... "Listen. I can't go to study hall after half a year of skipping. It'll fuck everything up."

"You could wait outside," Jesse said.

Shaun yanked his hoodie off and tossed it in the locker. He never took his clothes off for gym. "I'm not doing that. I'll meet you at your house when you get home."

Jesse pouted.

"It takes ten minutes to get home on the bus. You'll survive."

"You're a dick," Jesse said. He took his shirt off and tossed it in the locker. He didn't meet Shaun's eyes. He seemed upset.

Shaun kicked his grungy tennis shoes off and changed back into his boots. Jesse went the whole nine yards. He stripped down to his underwear before he put his jeans and T-shirt on again. Shaun avoided looking at him until he was completely covered. He didn't want anyone thinking he was checking him out. When Jesse was dressed, Shaun locked up.

"See you later," Jesse said. He smiled, but it didn't reach his eyes. He left to get to his last class of the day.

Shaun didn't want to wait. He didn't want to ride the bus home, either, but more than anything, he didn't want to upset Jesse. He'd wait fifty minutes for him to finish, if that's what Jesse wanted. It wasn't that big a deal.

He dropped his books off and grabbed his bag. He sat outside the front doors and listened to some music while he waited.

School was over sooner than Shaun had anticipated. Kids flowed out of the building and headed to the buses. Shaun stood up. He slung his bag over his shoulder and waited tensely for Jesse to appear. People were looking at him. Every person in the entire school filed past.

Shaun was scowling by the time Jesse came through the doors.

"You waited!" Jesse cried. He rushed to Shaun's side, and just like that, all the inconvenience was worth it. Jesse swayed on the balls of his feet. Shaun sensed Jesse wanted to hug him, but he restrained himself. He squirmed like a worm and beamed, happy as can be.

Shaun smirked. The excitement was palpable. "C'mon, let's get out of here."

They walked to the bus.

"Thanks, Shaun," Jesse said. "For waiting."

"Yeah."

They climbed on the bus. Kenny, Emily, and the rest of the gang did a double take when they saw Shaun. Shaun put his chin up and ignored them.

"I have to get off at my stop, so I can get the weed," he said as they sat in their regular seat at the back of the bus.

"You don't have to," Jesse said.

"What? You don't want to get high?!" Shaun hissed in disbelief.

"Fuck you." Jesse stuck his tongue out. "Fine. Go get your stupid weed."

"You act like I'm forcing you to smoke. You're the one that's addicted," Shaun pointed out.

They fought each other playfully the whole ride home. Jesse was fun to tease.

When the bus stopped outside Shaun's house, Jesse got off with him.

"Where are you going?" Sam asked as they passed.

Jesse responded with the finger.

It was a good thing they'd stopped at Shaun's place. He'd forgotten to pack the *Frist Blood* DVD. He'd promised Brian they'd watch it.

Shaun collected the weed from his room and a couple of movies from the shelf in the living room.

Ruth was watching Oprah in her favorite chair. She asked several nosy questions. Where were they going? What did they plan on getting up to? She even asked what they were eating for dinner. Shaun pushed Jesse out the front door before he could answer. What they did was no business of Ruth's.

It was still early. They stopped in the garage to smoke and fuck around on the guitar. Jesse wasn't a bad player. He remembered what Shaun had already taught him, and he took direction well, even though Shaun wasn't very good at giving it.

"No. Like this," Shaun snapped. He stepped up and forced Jesse's fingers into the correct position. Jesse batted him away with a giggle.

"I can do it."

"The fuck you can," Shaun muttered. He took another hit off the joint he'd rolled and watched as Jesse fucked up again. He released the smoke. "No, no, no. Try again. From the top."

"Give me a hit first," Jesse said. He gestured Shaun closer.

Rolling his eyes, Shaun held the joint out. "Here, you idiot."

Jesse leaned over the guitar to get a puff. He looked like a fish with his lips pressed out like that, a really cute red-haired fish. "Thanks," Jesse smiled as the pot did its thing. Smoke swirled around him in artistic billows. He closed his eyes and concentrated. His fingers flexed nimbly across the fretboard like Shaun had been trying to explain for the past hour. He nailed it.

"Good!" Shaun cried. "Finally!"

"That was good?" Jesse smiled uncertainly.

"Fuck yes."

They had to leave soon after that, but they both felt accomplished. They talked about it on the walk to Jesse's.

Sam was watching the twins in the living room when they came in the door. He glared at them.

"Give it a rest, Sam." Jesse said.

"Why do you get to slack off? Maybe I want to get high and hang out with my friends after school too," Sam bitched. "But no. I have to hurry home and wait for the twins."

"Like I didn't have to wait for you to get off the bus," Jesse spat. "I did it for *years*."

"Oh, so this is revenge?"

"No. It's called 'I have better things to do than babysit a thirteen-year-old.'"

Sam's face turned red. "I don't need babysitting, but I could use a hand with these two retards."

"Hey!" Tyler cried. He sat, quiet and well-behaved on the couch next to Allison, who was also on her best behavior.

Jesse rolled his eyes. "Looks like you've got it handled. And I'm back. I'm here, okay? Relax." He toed his shoes off and dropped his bookbag by the door. Shaun followed his example.

Sam wasn't done. He folded his arms and glared even harder. "Bet you're going upstairs."

"Damned right we are," Shaun sneered. "Neither of us wants to deal with your shitty attitude."

Jesse grabbed Shaun's wrist and pulled him to the stairs. "Let it go," he said.

"No, you're getting high again!" Sam shouted after them. "Fucking stoners."

"We already smoked a blunt," Shaun tossed over his shoulder. "We don't need your fucking permission."

"Oh my God," Jesse said once they were alone in his room. He shook his head. He climbed up to his bunk and sprawled out on the blankets. "Come lay with me?"

Shaun sighed, but he wasn't about to deny his friend. He followed Jesse up the ladder and lay beside him. "Your brother's a brat," he said.

"He's jealous," Jesse said. "I don't know what to do about it."

"It's a phase," Shaun said.

"Yeah, until he finds someone to smoke with." Jesse covered his face. "I was his age when I smoked the first time."

"I was younger," Shaun said.

"Ugh." Jesse rolled over. He looked into Shaun's eyes. "We're being hypocrites."

"I'm not smoking with your little brother," Shaun said through his teeth.

Jesse bit his lip. "I'm not asking you to," he said. "But I wish he'd stop hating me. I'm not kidding; I took care of that kid when he was a baby. I took care of the twins and Brian... I take care of Lissa all week long. It's nice knowing Sam's got the twins for an hour or two, so I can do my own thing. Just for a little bit. Christ, I'm always taking care of everyone! Why is it so bad I take a break here and there?"

"It's not," Shaun said.

Jesse closed his eyes and groaned. "I'm tired. I wish I could take a nap and not feel like a selfish loser for wanting to rest."

"No point going to sleep," Shaun said gently. "Your mom will be home soon."

Jesse groaned again. "Brian's going to be a bundle of energy."

"Yeah." Shaun smiled. The toddler was an interesting little guy.

And indeed, Brian was very happy to see Shaun. He shouted with excitement and jumped up and down.

After Monica dropped off the two youngest members of the family, Jesse was still feeling tired. He browsed through the pantry, muttering to himself. He pulled out a box of spaghetti and a can of sauce.

"I guess it's spaghetti tonight," he said. "Quick, simple, filling. It's mushy enough for the baby to eat too," he said.

Shaun felt bad for him. He watched Jesse whip up dinner with a practiced ease. He found some frozen garlic bread in the freezer and popped it in the oven while the water boiled. Shaun helped as much as he could. He kept an eye on Brian, who was dying to show Shaun his activity book from school, and Lissa, cooing and happy, strapped in her bouncer.

Brian continued to chat Shaun's head off during dinner. He ate, but he was barely paying attention to his plate. He got red sauce all over his face. Lissa got messy too. Jesse let her eat her noodles by hand.

When dinner was over, the twins went upstairs to play *Candy Land*. Sam followed them up. He said he would keep an eye on them, but they heard him slam the bedroom door. He was probably up there pouting.

Shaun offered to clean the kids up. He was in a good mood and wanted to be helpful. Jesse gave him a wet washcloth and smiled fondly as Shaun cleaned Brian's hands and face. When he got to the baby, he took her bib off to cut down on the sauce buildup. She had it everywhere though. It was in her hair, in her ears...

"I have to give her a bath," Jesse said with a sigh. He collected the dirty dishes everyone had left behind and carried them to the sink.

"Can we watch the movie now?" Brian asked hopefully, and Shaun glanced at Jesse for direction.

Jesse nodded. "Leave Lissa in her chair. We'll join you when we can."

"I don't know how to work your TV," Shaun admitted.

"Brian knows how to set it up," Jesse said, and Brian took that as permission. He grabbed Shaun's hand and yanked him into the living room. He found the remote on the coffee table and switched the television to video mode.

First Blood was an oldie, but a goodie. Shaun was glad to share it with someone who'd never seen it before. He and Brian got settled on the couch and waited eagerly for the movie to load up.

"Is this scary?" Brian asked.

"It's bloody," Shaun said. "And full of action. It's one of my favorite movies."

Brian snuggled into Shaun's side as he watched the blood and guts spewing on screen. Kids today really were desensitized, Shaun thought approvingly.

It was almost over when Jesse came downstairs with a clean baby in a onesie. He sat on Shaun's other side and held the baby to his chest.

"Dishes are washed and put away; the baby's clean and has a fresh diaper. The twins threw the pieces to *Candy Land* all over the place, but Sam has Mom's tablet and he's letting them watch videos on YouTube," Jesse sighed. "How's the movie?"

"Rambo is the coolest ever," Brian said. He didn't look away from the screen.

Jesse smiled wearily. "Did I miss much?"

"Only the entire thing," Shaun said. "It'll be over in five minutes."

"Aww, I want to watch another movie," Brian complained.

"I brought the original *Predator*," Shaun said. "It's like this movie, but it's got aliens."

Brian clapped his hands. "I want to see!"

When the movie ended, Brian put the next DVD in the player. He jumped back on the couch, and Shaun put an arm around his shoulders without thinking. Brian rested his head against Shaun's side.

Predator started, and within the first ten minutes, Jesse sprawled out on the couch and put his feet in Shaun's lap. He looked like he was halfway to dreamland already. The baby snuggled into his chest, and Jesse hummed her a lullaby. Shaun could barely hear it over the movie, but the baby felt the vibrations. She stopped moving and Shaun knew she was asleep.

Jesse was next. His eyes closed gradually. His face smoothed. He looked peaceful and angelic, and Shaun had seen this movie a million times before; he watched Jesse sleep, enjoying the simple domesticity of it.

Brian lasted the longest, but he too petered out before the movie ended. He shifted to drop his head onto Shaun's thigh and drifted to sleep easily.

He looked so much like Jesse. They both had the same pretty blue eyes, the same cute upturned nose and soft pale skin. They both looked incredibly sweet in their sleep.

Shaun had never wanted a brother. It'd just be someone else to hate, he'd figured. But when he looked at the little boy asleep in his lap, he wished he could have grown up with a kid brother half as cool as Brian.

Looking at Jesse, though...well, Shaun felt something quite different than the swell of brotherly affection he felt toward the blond toddler. Something he'd rather not think about just now.

When the movie ended, he picked Brian up. He marveled at the way the little boy clung to him, completely trusting.

"I'm not tired," Brian muttered sleepily. He pressed his face into Shaun's shoulder and promptly fell back to sleep.

Shaun carried him upstairs.

He placed Brian in the top bunk and covered him in one of Jesse's blankets. As he climbed down, a voice startled him into missing the last step.

"What are you doing with my brother?"

Shaun stumbled. He whirled around and glared at the teenager in the doorway. "I'm putting him to sleep," he sneered. He tried to cover his misstep with a vicious glare.

Sam was doing his best to match Shaun's viciousness. He stared at Shaun hatefully.

"I meant with Jesse."

Shaun narrowed his eyes. "We're friends," he said.

Sam continued to glare death at him, and Shaun wondered if that was all Sam was going to say, but then he spoke again.

"I've heard the things people say about you. You're a *monster*."

Shaun grunted. He'd certainly heard that before. The word had been tossed around quite a bit before he'd started punishing people for saying it.

"You don't know anything, you little shit head."

"I know you killed your parents," Sam said. "You made Jesse hate me, and now you're trying to turn him against the whole family." He poked a finger at Shaun.

"Wrong on all counts," Shaun said boredly.

Sam sucked his teeth. "As if you'd admit it. What's your plan? Are you going to drug Jesse until he agrees to murder us in our sleep?"

With one quick step, Shaun was in Sam's face. He jerked his head back with a fistful of hair and forced the boy to meet his eyes.

"Let's get the story straight, kid. Since we're spending so much time together," Shaun hissed, ignoring Sam's frantic hands clawing at him, desperately seeking a release. He held tight. "I didn't kill my parents. I watched them die though. And if I really wanted to turn Jesse against your family, I wouldn't be helping him babysit you little brats every night. Oh, and the reason Jesse hates you right now is because you're a fucking—" Shaun yanked Sam's head back at a painful angle. "—punk-ass bitch, who specializes in being a nasty little cunt."

As suddenly as he'd grabbed him, Shaun released Sam. The boy lost his footing and stumbled into the hall. Sam stared at him for a full five seconds, his eyes wide with shock. Then he bolted back to the twins' room. He slammed the door with a bang.

Surprisingly Brian had slept through the commotion. Shaun checked on him first, peeking into the bed. Then he went down to see Jesse.

The movie had ended. The credits were rolling. He went to the DVD player and took his movie out. He put it back in its case, then turned the TV off.

"Wha..." Jesse stirred.

"You're awake," Shaun said. He smiled gently.

"I guess," Jesse laughed. He sat up, cradling Lissa to his chest. "Did you put Brian in my bed?"

"Yeah."

"Mmm." Jesse got up. "I'm going to put the baby down. Don't go away."

Shaun nodded. He watched Jesse trail up the stairs and hoped Sam wouldn't blab and get him in trouble. He'd been harsh. Way too harsh.

He waited on pins and needles for a good two to three minutes. But Jesse looked totally oblivious when he came down. Sam must not have said anything.

"Sorry I fell asleep," Jesse said. "I wasn't much fun tonight." He still looked pretty tired, but he didn't lie down again. He sat with his legs folded under him. "Wonder what's on," he said. He turned the TV on and picked a boring sitcom.

Monica was unusually late. It was already half past nine. She was usually home by now.

Jesse didn't seem worried though, so Shaun didn't mention it.

"You okay?" Jesse was looking at him, concern on his sleepy face.

"Yeah. Fine," Shaun said, a little too quickly.

Jesse scooted closer and leaned into Shaun's side a lot like Brian had been doing earlier. He sighed and his soft breath blew through Shaun's hair.

They watched TV for what felt like forever. Shaun was afraid to move. He was pretty sure Jesse was asleep again. He couldn't take this much longer, though...being close like this. Jesse made sweet noises in his sleep, and his breath was hot on the back of Shaun's neck. It was doing things to Shaun's body he wasn't comfortable with.

The sound of keys in the door had Shaun up in an instant, upsetting Jesse from his slumber. Monica walked in the room just as Jesse did a nose plant on the couch cushions.

"Er...hi," Shaun said. He knew his face was bright red, even though Monica hadn't seen them. She'd been looking at her cell phone when she'd walked in.

"Oh. Shaun." Monica looked up from her screen. "I hope you boys weren't waiting up for me. Sorry I'm so late."

Behind him on the couch, Jesse moaned. Shaun blushed harder. "I'd better go," he said quickly. He sprinted for the door and slid out into the cool night air. At least out here, nobody could see his burning cheeks.

*

Shaun kept waiting for Jesse to get over his clinginess. Waited for him to crawl back to Emily, Kenny, and their ilk, but if anything, Jesse focused on Shaun even more. He hung off him at every opportunity, followed him everywhere, made Shaun talk unendingly...

Shaun wasn't happy about it, but he rode the bus home with Jesse every day. He hated sitting around and waiting for the end of the day to come, but it was always worth it when he saw Jesse's smiles and his badly restrained affection.

They practiced guitar every afternoon before Brian and Lissa came home. Shaun didn't know how much Jesse was learning, but it was always fun.

Jesse never brought up Shaun's run-in with Sam. Sam had kept his mouth shut, but whenever Shaun saw him and Jesse interact, Sam seemed bitchier than ever.

On Wednesday, Jesse didn't mention going to church. Shaun didn't show it, but he was thrilled. They hung out all night, watching movies and playing with Brian and the baby. They didn't even speak Emily's name.

So, Shaun really shouldn't have been surprised when Jesse asked what they were doing on the weekend.

"What do you mean?"

"Well...my mom tries to give me the weekends off, you know. So hopefully when she comes home tonight we'll be able to do something on our own," Jesse explained. "Unless you have to go to band practice."

"Don't you have something better to do? Like be with your girlfriend or something?" Shaun sneered, but not because he was mad. There were butterflies in his stomach again. It was all so fucking gay. He hated it.

"No," Jesse said as if the idea of spending time with Emily was the most ridiculous thing he'd ever heard. "So, can we do something tonight?"

"I guess." The fluttery feeling stuck around. It refused to leave.

"Good." Jesse casually touched Shaun's knee, playing with the worn hole in his jeans. "So, you don't practice with your band on Fridays?"

"No, that's tomorrow." Shaun flicked Jesse's hand away, covering the hole and effectively putting an end to the wandering hands. They were still on the school bus after all. People could see them.

"Can I come?"

Shaun snorted. "Seriously?" There was *no* way Shaun could bring Jesse to practice. He could picture it now. Jesse touching him, holding his hand, snuggling up to him like a cat in heat. "*Hell* no."

"Why?" Jesse pouted immediately. "C'mon. Please! I want to see you guys play again!"

"Then come to the next show." That wasn't much better, but at least Shaun could duck out of the venue and get some privacy. There'd be none of that at Will's house.

"Shaun!" Jesse pleaded, and Shaun was usually kind of a pushover when it came to Jesse begging, but this time, he had a good reason to refuse.

"No."

Jesse pouted and whined to come to band practice for the rest of the day. He did it through chemistry, lunch, gym, and the bus ride home.

Shaun waited until they got off the bus to tell Jesse he was serious. He pulled him into the garage.

"Fucking stop! Shut up, already!" he yelled as soon as they were alone.

Jesse shut his mouth.

"I don't want you coming with me because..." What was a nice, and not completely stupid way, to tell Jesse he couldn't come around because he couldn't keep his hands to himself? "Because you..." Fuck it. "Because you keep acting like a fucking fag!"

"What?" And of course, Jesse had to look completely confused, as if he'd been possessed this past week and someone else had been molesting Shaun without Jesse's knowledge.

"You keep...touching me!" Shaun said, flushing an ugly red as he did. This was *so* embarrassing. "Danny called us gay last week because you were hugging on me and crap!"

"Who's Danny?" Jesse asked sourly. "He sounds like a prick."

Shaun snorted at the comment. "Danny's the drummer. And he is, by the way," Shaun said. "A prick."

"I won't hug you then," Jesse said quickly. "I won't touch you at all!"

Shaun didn't want to say it out loud, but he disliked the prospect of no further touching. It wasn't a big deal, really, but he knew people would see it the wrong way.

"You know...just when we're around the band," Shaun said.

"Okay. Just when we're around other people. Like you said," Jesse said softly. He poked Shaun in the stomach with a goofy smile. Shaun knocked his hand away with a half-hearted scowl. "People just don't get it."

"No, they don't," Shaun said solemnly.

"I'm sorry I'm so touchy-feely, but...you're the best friend I've ever had," Jesse said. He smiled when Shaun's expression remained serious. "Do you forgive me?" He slid his arms around Shaun's waist and hugged him tight.

Shaun sighed. Well, it looked like he didn't have to worry about Jesse getting over his clinginess. That stupid fluttery feeling came back in full force, and Shaun felt his arms wind around Jesse's shoulders of their own accord. His long fingers threaded through Jesse's incredibly soft hair.

"Mmm," Jesse murmured. He buried his face against Shaun's chest, effectively pushing his head into Shaun's hands. "That feels nice," he said in a muffled voice.

This was getting too lovey-dovey. Shaun rubbed his knuckles into Jesse's scalp and gave him a noogie.

"Hey!" Jesse ducked away with a laugh. "Cut it out!"

The fluttery, butterfly feeling left. Shaun relaxed. "Do you want to practice or not?" He gestured to the guitar they'd left on boxes yesterday.

"Yeah!" Jesse cheered. He rushed to set everything up.

They didn't end up doing anything special that night. Once Monica came home, they tried to escape back to Shaun's, but Brian threw such a huge fit that they—or rather Shaun—decided to stay put. Jesse rolled his eyes and called Shaun a pushover.

The three of them went to Jesse's room and played with a bucket of Legos. It was far from thrilling, but Shaun didn't mind playing as much as he'd thought he would. He liked the stupid kid.

They made a game out of it. Shaun showed Brian how to make a gun out of blocks, and Brian assassinated Jesse with it. Shaun laughed. The kid was pretending he was Rambo.

They put Brian to bed after ten. Shaun helped Jesse clean up his room while they talked and laughed about their evening with the energetic toddler.

"We shouldn't let him watch Rambo," Jesse said as he tossed the last of the blocks into the bin. "He'll turn into a serial killer."

"Like me?" Shaun joked.

Jesse sucked his teeth. "No. You're a big softie. I don't think you'd ever hurt anybody."

"Fuck you. Yes, I would," Shaun grunted. "I've hurt lots of people."

"So you say." Jesse sounded superior, like he knew everything. He climbed up to his bunk. "Are you coming up?"

Shaun shook his head. "It's getting late. I should go."

"No. Stay the night."

Jesse made it sound so casual, so normal. Just two guys sleeping in the same bed. Completely normal.

"Jesse—"

"What? It's not a school night. You can stay if you want," Jesse said earnestly.

"No. That's weird."

"Is not."

Shaun rolled his eyes. "We'll probably crash at Will's house after practice," he said. "We'll hang out tomorrow night."

Jesse pouted. "But what about tonight?"

"Jesse, c'mon." This was getting weird. Jesse never wanted Shaun to leave. Their relationship was already abnormal, but sleeping together? That seemed like a whole other level.

An incredibly, irreparably gay level.

"You're no fun," Jesse said. He lay down on his stomach and looked over the edge of his bed with sad eyes. "So, when are you coming to pick me up tomorrow?"

Shaun shrugged. He didn't want to get to Will's place too early since he didn't know how the band would react to him bringing a friend along. So, limiting the amount of time they were there, sitting around, sounded like a good idea. And if Danny and Will were really being obnoxious about Jesse, then they could just wrap up practice and leave early.

"Around five maybe." That'd give them an hour to get there. Practice started up around six.

"Okay." Jesse seemed disappointed. Shaun nodded curtly and turned to leave. "Do you want me to come with you?" Jesse threw out, stopping Shaun in his tracks.

The fluttery feeling, like butterflies tickling him from the inside, started up again. He imagined Jesse in *his* bed, and the thought was so ludicrous he could barely stand it.

"No," he said without turning. "I'll see you tomorrow."

Jesse didn't respond and Shaun left in peace. Only he wasn't in peace. He was upset.

Why couldn't Jesse let him enjoy anything? Every time they had a little fun, Jesse insisted on making it weird. All the touching and the affection made that fluttery, butterfly feeling start in his stomach, and Shaun hated it. He wished they could go back to the way they were, cautious friends, who knew very little about each other and never fought over what day they were going to sleep together.

Shaun had never been so confused in his life. He didn't know how to take the new feelings Jesse stirred up. The more he repressed them, the more he longed for Jesse's approval and attention, and Jesse was certainly happy to provide it. He was completely overwhelming Shaun.

The walk home did little to calm him down, and when he got home neither did the sight of his grandfather, asleep in his armchair and apparently waiting up for him.

Eli dropped odd comments about Jesse whenever Shaun was around, which wasn't often nowadays. It was infuriating. He kept insinuating something was going on between them, and Shaun didn't like how close to the truth he was getting.

He passed Eli silently on his way to his room.

Shaun took his boots and his jeans off. He lay on top the covers and stared at the dark ceiling. He lay there for a while, thinking.

At first, he was able to keep his mind off dangerous topics. He thought about the band, about the new song ideas bouncing around his head. He thought about school and how he hadn't started the poem for English class. It was due next Friday.

Then, helplessly, he thought about Jesse.

He thought about Jesse's goofy smile when he learned a new trick on the guitar. The way his nose would wrinkle up when he thought something was funny in class. His insistence that he put his feet in Shaun's lap every time they watched TV before the kids' bedtime.

The fluttery feeling started again, and that was unacceptable.

Shaun took his father's knife out of the bedside table. He yanked his shirt up and pressed the blade into his stomach, right over the traitorous fluttery feeling.

Jesse's face appeared in his head, gazing at him adoringly, repeating the words from earlier.

"You can stay if you want."

Shaun's sick mind forced him to imagine if they'd stayed together. If Shaun had climbed into Jesse's bed like he'd suggested.

They'd be lying there right now, facing each other like they had Sunday night in the back of Ruth's van. There'd be no stars to distract Jesse this time, just the two of them, covered in darkness, pressed together because Jesse was having a hard time with personal space.

The mental picture conjured up something a bit stronger than the butterfly feeling. Instead, he felt the stirrings of arousal coiling in his belly.

Shaun was horrified. He forced the knife into his stomach.

The blade was incredibly sharp. Shaun gasped as blinding pain shot through his abdomen. The knife slipped from his hand.

He hadn't cut deep; at least, he didn't think so. He'd stabbed himself in the stomach though, and blood leaked through his fingers.

He cursed and ripped his shirt off. He wadded it up and pressed it gingerly to the wound.

The fluttery feeling was gone. And the beginnings of arousal had been chased away.

All that was left was pain.

*

Shaun slept like crap. In the morning, he was woozy and feverish.

The knife wound was disgusting to look at. It was an inch-wide hole to the right of his belly button. It was red and inflamed.

He'd bled through his sheets. The hem of his boxers was stained a sticky brown. The shirt he'd used as gauze was completely ruined.

Shaun had no experience in gut wounds. He had no idea whether he should be concerned or not. He figured he'd treat it the same as all his other cuts. He dragged himself out of bed, picked a clean shirt and ventured into the bathroom. It was too painful to directly wash the stab wound, but he splashed it clean with warm water and taped some heavy gauze over it.

It took care of the bleeding at least.

There was a knock on the door. Shaun jumped. "What are you doing in there?" It was Eli. Shaun scowled at his reflection in the mirror.

"Nothing!" he cried. He yanked the shirt over his head. He winced when the fabric caught the mass of tape. "What do you want?"

"Can we talk?"

"I'm taking a shower," Shaun said. He strode to the tub and turned the water on. It drowned out whatever Eli said next. He gave up. He knew better than to just barge in.

Shaun sat down on the toilet and let the water run. There were hours to go before Shaun picked Jesse up. He didn't know how he was going to avoid Eli until then. He couldn't run the shower all day, though it was tempting.

Once he was sure Eli was gone, he shut the water off and escaped back to his room. He blocked the door with his desk chair and turned some music on.

Normally he liked it loud, but today it was giving him a headache. He lay back on his bed and put a pillow over his head.

He was roughly shaken awake. He pulled the pillow off his face and sat up with a groan. His stomach radiated pain. The music had stopped, and Eli stood over him, his face grave.

"What?" Shaun snapped.

"You're bleeding." Eli sat on the edge of the bed. He stared at Shaun's stomach. With a feeling of dread, Shaun checked himself. The bleeding had started again. There was a sizable patch of blood through his fresh T-shirt.

"Fuck," Shaun said under his breath.

"Jesse's here," Eli said. His hands fluttered uselessly over Shaun's abdomen. "He said you were supposed to pick him up at five."

"Shit. What time is it?"

"Quarter to six."

Shaun hauled himself out of bed. The pain was severe, but he did his best to ignore it. He had to get to practice. He had to pretend everything was normal and that he hadn't stabbed himself. He didn't want anyone to worry. Especially Jesse.

He grabbed another set of clothes. He'd change in the bathroom after he reapplied some gauze.

Eli was hot on his heels. "What's going on with you!" he hissed as Shaun hurried into the hallway.

"Shaun?" Jesse stood at the end of the hall, in the living room. His carefully blank expression turned into a grin when Shaun met his eyes.

Shaun turned away before Jesse saw the blood. He slipped into the bathroom.

Eli forced the door open and squeezed into the room behind him. He shut the door. "What's going on?" he asked. He guarded the door like a sentinel. Shaun ignored him. He got the roll of gauze from the cabinet over the sink. Eli grabbed his arm. "Shaun? Please," he pressed.

"Nothing's going on!" Shaun snatched his arm away. His eyes flashed dangerously. Eli didn't back down. "Jesus Christ! I'm trying to get ready!"

"Why are you bleeding?" Eli gestured to the bloody stain. "What are you doing to yourself?"

Shaun pulled his shirt off and pressed his lips together as he peeled the bloody gauze from his wound. Eli gasped and tried to get a look, but Shaun twisted out of the way. It really looked infected, but Shaun didn't have time to worry about it. He sloppily applied the new gauze and plastered it over with surgical tape.

"I have to go to practice," Shaun muttered, his back to Eli.

"I don't think—"

"I have to go," Shaun said firmly. "I'll be fine."

Eli thought it over in silence. He sighed.

"Do what you want, Shaun. I can't stop you," he said tiredly. "But when you come back, we really need to have a talk."

"You've been saying that for days now," Shaun sneered. "Didn't we just talk?"

"Hardly."

"You want to make sure I'm okay, right?" he taunted. "Well, I'm great. I've never been better, actually."

"Shaun..."

"You don't need to worry about me, because I have everything under control." Shaun threw his bloodied bandages into the trash before he pulled his thermal shirt over his head. He met his grandfather's troubled gaze. "Thanks for the concern," he said sarcastically.

Eli moved aside as Shaun stepped into his cargo pants. He was ready to go.

"I'll see you very soon," Eli said as if to reassure himself.

"Whatever."

Shaun grabbed his boots from his room and kicked them on. Jesse waited at the end of the hall, where Shaun had left him. His expression was a mix of excitement and concern.

"Everything okay?"

"Yep. Fine," Shaun said, trying for a cheerful tone, but falling short. Jesse looked even more concerned. "Let's go," Shaun said quickly before Jesse could ask again.

Shaun took Eli's car, like always. He was afraid to load his guitar and amp himself though. He didn't want to risk bleeding through his fresh bandages, so he ordered Jesse to do it. Luckily, Jesse was eager to please. He did as asked without complaint. Shaun started the car and found a suitable song on the radio while he waited.

Jesse was mercifully quick. He packed everything in the back, then hopped in the passenger seat.

"Thanks," Shaun said. He backed the car into the street and took off. He could feel Jesse's eyes on him, watching him meticulously. He didn't dare look over.

"You're welcome."

There was a long silence as they drove, top speed, to Will's house. Being an hour late wasn't a huge deal. There was a good chance the band hadn't even noticed Shaun was late, but Shaun was sure he'd fucked everything up. His stomach throbbed and itched. He wasn't sure he'd even be able to play when they got there.

But the knife had done the trick. He didn't feel anything for Jesse, at least not now. He'd barely looked at him, he hadn't said much to him, and there were certainly no fluttery feelings in Shaun's aching belly. He was so wrapped up in his own little world there was no way for Jesse to worm his way in.

"Something's wrong," Jesse said, obviously sensing that, in Shaun's mind, he was a thousand miles away.

"Everything's fine."

"You've already said that," Jesse said.

"I did," Shaun said flatly. "And I meant it." At this point, he didn't care what happened. He just wanted to get through practice without embarrassing himself and being cross-examined.

"Shaun!" Jesse cried, and Shaun grudgingly looked at him.

Jesse had his back to the window and his legs tucked up underneath him. His pretty eyes were wide with hurt and betrayal. His mouth was open, and his lips were red and soft looking.

Shaun zeroed in on that piece of anatomy. Mouth. Hot. Wet. Tongue flicking out to taste a pouting lower lip...

Shaun tore his gaze away. He clenched the wheel in a death grip.

"What is going on? Did something...happen last night? Did your grandpa say something to you?" Jesse asked. "Why are you so distant?"

Shaun hated that he cared so much about Jesse. Before, he hadn't cared if he'd hurt Jesse's feelings, but now it was painful to listen to his distress.

But what was Shaun going to say? He wasn't going to tell him the truth...

"Nothing happened, nobody said anything, and I'm not acting any different."

Jesse's eyes widened. "Did I do something wrong? You're acting like you hate me."

Shaun couldn't help but laugh. On the contrary, *I like you too much*. Of course, Shaun didn't say that. "Do you want to go home?" he asked instead, a tad harsher than he'd intended, but maybe that was for the best. "I'll take you home if you don't want to do this."

"No," Jesse said immediately. "I just wish you'd talk to me," he said softly.

And maybe if it had been about something other than his developing homosexual feelings, he would have. Shaun shook his head, muttered that nothing was wrong, and continued driving.

Jesse didn't say another word.

Shaun had never been so glad to get to Will's in his life. The forty-minute drive had been unbearable. They'd sat in an awkward, stifling silence while Jesse shot him little glances, pleas for Shaun to talk to him. Shaun ignored him and Jesse kept his mouth shut.

"Do you want me to get your stuff?" Jesse asked shyly when they pulled up outside Will's house.

"Yeah."

For some reason, that seemed to make Jesse sad. He turned his face away and looked out the window for a moment. Then he got out and went around to the back to get the equipment.

Sighing, Shaun reached over the seat and snatched his guitar before Jesse could. He could carry a guitar without killing himself, he reasoned. It was the amp he thought might hurt.

"Hey," Danny called as Shaun walked in the front door. He was sprawled on the couch, alone in the living room. Football was on TV. Danny held a beer and his face was flushed. He was drunk.

"Is that Shaun?" Will appeared in the doorway to the kitchen. He had a beer too, but he didn't look intoxicated. He spotted Shaun at the door and narrowed his eyes. "It's about fucking time."

"Sorry," Shaun muttered. He stepped aside as Jesse maneuvered the amp through the front door. Shaun cringed internally when both Will and Danny turned their gazes to the newest arrival.

"Who's this?" Will asked. He furrowed his brow in confusion.

Danny almost dropped his beer as he started to laugh. Shaun clenched his teeth, furious. "That's Shaun's little friend. From last week," Danny said. "Remember? I told you about him."

Will gave him a blank look.

"The kid that hugged Shaun?"

"Oh." Will laughed, and Shaun flushed an ugly brick red. Ben appeared in the door behind Will. He pushed his way into the room.

"Hey. You're here." Ben shot a glare at Danny but otherwise didn't acknowledge him. He flashed a smile at Jesse. "Hi," he said. "I'm Ben."

"Hello," Jesse said shyly. "I'm Jesse." He put the amp down and shook Ben's hand. "You're an amazing bass player. You're all great musicians," he said, totally sucking up. He glanced at Shaun, uncertainly written on his face. Shaun had no direction for him. He didn't know how to make his band mates like Jesse. They barely liked him.

Jesse seemed to be doing well on his own anyway.

"That's fucking right," Will preened.

"At least your boyfriend's got good taste," Danny joked.

Shaun bristled. "Are we going to practice or not?" he grunted. He dragged his guitar into the garage.

The others followed momentarily. They were distracted by Jesse. He talked a mile a minute, asking about upcoming shows and new songs. Will answered his questions in the arrogant way he had for fan-types. Danny watched the proceedings with a vague amusement. Ben seemed particularly taken with Jesse. He pulled him aside when Will got sick of the never-ending questions and dismissed Jesse with a wave.

Ben and Jesse talked in low quiet tones as Ben set up his bass. Shaun couldn't hear what they were talking about over the sound of Danny warming up his drum kit, but he could tell they were hitting it off.

Shaun didn't like it, but he didn't know how to stop it either.

Will bitched at everyone to hurry up. "Let's get started sometime this century."

Ben gestured to the threadbare couch against the far wall, and Jesse flounced off to have a seat.

It was an uncomfortable practice for Shaun. He was in pain, of course, but he was also hyperaware of his every move thanks to Jesse's intense stare. Shaun was tempted to stop playing and demand Jesse look at someone else for a change, but he didn't want the others to know what was up.

"What the fuck's wrong with you?" Will halted practice after twenty minutes. He glared at Shaun. "You're playing's for shit today."

"He's got performance issues," Danny snorted from behind the safety of the drum kit. "He can't do it when his boyfriend's watching."

Shaun sent Danny a dark and malevolent glare, shutting him up effectively. Ben defended him anyway.

"Shut up, Danny," he ordered.

"Are you ready now, asshole?" Will asked, ignoring the side discussion. "We've got another show coming up soon." He proceeded to start the next song without waiting for a reply, which was typical.

Shaun played his heart out. He worked up a sweat which was only partially due to effort and mostly from the strain he was putting on his injured body. They were an hour in, and nobody was impressed.

"You suck." Danny flicked Shaun off.

"Yeah. Maybe we should call it a night," Will frowned. He bent over to pick up his bottle of beer. He gulped it down and headed back inside for more. Danny ran after him.

"You okay?" Ben asked. He was one of the last people in the room. Jesse was still on the couch. He watched them with wide eyes.

Shaun sighed. "I guess," he said. He wanted to sit down.

"C'mon. Let's get something to drink." Ben waited for Shaun to put his guitar down. He put an arm around his shoulders and led him into the living room. Jesse followed them.

Shaun was exhausted. He flopped into the armchair and stared at the football game on TV. He could hear Jesse and Ben whispering behind his back, but he ignored them.

Some stuff happened, but Shaun was too out of it to care. Will and Danny went on a beer run while Ben and Jesse got comfortable on the couch. They talked in hushed voices. They snuck glances Shaun's way; it was obvious they were talking about him. He wondered what they were talking about, but he was busy thinking about how he was going to get out of here. He felt really fucking sick.

It felt like hours passed before Will and Danny were back, carrying a couple cases of beer. They threw one at Shaun and he drank obligingly.

When he'd finished the first one, Ben brought him a second, leaving his cozy seat with Jesse to do so. And when he'd finished the second, Jesse brought him a third. He was feeling a little better by this point, numb anyways. Then Jesse sat on the arm of his chair.

"Is it okay if I'm worried about you?" Jesse whispered. He leaned into Shaun side, practically falling into his lap. He nudged Shaun's aching wound, and Shaun bit his lip to keep from cringing overtly. Then Jesse slid his arm around Shaun's shoulders. He stroked his hair.

Shaun jerked up straight, feeling frantic. He looked around the room.

They were alone. Shaun didn't know how long they'd been the only ones in the living room; he knew the guys had been watching the game just a second ago, so they couldn't have gone far.

Jesse nodded toward the kitchen. "They're in there," he said. "But I want—need to talk to you."

"You need to get off me," Shaun said, trying to sound firm and threatening. His voice was weak though. He was half-awake and totally out of it. He wasn't convincing anyone.

"Why are you being so mean to me?" Jesse asked. He pet Shaun's hair, like he was his girlfriend or something. "I thought we were best friends?"

"We *are*," Shaun hissed through his teeth.

"Then stop pushing me away!" Jesse hissed right back. "If you don't want to talk about it...fine. But you need me—"

"Like a hole in my head," Shaun finished sarcastically. *Or a hole in my stomach*, he thought darkly.

"Stop pouting." Jesse playfully yanked a lock of Shaun's hair to get his point across. Shaun growled. "Stop moping over here and come watch TV with us."

"I can watch it fine from here."

"Well, then I'll just have to sit here with you, won't I?" Jesse threatened. He snuggled into Shaun's side to drive home how embarrassing their current positions were.

"You're a fucking brat." Shaun scowled, but Jesse smiled brightly. He wasn't deterred in the least. He leapt up and held out his hand. Shaun took it reluctantly.

His face contorted with pain as he got up, the edges of his stab wound pulled this way and that. Jesse totally missed it. The moment Shaun was upright he wrapped his arms around Shaun and nuzzled his face into his chest. It hurt. Immensely. But Shaun took it stoically.

"Stop being so mean to your friends, Shaun," Jesse chided. His voice was too breathy and soft to be reprimanding. He hugged Shaun once more before he released him and led him to the couch.

As they sat down, Jesse uncomfortably close, almost in his lap again, the others came back into the room.

Ben sat on the other side of Jesse. They shared a conspiratorial smile. Ben asked if Shaun was feeling any better.

"Never better," Shaun growled. He was deeply uncomfortable, in pain, pissed off... Jesse and Ben seemed amused. It wasn't right.

Will sat in Shaun's abandoned armchair. He passed out joints, which he and Danny had been rolling in the kitchen. "Here, you fucking need it," he told Shaun as he pressed the drugs into his palm.

"Fuck you," Shaun muttered, but he couldn't have agreed more. Ben passed him a lighter, and he toked up.

Will had cut something nasty into the weed again. Shaun was sick almost instantly. This time he managed not to throw up, but he ended up lying on the couch with his head in Jesse's lap. Jesse smiled down at him. His eyes were off; his smile was weird. He was obviously reacting to the drugs.

"Poor baby," Jesse said. He slowly stroked Shaun's hair and his face, even his chest and arms occasionally. He was entranced. He didn't go below Shaun's waist, which was lucky, because Shaun was pretty sure he had a raging erection.

The game ended, heralded by the sound of Will and Danny cheering obnoxiously. They promptly left to pick up some girls from the bar down the street. For a while, things were quiet and nice. Shaun was close to sleep. The sound of Jesse and Ben murmuring to each other was soothing.

But Will and Danny returned, and a slutty girl accompanied them. They took her straight into the bedroom and started fucking at the top of their lungs.

Ben made his excuses and ducked out. Shaun wanted to leave too. He wanted to crawl into his bed and sleep for days, but he was in no state to drive. He had to go to the bathroom at one point, and Jesse had to help him get there.

When Will and Danny quieted down, Jesse turned the TV off and rearranged Shaun on the couch. He let him lay the full length. As Shaun stretched out, he wondered where Jesse was going to sleep. Then Jesse lay beside him on the narrow couch. He pressed his entire front to Shaun's side and threw an arm over his waist. He was dangerously close to Shaun's stab wound, but Shaun was too far gone to feel the pain.

"Good night," Jesse whispered. His head was buried in the crook of Shaun's neck.

Shaun was too out of it to reply. He was embarrassingly turned on, confused, and sore, but he was sure he felt Jesse's lips on him, kissing him chastely.

Morning was only a few hours away. It dawned bright and clear.

Sunlight poured through the living room window, and Shaun winced and shielded his eyes. He had to throw up. He opened his eyes cautiously.

Jesse still clung to him. His face was very close.

Pain and nausea warred for dominance. Shaun had to get to the bathroom.

He tried to extract himself gently, but the second he tasted bile his initiative went from "trying not to disturb" to "trying not to throw up all over Jesse."

Jesse was knocked from the couch with a thump. "Oomph!"

"Sorry..." Shaun murmured. He jumped over Jesse and dashed for the toilet. He should know better by now than to take anything Will gave him.

Shaun emerged from the bathroom after he threw up a gallon of yellowish liquid. He hadn't checked his stomach, but it throbbed horribly and burned. He was anxious to get home.

"Are you okay?" Jesse asked.

"Yeah," Shaun said wearily. "I want to get out of here before those assholes get up." He nodded toward the bedroom.

"Want me to drive?"

Shaun shrugged. He wasn't up for the long drive back, but he had no idea if Jesse could be trusted behind the wheel. He was willing to find out though.

"Sit down," Jesse soothed. He took Shaun's arm and led him to the couch. "I'll pack up your stuff. I'll be right back." He smoothed Shaun's frizzy hair down, smiling when it sprung back up again in a cloud of disarray. "Right back," he repeated. He rushed through the door to the garage.

Shaun closed his eyes and rubbed his temples. His fucking head hurt. Hangovers, open bleeding wounds, drug-induced nausea...he'd really done a number on himself.

He listened to Jesse run to and fro, fetching his guitar and running it to the car, then back again for the amp. He came for Shaun next. He helped him up.

"C'mon," Jesse urged. His arm slipped around Shaun's waist as Shaun leaned into his side for support. Jesse's voice grew exponentially more cheerful. "It's a good thing I was here to help you," he said. "Where'd you be without me, hmm?"

Shaun laughed at the irony.

Without Jesse, Shaun would currently be in much better shape, but he didn't say that. He wasn't going to explain himself.

"What's so funny?" Jesse asked. He opened the car door and awkwardly helped Shaun into the car. Shaun pushed him away the second he didn't need him anymore and shut the door behind himself. Jesse hurried around to the driver's side and got in.

"Nothing."

"But—"

"Jesse." Shaun said the name warningly.

Jesse frowned, but he started the car and pulled away from the curb.

They drove in silence. Shaun had to remind Jesse of the way more than once, but other than that, they didn't talk. It wasn't as awkward as yesterday though. Jesse was quiet out of consideration for Shaun. He mentioned a few times he'd be fine if Shaun wanted to rest his eyes, but Shaun didn't sleep. He was uncomfortable. He just wanted to get home.

When they arrived, Jesse insisted on following Shaun inside.

"I'm going back to sleep," Shaun said as Jesse helped him to the front porch.

"That's okay," Jesse said. The door was unlocked, but he fumbled with the latch.

"You can't stay, Jess," Shaun told him.

"Why not?" Jesse was pouting. Shaun could hear it in his voice. "Are you seriously going to make me walk all the way home?"

They knocked into the kitchen table and stumbled through to the living room.

Ruth sat in front of the TV. She was knitting. She glanced up as Shaun and Jesse bumbled through. She scowled at the sight. "Nice to see you got home in one piece." She dismissively returned to her knitting.

"You're not staying," Shaun repeated as if Ruth hadn't spoken.

Jesse led Shaun back to his room. Shaun decided to take the silence as agreement, but as soon as Shaun's door closed behind them, Jesse started complaining again.

"But we slept together last night," he pointed out as he helped Shaun to the bed.

"We didn't sleep together." Shaun cringed. He sat down gingerly and rubbed his face. Most of last night was hazy, but he remembered quite vividly the persistent erection he'd maintained most of the night. The memory combined with Jesse's easy admission of "sleeping together" scared the fuck out of him.

"We slept on the couch together," Jesse said. "You know what I mean." He knelt in front of Shaun and casually untied his boots. He pulled them off like he undressed his close friends all the time.

"What is it with you and sleeping with me?" Shaun grumbled.

"You're the one who's always making a big deal about it," Jesse said.

"Me?!" Shaun glared at him. "You're obsessed with it! You want me to sleep in your bed every single night!"

"So? I've had lots of guy's sleep over before," Jesse said primly. He stood over Shaun, his arms crossed.

"I'm sure you insisted on cuddling up to them too," Shaun sneered. He was pissed. The thought of Jesse cuddling with anyone other than himself enraged him.

Jesse frowned. He gestured for Shaun to stand up.

Shaun scowled and got up. He winced, but he played it off with a rude question. "How many guys have you slept with?"

Jesse blinked. "What the fuck is that supposed to mean? None."

"See! My point exactly. You're not *staying* here in my bed," Shaun growled.

Jesse threw his hands up. "Fine. But you need help. Let me help you get undressed." He reached for Shaun's fly before Shaun had even registered his words.

"Wait..."

But Jesse was already undoing Shaun's pants. He brushed against his stomach as he popped the fly. Shaun forgot for a moment that he was being undressed like a child and sucked in a pained breath at Jesse's careless move.

"What's this?" Jesse reached under Shaun's thermal to feel the mess of bandages the back of his hand had brushed against. "Shaun, what is this?"

Feeling like it was inevitable, Shaun didn't stop Jesse from lifting his shirt and exposing his stomach.

Jesse gasped. He looked deep into Shaun's eyes. "What happened?" he asked.

Shaun didn't answer. He waited for Jesse to figure it out himself. He was investigating. He bent closer and tried to peel the gauze back. It stuck to the surrounding skin, and they both gasped as yellow pus leaked out of the wound.

"Oh my God..." Jesse moaned. "This needs...you need to go to the fucking hospital!"

"It's fine," Shaun said calmly.

"It's infected!" Jesse cried. "How long have you had this?!"

"Since Friday."

Jesse groaned in distress. His hands shook. He released the edge of Shaun's shirt. "C'mon. Let me get these off," he said, returning to the half-discarded pants. He crouched and worked them down. "I can at least clean it out for you. Maybe my mom can—" But Jesse stopped short as he noticed all the other cuts on Shaun's legs. The partially healed wound on his thigh, old scars above his knees, climbing his legs like ladders. There were bigger slashes here and there and quite a few more were still hidden under his boxers, but Jesse looked horrified enough without seeing everything. "When you hurt your arm the other day...was it really from hunting?" he asked in a soft voice.

That hadn't been the question Shaun was waiting for. He answered honestly. "No."

"Did you do it...yourself?"

"I wanted to. It wasn't an accident," Shaun said defensively.

"You did all this?" Jesse gestured to the mess of scars.

"Didn't I already say that?" Shaun snapped.

"You—you're hurting yourself? Cutting yourself?!" Jesse straightened up to look Shaun in the eye.

"Yes, all right!" Shaun didn't want to have this conversation with his pants around his ankles. He pulled them back up, wincing as he buttoned them.

"You did this?!" Jesse laid his hand over Shaun's arm, just above his gash.

"Yes!"

"And this?!" Jesse jabbed a finger at Shaun's thigh.

"Yes!"

"And you did this. You stabbed yourself in the stomach?!" Jesse pulled on Shaun's shirt, a mixture of disbelief and betrayal on his face.

Shaun glared at him. "So, what if I did?"

Jesse stared at him for a long, breathless moment. Then he punched Shaun in the shoulder. "You asshole!" he cried, literally cried. His eyes filled with tears. A few escaped and rolled beautifully down his cheeks. He hit Shaun again, not as hard—though the first had barely hurt—and again. "Are you trying to kill yourself?!"

"Jesse—"

"No! Tell me right now! You owe me an explanation at least!" he demanded. "Tell me why you'd do this to yourself!"

"I don't owe you anything!" Shaun yelled, and Jesse gasped out another sob, the tears really falling now, completely unhindered.

"You can't do this! You promised we'd stick together!" Jesse cried. He was hysterical. "You can't kill yourself!"

"I never said I was going to!"

"Well, then why are you doing this?! You could have hurt yourself so much more! You could have died!" Jesse whimpered. "Oh God...oh, Shaun...oh—"

Jesse was perfect in his anguish. He was gorgeous. His tears were real and beautiful and all for Shaun... Shaun's heart beat quicker in his chest.

He couldn't help himself. He grabbed Jesse by the front of his shirt and pulled him up until he swayed on the tips of his toes.

"Shut up," he growled. He smashed their lips together. Jesse's mouth was open and wet, and Shaun thrust his tongue inside with a moan.

Jesse tasted like stale smoke and old beer, but that made everything more real.

This was really happening...

Shaun's free hand sifted through Jesse's auburn locks and clutched him tight. Jesse was limp and unresponsive in his arms. Shaun refused to open his eyes. He used his handhold to deepen the kiss. *God*, he wanted this so badly.

He twisted his tongue around Jesse's and sucked the spit out of his mouth. It was a horrible kiss, but Shaun's cock was rock-hard. Jesse's whole body trembled, and Shaun bit down on his lips, frustrated and horny and not knowing what to do about it. He was desperate for Jesse to respond.

Jesse whimpered, and Shaun shoved him away. He panted for breath as Jesse tripped over his own two feet. He caught himself and looked up with huge eyes.

There was spit smeared on Jesse's face. A bit of blood stained his lower lip. He gingerly touched his kiss-swollen mouth.

There was a single moment of silence as they stared at one another. One moment for Shaun's fear of rejection to bubble up inside him. His throat constricted as a thousand different thoughts rushed past, adding to his confusion and dread.

And then Jesse's face twisted, his mouth—that fucking mouth!—opened, and all of Shaun's confusion coalesced into a single thought.

"Get out," Shaun said. Jesse deserved to hate him for what he'd just done—kissing him...practically raping his mouth for fuck's sake! But he didn't want to hear it. He wanted to be alone. Alone with his humiliating thoughts and his shameful erection.

How could he have fucked up so bad? It was one thing to lust after a boy...after a boy who had tried to be his friend no less! But he couldn't believe he'd acted! He hadn't been completely honest when he'd told Jesse he wasn't interested in killing himself. He was seriously considering it. Just a quick clean cut along his jugular vein, and he could bleed out, staining his freshly changed sheets a nice dark red.

"Shaun—"

"I said get out!" he shouted. Jesse's face was completely drained of color; the disgust he felt was clear as day. Any minute now he'd start to laugh. He'd tell Shaun how much he hated him, how horrible it had been to have an erection pressing into his stomach, how completely revolting it had been to have Shaun's tongue in his mouth, licking his tonsils. Shaun couldn't listen to it. He'd have to kill someone if he did.

Jesse must have saw something in his eyes that conveyed Shaun's murderous mindset, because he backed out of the room without another word.

Shaun listened for the slam of the front door. He sank onto his bed.

Oh, God. He'd be a laughingstock by Monday. Jesse would tell Emily and her brother. He'd tell everyone what a sick freak Shaun was. Everyone would know and he'd be worse than a pariah. He'd spent most of his life being feared and avoided, but now…

And Jesse…he'd lost him forever. The best friend he'd ever had was gone because he hadn't been able to control himself and his desire.

What had he done?

"Shaun? Jesse ran out of the house like someone had lit a fire under his ass. What was that all about?"

Shaun's head snapped up. His face had been buried in his hands, and if he could have cried, he would have, but his eyes were dry, hard, angry—mostly with himself, but also with the world in general.

Eli stood in the doorway. He looked like he was settling in for a long conversation. "How about we have that talk now?"

"Whatever." Shaun had wanted to be alone, but with the direction his thoughts were heading he wasn't sure it'd be a good idea. The knife in the bedside table was calling to him, and as much as he longed for the release, he was too ashamed to touch it.

"Why don't you start by telling me what's going on?" Eli said. He walked into the room and sat gingerly beside Shaun. "Why the long face?"

"I kissed him," Shaun blurted. He dropped his face into his hands. If he could talk to anyone about this, it'd be Eli. Ruth wasn't one for heart-to-hearts. She was more like Shaun in that regard; plus, he felt she'd react unfavorably. Eli immediately put his arm around Shaun's shoulders.

"And he ran out?"

"He hates me now," Shaun said into his hands. "I could see it in his eyes."

"Son, I find that hard to believe."

Shaun raised his head. "What?"

"Well, I've only seen you together a few times; you're both so reclusive. I honestly thought you were already an item."

"An item?!" Shaun hissed.

"I walked in on you boys snuggling on the couch," Eli deadpanned. "I took Ruthie out to dinner because I thought you'd want some time alone."

"Oh God..." Shaun moaned, humiliated. "It wasn't like that. He just—"

"What? Was cuddling on you because he hates you?"

Jesse had been awfully clingy lately. But that was just because...well...Jesse hadn't explained why. Shaun had gone along with it because he was a pervert.

"Did he actually say he hated you?" Eli asked.

"When I..." Shaun trailed off, his face flushed with embarrassment. "He didn't kiss me back."

"Maybe he was surprised."

"Horrified, more like."

Eli chuckled. "Did you even let the poor boy get a word in edgewise?"

"No. I know what he was going to say," Shaun grunted.

"Why don't you—"

"Grandpa?" Shaun asked. "Can we stop talking about this?"

Eli looked like he was going to say something but changed his mind. "If you want."

"Can you do me a favor?"

Shaun lifted the hem of his T-shirt. Eli gasped as Shaun exposed the wound on his belly. "Can you help me?"

Eli shook his head. "Oh, Shaun. When are you going to stop doing this to yourself?" But he stood up and gestured for Shaun to follow him.

His grandpa wasn't a nurse, but he did know a fair bit about first aid. Shaun was in for a few painful minutes of treatment, a prescription antibiotic, and then he was sent to bed. Ruth brought in some lunch, and Eli came in with some Tylenol.

Shaun hadn't felt so weak in a long time. He let himself be babied. It felt good to be cared for. This was going to have to tide him over until he could get out of town, because no matter what Eli said, Shaun was convinced his life was about to change for the worse.

About the Author

C.R. Scott is a self-taught writer with a BA in psychology. Her characters are flawed and imperfect and she loves them for it. They urge her to write their stories. She currently resides in the ever-changing climates of Ohio with her husband and two children. This is her first published book, with more to come.

Email: crscottnsp@gmail.com

Coming Soon from C.R. Scott

Scars; Permanently Black and Blue, Book Two

Also Available from NineStar Press

Connect with NineStar Press

www.ninestarpress.com

www.facebook.com/ninestarpress

www.facebook.com/groups/NineStarNiche

www.twitter.com/ninestarpress

www.tumblr.com/blog/ninestarpress